Journey

Journey

A Novel

Andrew Zimmerman

Radius Book Group
New York

Distributed by Radius Book Group
A Division of Diversion Publishing Corp.
443 Park Avenue South, Suite 1004
New York, NY 10016
www.RadiusBookGroup.com

For more information, email info@radiusbookgroup.com.

First edition: March 2020
Hardcover ISBN: 978-1-63576-664-6
eBook ISBN: 978-1-63576-663-9

Library of Congress Control Number: 2019909292

Manufactured in the United States of America

10 9 8 7 6 5 4 3 2 1

Cover design by Rodrigo Corral
Interior design by Scribe Inc.

New Year's Eve

One

Paul Moore stared at the mirror—dressed in his crisp shirt, red tie, and dark blazer—preparing for his last cocktail party of 2009, New Year's Eve in Sea Island, Georgia. A hint of tan from playing golf that day set off a missed spot of shaving cream. He rinsed his face again. The day's color disguised puffy rings under his eyes. Propped against the sink, water dripping from his face, he realized what he really wanted to do was crawl into bed, pull the covers over his head, and sleep.

He closed his eyes and saw himself a decade ago, holding his five-year-old son's hand as they left the theater. They had seen the movie *FairyTale*, its title flashing above their heads. *FairyTale* was a true story about children in England who took photographs of ghostly people with wings—the so-called Cottingley Fairies. In the early twentieth century, the world debated whether or not the pictures were of real fairies or doctored photographs. Two famous men had opposing views. Sir Arthur Conan Doyle, creator of rationalist Sherlock Holmes but a spiritualist later in life, believed they were real. His friend Harry Houdini, master illusionist, who later became the debunker of false mediums and quackery, believed the

3

photographs had been faked. The ending left the answer to the viewer's imagination.

Paul watched his five-year-old son walking next to him. Simon always smiled, his imaginary world overflowing with happiness. Paul kneeled and put his hands on his son's diminutive shoulders. "Tell me, Simon, after seeing that movie, do you believe in fairies?"

Simon's face wrinkled into a mask of deep thought. He deliberately took his time, determined to get the answer right. Then his smile reappeared. "I believe in everything."

Paul bent down and hugged his son, feeling Simon's warmth against his cold body. He wanted to hold him forever. Other moviegoers passed by. Some had enjoyed the two-hour respite with their children; others checked their watches, late for dinner reservations or other plans. A few wondered whether or not fairies were real. Paul did not know why he remembered that exchange with his son. It happened more than ten years ago but seemed like yesterday. Today, Simon was a teenager and believed in fewer things, but what he did believe in, he did with greater passion.

If his son had believed in everything, Paul tended to believe in nothing at all. Life was a game, and he played with other executives chasing the brass ring. Everyone was a pinball, pinging inside an arcade machine, racing through life before disappearing down the drain. Paul was thankful when the ball sat in a hole for the moment, ringing up a score: *ching, ching, ching*. Time counted down. At the final *ching*, the ball popped out, bouncing off bumpers, rotating through spinners, plunging through rollovers, falling into the drain, flippers flopping helplessly, waving goodbye. No more *ching*.

Paul was a top executive at Ascendant, the world's largest technology services company. He advised companies making bets on the next new thing in tech. The game was changing. Ideas coursed through a knowledge network like a swarm of angry bees. Younger gurus appeared with pithier ideas, sometimes reduced to 140 characters. Paul struggled to keep up. He felt like the ball hiding in a hole, enjoying a brief respite. The chimes rang more quickly, and he feared the next leg of his journey could be his last, disappearing like every other ball.

Paul patted his face dry. He and his wife, Mary, were spending the holiday weekend with friends. Bill and Marybeth were their hosts, and the other two guests were their friends from England—Edward and Jeanne. It was Paul's first time visiting Sea Island, a narrow dune miles long and a few homes wide. Their hosts' home was surrounded by moss-covered trees overlooking a pool and fifties-style cabana. It was not an oceanfront property; for that reason, it was considered a starter cottage, worth less than $2 million.

Paul had walked with Bill on the beach that morning. Bill pointed out the grander homes. "This one's owned by John Portman, the architect and developer—worth twenty million dollars. This one's owned by John Smoltz, the Atlanta Braves all-star pitcher." And so it went until they reached the last house and Bill gestured to another smaller island in the distance. "And that island—the whole thing—is owned by Henry Paulson, former CEO of Goldman Sachs and US secretary of the treasury."

The game was Monopoly, but even the people on Baltic Avenue were doing pretty well. At least that's how Paul felt. He hadn't earned his "fuck you" money yet. But he was well on his way if he could keep the chimes going a little while longer.

Paul was startled out of his reverie. "Paul, you're taking forever! I need to get in there," Mary said. "You're worse than a woman."

Paul came out of the bathroom. Mary sat on the bed, pulling up her black pantyhose. "You sizzle in that outfit," Paul said. "I like you in black."

Mary rolled her eyes. "You say that to all the girls. Help me zip up." The dress opened to the small of her back. For a moment, Paul thought how sexy she was. He wanted to pull off her dress and push her onto the bed. He moved his hands inside her dress. "Paul, stop. We're going to be late."

"Late for what? We have time."

She pushed his hands away and kissed him quickly on the cheek. "I have to put on makeup. You spent too much time in the bathroom. Fix yourself a drink, and I'll be out in ten minutes."

Paul walked into the living room. The fire was going, and Jeanne was sitting near it, reading a book. He notices her pretty blue eyes and pale skin. He realized he barely knew Edward and Jeanne, meeting them once before at a party with their friends in Atlanta. "Where is everyone?" Paul asked.

Jeanne looked up. "It's about time someone showed up. I'm feeling lonely. And waiting for a man to pour me a drink."

"Consider it done. What would you like?"

"White wine, please."

Paul fetched drinks for both of them. "I can understand why the ladies may be a little late, but what are Edward and Bill doing, blow-drying their hair?"

"Between you and me, Paul, I think you gave Edward such a thrashing on the golf course, he needed a nap to recover."

Paul gave Jeanne her wine and held up his cocktail glass. "Cheers."

"Cheers." Jeanne smiled at Paul, her eyes glowing.

Paul said, "You look younger than the last time I saw you. It's been a couple years. What's your secret?"

Jeanne put her book down. "I try to eat well, I do cleansings and meditation, and I try to get enough sleep." She clinked his glass again and winked. "Tonight being an exception, of course."

"Well, it's working, that's for sure." Paul sat down next to Jeanne. "I heard that you've opened up a bed-and-breakfast in the English countryside."

"Yes, it's a small place with four rooms. Provides us with a little pocket change and keeps us busy."

"Whereabouts?"

"In a village called Glastonbury. It's a two-hour train ride west of London."

"What attracts people to Glastonbury? Other than your bed-and-breakfast, of course," Paul teased.

"It's a very historic place, and it's not far from Stonehenge. There's a hill called the Tor at the edge of the village. It's said to have a special energy. Some believe it's the Isle of Avalon, where goddesses and fairies lived. We get all kinds of guests." Jeanne's eyes twinkled. "Last month, we had two witches."

"Witches, huh?" Paul smiled.

"There's a Wiccan festival every year. These guests were from the North Country and seemed very nice, though somewhat standoffish. When they left, our cleaning lady rushed out of the room screaming, 'The witches cursed the room! They hid dead spiders and a cat's hair ball in the back of the closet!' She refused to clean it until the 'curse' was removed."

"What did you do?" Paul leaned forward.

"Well, we hired a witch to remove the curse. She spread salt and herbs on the floor and in the closet, did a few chants, and then vacuumed everything up." Jeanne laughed at Paul's bewildered expression. "We've lots of interesting guests. It's a steady flow of seekers. Some believe they're Druids or goddesses. Some are people like you."

"What do you mean like me?"

"I don't know." Jeanne looked at Paul intently. "Seeking something different. A businessman from Denver visited a few years ago, not really knowing why he came to Glastonbury. He was dissatisfied with his life. Booked a single night, and he ended up staying for a week. Now he returns every year for a recharge." She continued to weave the story about this utterly strange place—and Paul, entranced by her soft voice, fell under her spell. Suddenly, he realized she had stopped talking and was looking at him, almost daring him to ask a question. She smiled as if she knew he didn't know what to ask. By this time, the others had joined them in the living room.

"Edward, do you believe any of this?" Paul asked.

"What?" Edward's booming voice filled the room. He was a retired barrister. His pants clung to his large waist, held up by wide suspenders. He walked over, gin and tonic in hand. Jeanne smiled and reached for her husband's hand. "Do I believe in what? What's this girl telling you?" Edward asked with a big grin. It was clear Edward was on his second gin and tonic.

"Jeanne's been telling me about Glastonbury and all the unusual visitors—like witches—who stay at your bed-and-breakfast. It sounds amazing. What do you think?"

"It's all rubbish," he said, licking the last drops of gin from the ice cubes. He laughed. "They're all nuts, but they're our guests. Would you folks like another drink?" He returned to the kitchen.

Jeanne shook her head. "Edward doesn't believe in any of it. Don't pay attention to him."

Paul asked, "Do *you* think it's rubbish?"

"There're a lot of charlatans," Jeanne admitted. "And troubled people. But there's something there. An energy . . ." She looked down, as if confessing. "My girlfriends and I went to a soul reader one day."

"I've never heard of a soul reader. What do they do?"

"She looks inside you, accesses your soul. She tells you what she sees and records it for you so you can listen to it later. I've recommended her to some guests at the bed-and-breakfast and have seen the effect she can have. The man from Denver that I mentioned? He had a session with her. Changed man."

"Interesting." Paul noticed that Jeanne did not talk about her own visit with the soul reader.

"I think," Jeanne said, "there are people out there who are truly gifted in ways we don't understand."

Edward returned, holding up his hand. "Children, we must be heading out or we'll be late for the festivities. Who's driving?" He winked at Paul. "Unfortunately, the broomsticks are on strike tonight."

Jeanne leaned over and whispered in Paul's ear, "You and Mary should visit us in Glastonbury. And maybe have a soul reading." She rose. Paul watched her join Edward and Mary, and they laughed at something Edward said as they walked out the front door.

The door closed behind them, leaving Paul alone in the living room. Paul wondered when they would realize he was left behind. The room was silent but for the crackling of the dying embers of the fireplace. He heard a faint fluttering sound, like the wings of a bird. Was it coming from the chimney? Suddenly, the air felt ancient, and something stirred inside Paul. He shivered and hurried to join the others, shutting the door behind him.

The Davos Man

Two

The next day, Paul and Mary sat together in the airport lounge in Atlanta, waiting to board the flight to New York. From a distance, an observer would not know they were a couple. Paul's head leaned forward into his laptop. Mary hid behind the *New York Times* Real Estate section.

Mary put down the paper and crossed her freshly tanned legs. A few colored sprinkles from the New Year's Eve party clung to her skin despite her best efforts to clean off this morning. They sparkled in the harsh fluorescent airport light. The trail of dots meandered up her leg, disappearing under her skirt, its hem laced with a pattern of stars.

"You look like a fairy," Paul blurted.

"What?"

"With the party sprinkles sticking on your legs and your lace dress, you look like a fairy."

"Is that a compliment?" Mary said, confused.

"I guess. Jeanne told me about Glastonbury—where they live—and the strange guests they have at their bed-and-breakfast, including witches. I noticed the sparkles and thought of a fairy."

Mary was nonplussed. "I'll take it as a compliment then. It's better than looking like a witch. Plus, anything that takes your eyes off that computer screen . . ." Her phone rang. "It's my sister." She answered, "Hey, Janet."

Paul's phone also started ringing, and he stood up. "Steve?" It was his boss, the CEO of Ascendant.

Steve's voice boomed, drowning out the airport announcements. "Where the hell are you? What's all that noise?"

"I'm at the Atlanta airport. Mary and I spent a weekend at Sea Island with friends."

"I wish *I* had friends in Sea Island."

"They're old friends. It was a fun weekend."

"You know how I spent my weekend? Closing the quarter." Steve's voice grew sarcastic. "Wait a second—why didn't I take off this weekend? Because I'm actually *running* a company."

"Steve, all my stuff was closed. We blew past the forecast, and you know that."

Steve laughed. "I'm just fucking with you. You are so easy to wind up, I swear."

"OK."

"I'm working this weekend because you're the *only* division-beating forecast."

"Well, I'm glad it wasn't—"

"Paul, I'm calling because the World Economic Forum in Davos, Switzerland, is coming up, and I can't go. So you're going in my place."

"I'm flattered." Paul walked over to the airport lounge window. He watched Mary sitting next to their bags, absorbed in her conversation with her sister.

"Don't let it go to your head, Paul. I don't want rumors starting because of this. 'What does this mean? Is Paul lined up to take the CEO job?' It means nothing, OK? I'm asking you to do it because you're a smooth, fast-talking wizard. But nobody's taking my job. Plenty of time before that happens. I have to squeeze every drop of blood out of you first, and you probably won't get the job anyway, because I really like fucking with you."

"I understand. But I really appreciate—"

"Marketing will prep you. You'll be fine. Have a good time. You'll meet a bunch of assholes there. Rich assholes. Though you might fit in with them!"

"Steve, you know I don't come from money. I came from—"

"I'm giving you a hard time. Listen, gotta go. Remember, touch base with marketing. And you're not getting my job."

Paul was excited. Davos was the Olympics of the global elite. He looked for Mary; she was still talking to Janet—what could they be talking about?

*   *   *

Janet complained to Mary, "Are there any men in New York who can put together a few coherent sentences before they try to get into your pants?"

Janet was an investment banker on track for partner, one of the few women at that level. But the financial crash was slowing down her progress. And her biological clock was ringing in her ears. She was feeling pressure from all angles.

Mary watched in horror as a little boy dropped his candy bar on the airport lounge floor, picked it up, and took another bite. "I'm sure there are—"

"On New Year's Eve, I was feeling a little lonely and wore a hot outfit, which I guess is equivalent to having a billboard on my back that reads, *Yes, I want to get laid tonight.* But I have a threshold, you know what I mean? Slugs and cockroaches are below that threshold."

Mary interrupted, "Glenn would've been a good date."

"Boring. Boring. Goodbye, Glenn, you bore me to death." Janet sighed.

"Are you hungover?" Mary asked.

"A little."

"A little?"

"I did sleep with someone last night."

"I can't believe you! You just told me you couldn't find any men—"

"He barely made it over the threshold, but he was so good looking! Didn't have to talk. He was like a very pretty lizard. It was like having a pet for the night."

"Janet, you better take precautions."

"Listen, just because you are my older sister doesn't mean you can lecture me. Do you think I'm an idiot? Speaking of lecturing, how's my favorite nephew?"

"He stayed with a friend this weekend. The parents didn't call once, which is a good sign."

"Is he still growing?"

"You know he's sensitive about his height." Simon was already 6'5" and showed no signs of stopping. "He drives me crazy."

"What did he do now?"

"I found out he's the only junior who hasn't met with a college counselor. Now I have to fix that."

"I wish you could fix me."

"You OK?"

Janet sounded like she was going to cry. "It was a pretty bad start to the new year—I'm too old for this."

"Let's get together this week," Mary suggested. She felt a hand on her shoulder. It was Paul.

"Come on, fairy—it's time to board the plane," Paul joked.

"What did he say about fairies?" Janet asked.

Mary laughed. "Don't mind him. He's been thinking about fairies and witches too much lately."

"Maybe I went to the wrong party."

"Let's get together soon."

"Love you." Janet sounded tired. Mary felt bad for her—a single, high-powered professional woman in New York City had few single men to match her success and wit.

"Let's head over," Paul said, beaming.

"You look like you have good news. What's up?"

"That was Steve. He asked me to go to the World Economic Forum."

"Sounds familiar. What is it?"

"It's a big conference held in Davos, Switzerland. All the heavy-weights are there—heads of state, Bono, CEOs, and Bill Gates. Everybody. Now I'm going."

"Oh!" Mary's eyes opened wide. "That's a big deal! Can I come?"

Paul's face dropped. "Well, no, it's not that kind of conference."

"Isn't it great skiing there?"

"I guess, but you don't ski."

"I can learn."

"Mary, it's not a vacation. I'm substituting for the CEO. This hardly ever happens."

"But he expects you to go to Davos and not take your wife?"

Paul shrugged. "Anyway, it was a pleasant surprise." They joined the line at the gate.

"Well, I'm happy for you," Mary said unconvincingly. The line was moving slowly. "You know that Simon still needs to meet with his guid-ance counselor to pick his target colleges? He's the only junior not to have that meeting."

Paul wondered why Mary changed the subject. "I thought we had a consultant helping Simon."

"And who's going to work with the consultant?"

"Simon?"

Mary's voice rose. "Do you even know your son? We'll be lucky if he'll say hello to the consultant. It's all down to me, as usual."

Paul closed his eyes, hoping the conversation would just go away. Simon resisted any form of instruction, and Mary was full of instructions. He would talk to Simon when they got back home.

The boarding line started to move. Mary walked ahead of Paul, not looking back.

Three

"I can't believe Simon won't text back. Where is he?" Mary spent half her life chasing down her son. Paul and Mary had arrived at their apartment in New York after landing at JFK. Simon was staying with a friend for the weekend but was supposed to be home by now.

"Do you want to eat out?" Paul called out from his home office.

"I bought a nice sea bass at Citarella's," Mary said, her phone next to her ear. "He's not answering his phone." Mary called Simon's friend's mother. "Hi, Chernique, thank you so much for watching Simon. I hope he wasn't any trouble. Yes, they do tend to keep to themselves." Mary unwrapped the fish in the sink. "We had a great time; Sea Island was beautiful. But it's good to be back. I was wondering if I could talk to Simon. He needs to come home for dinner." Mary searched for the olive oil. "He left this morning? Hmm, wonder where he is. No, no worries. He's a big boy. Chernique, could you hold a second?" Mary pressed mute and called out to Paul, "Chernique says Simon left their apartment this morning!"

"Did you check his room?"

"Of course I checked his room." Or did she? She went to his room and tried the door—it was locked. "Paul, could you help me here?"

Paul's voice floated from the office. "What?"

"Simon?" Mary pressed her head against the door. "Simon, are you in there?" Silence. "Simon?" She tried the doorknob again. "Paul?"

"What!"

"I think Simon's locked in his room." Mary knocked on the door. "Simon?" Her frustration grew, and she pounded on the door. "Simon!"

Paul ran out of his office. "What the hell—"

Mary shouted, "Simon, are you in there?"

A voice came from deep within the room. "What?"

"Are you in there?"

"Yeah, I was taking a nap."

"Oh, for Christ's sake." Mary glared at Paul. "What's wrong with him?" She realized she was still holding her phone in her hand, and in the chaos, she'd turned off the mute—Chernique had heard it all.

Mary lowered her voice. "Chernique, are you still there? It turns out Simon was in his room asleep." Paul heard Chernique laughing. "Yes, that boy could sleep through a nuclear attack." Mary sighed. "Absolutely, he can be so funny. I wonder where he gets those ideas. Well, I'm glad you enjoyed having him. I owe you lunch. Sorry for the outburst. OK, thanks again and talk to you soon." Mary looked at Paul and pointed at Simon's door. "You need to fix this. I'm making dinner." She stormed off to the kitchen.

Paul wasn't sure what she meant, but he was smart enough not to ask. What did he need to fix? Simon's door slowly opened, and he peered out, his hair standing up in patches. He had dark circles under his eyes, and he squinted at Paul as if through the slits of a window blind. Being nearly a foot taller than his father, he hovered over him like a giraffe. "Dad, what's going on?"

"Did you hear your mother screaming your name?"

"I was sleeping. I didn't hear anything until the door started coming apart."

"Well, if you wouldn't lock your door and you actually answered when your name was called, life would be easier."

"I'm surprised she didn't put a hole in it."

"Let's not talk about the door. Take a shower—a quick shower, not an hour-long shower. Save water, remember? Mom's making dinner now."

Simon smiled. "Got your back, Dad." He closed the door, and Paul could hear the lock clicking shut inside.

"Be out in ten."

Paul heard the muffled "No worries" through the door.

Paul retreated to his office and closed the door. Another ten emails had dropped into his mailbox during the short interruption. Sunday nights were stressful. Everyone—even his colleagues who aspired to a healthy work-life balance—fired and returned fire in email war games on Sunday night. The new week emerged like a giant sea monster, and everyone was treading water, at its mercy. The sea monster grabbed Paul's legs with its tentacles—hardly a fair fight. Paul took Ambien every Sunday night just so he could sleep through the night without drowning in emails.

Cynthia, the head of marketing and his nemesis, sent him an email, which he decoded in his head:

Paul,

I heard from Steve you're taking his slot at Davos this year. [Translation: *Steve told me to help you, which is the only reason I'm reaching out, because otherwise, I wouldn't help you.*] Steve's schedule is tight, and I know his priority is preparing for the board meeting next week. [Translation: *The only reason you're going to Davos is that Steve has more important things to do, which I know about and you don't.*]

He asked me to help you prepare (not that you need any, I'm sure!), and my team is setting up a call tomorrow and sending you background materials. [Translation: *You need my help, and even if you don't, I'm going to appear to help you so that, if things go well,*

Steve will give me the credit for shepherding you through an event that you're clearly not qualified to attend.] Davos can be tricky, and I'm sure you want to have a good showing as our company delegate. I thought it might be useful for you and me to touch base one-on-one before our group call tomorrow so I can give you some color commentary. [Translation: *I want to talk to you one-on-one to figure out how you're going to play this. Your opening move for Steve's job? Are you going to push me aside, confirming my suspicion that you don't like me and we're enemies? I'm trying to make you feel like you can trust me through the clumsy approach of suggesting a one-on-one call, as if we are in this together.*]

Let me know when you can talk. [Translation: *I'm suggesting a call tonight to let you know that I'm always armed and ready for battle, and being a single woman beyond childbearing years, you should fear me day and night, especially Sunday night. If you look away from me for a moment to waste time on your wife and children, consider this—they're just anchors wrapped around your neck, I'm the sea monster, and it's Sunday night. Do you feel my tentacles tugging at your leg?*]

Best,

Cynthia

Paul hesitated. He could feel her out by having the call. He hit reply. On the other hand, what message would he be sending by talking to her tonight?

There was a knock at the door. It was Mary. "Come join us for dinner before things get cold."

Paul replied to the email:

Dear Cynthia,

Thanks for reaching out. I did have a chance to talk to Steve earlier today, and he briefed me on the Davos trip. Let's have the group call tomorrow and then see if we need to connect separately.

I'm jammed tonight, the usual social commitments. Can't wait to get back to work so I can relax!

Talk to you tomorrow,

Paul

He sent the message, which pinged like a rifle shot.

When he walked into the dining room, Mary said, "Sit down. We've been waiting."

"This is great. Dinner with the family on a Sunday night." Paul smiled. "So, Simon, how was your weekend?"

"Good." Simon looked preoccupied, moving his food around the plate.

"I mean, what did you do . . . you know, with your friend?" Paul racked his brain for the kid's name.

"Henry," Mary said.

"With Henry. Did you do anything? How were his parents? They seem like nice people," Paul persisted.

"They're nice," Simon said agreeably.

"Henry's mom had said something about taking you to a movie. Did you go?" Mary offered.

Simon looked at his mother as if she just suggested that he robbed a bank. "No, we just hung out."

"For the whole weekend?" asked Paul.

"Pretty much."

"I'm just wondering if there was anything that you did this week-end you can—"

"Paul," Mary intervened, "don't start interrogating him."

"I'm not interrogating—"

"If he doesn't want to talk about it, let's respect that."

"I'm just trying to have a conversation. I'm not interrogating."

"We really didn't do anything," Simon offered.

"And there's nothing wrong with that." Mary covered Simon's hand like a mother duck sheltering a young duckling. Simon pushed his chair back and stood up.

"Thanks for dinner."

"But you didn't eat."

"I had a lot to eat at Henry's. I've got homework for tomorrow. Outline for a big paper."

"What's the paper about?" Paul asked.

"Paul, leave him alone. He doesn't want to answer your questions, and we can't even have a civil family dinner without—"

"Maybe I can help him, that's all." Paul shrugged.

"Thanks, Dad, I got it." Simon started toward his room, then turned. "Oh, let me know if you want me to walk the dog tonight." Simon went into his bedroom and locked the door behind him. He loved his parents. They were so nice to him. He knew he frustrated them, but that was part of being parents of a teenager. Simon observed himself and others with a dispassionate eye. "You're an old soul," his teacher told him when he was in kindergarten. He was a tall, old soul, and that was a heavy burden. His height drew attention to himself, and nothing could be less attractive to him. He wanted to stand in the corner and watch the world turn in front of him. Often, however, it noticed him and tried to draw him in. Simon's favorite pastime was thinking. Why was the world the way it was? Who were these people? Why was he so shy yet fearless? He flopped on his bed with his computer. The paper outline was done, but his friend Henry showed him a couple of really cool porn sites over the weekend, so he opened his laptop . . .

Mary and Paul finished their meals in silence. "I'll do the dishes," Paul offered.

"Don't bother; there's not much to clean. You take the dog out."

"OK."

"I'm going to watch some TV and have a glass of wine—I'm sure you can't join me."

She was right. He had to work. "Maybe later."

No email from Cynthia. She must be puzzling out her next move, he thought. Paul returned other emails like a professional baseball player at batting practice, sending them back into the seats, along the ground, or high into the air.

Snuffy, their dog, crawled onto his lap, ready for a walk. He patted Snuffy and said, "OK, girl," and got up and headed out of his office, Snuffy trailing behind. He paused in front of Simon's room. The sounds of Simon playing the flute floated just behind his closed door. Paul paused to listen. Simon attended Juilliard on weekends and was one of the leading flutists in the city—an excellent addition in his college applications. Snuffy scratched the door. The music stopped, and Simon's disembodied voice came from behind the door. "Are you walking the dog?"

Paul smiled. "Yeah, come with me."

"Hold on."

Paul and Simon walked along the river in Riverside Park in silence. They rarely talked, but when they did, the conversations often stayed with Paul in the Simon Moore Museum of Memories—exquisite moments like that night they saw *A FairyTale*. Or not long after that, when Simon said he wanted to have a lot of money so he could buy a good job. As a teenager, Simon said even less but had deeper thoughts. Paul was sure of that.

"Did you ever think of being a minister like Grandpop?" Simon's voice startled Paul.

"Not really. Why do you ask?"

"Because some people follow in their parents' footsteps and some don't. And I wonder why."

Paul did not want to tell his son that he was afraid of his father and his fire-and-brimstone view of the world, that he wanted to run away from it as soon as he could. His father was a God-fearing Christian who embraced his own personal hell, particularly after Paul's mother died from cancer ten years ago.

"Mom told me you left Grandpop's church and became a Quaker when you were still in high school."

"That's right. I was about your age. I was protesting their religion." They stopped and watched Snuffy circle, getting ready to do her business.

"I should go to church in protest of your atheism." Simon grinned.

Paul laughed. "You're going to get up on Sunday morning?"

Simon bent over to use the poop bag. "Good point. Do they have night services?" They started to walk back toward the apartment. "Do you miss religion?"

Paul was uncomfortable. "I wouldn't say I'm an atheist. You don't have to go to church to be religious."

"It can't hurt," Simon noted. "Was your first wife religious?" Paul was married for a short time to Samantha, his college sweetheart.

"This is turning into Twenty Questions—what's gotten into you?" Paul asked, surprised that Simon even took an interest.

"I'm taking psychology this semester, and we're looking at how a family's cultural and religious backgrounds affect the children, that's all." Simon kicked a half-eaten pastry off the sidewalk before Snuffy could grab it.

"A psychology course already? You *are* growing up." Paul thought about his first wife for the first time in a long time. "Samantha was not religious. She was sort of antireligion, actually. Her parents were very Catholic, and I think she was reacting to that. But she *was* spiritual."

"What do you mean? Did she trip? Did you guys do acid in college?" Simon asked excitedly.

Paul laughed. "You know I do not answer these sorts of questions."

"So the answer is yes." Simon grinned.

Paul looked at his watch. "We'd better start heading back. It's late."

"I'm thinking I might pick up a slice on the way back. I'm feeling a little hungry."

"Sure. Go ahead. I'll meet you back at the apartment." *Get high and get a slice of pizza*, Paul thought. *I get it.* His son walked briskly toward Riverside Drive. He stood out among the passersby with his tall, gangly frame and his hair shooting above his head like a troll doll. How much taller will he grow?

Paul enjoyed walking the dog in Riverside Park. He stared at the teardrop luminaires on the row of vintage-style lampposts. The glow from the lamps illuminated the trees, their shadows looming threateningly on the sidewalk like creatures leaping over the stone wall lining the park and running into the street. Paul tightened his grip on Snuffy's leash.

He watched a solitary jet glide high above the Hudson River, its faint rumble sounding like someone blowing into a funnel. The jet reminded him that he had more work to do tonight. The Davos trip wreaked havoc with his travel schedule; he'll probably be in Europe for the entire week.

Paul felt a tug on the leash and realized he'd stopped walking. Snuffy wanted to get home for her treat. Then Paul had a thought. Could he visit Jeanne and Edward in Glastonbury after Davos? What a great idea. He started walking faster, and Snuffy struggled to keep up.

Four

The car slowed down as it approached the first security checkpoint for the World Economic Forum (otherwise known as WEF) in Davos. Paul was traveling with Roberto and Kristoff, his European heads of marketing and sales, respectively. The guards checked their passports and letters of invitation and waved them through. Roberto, who was sitting in the back, announced with mock solemnity, "Paul, you're becoming a Davos man. How do you feel?"

Kristoff, who was sitting next to Roberto, said, "He'll know how he feels when we add up the sales leads." He reached forward and patted Paul on the shoulder. "Right, Paul? How many leads? That's what it is about."

Roberto ignored Kristoff's cynicism and leafed through a briefing paper, reading out loud, "Attendees this year include everybody from Bono, to a cardinal, to forty-two heads of state. Amazing!"

Kristoff said, "We're up to twenty-two CEO meetings in three and a half days—pretty cool. And still counting."

Roberto ignored Kristoff. "The theme of this year's conference is the 'Reshaping of the World: Consequences for Society, Politics, and Business.'"

"Which means you better spend a lot of money with us," Kristoff offered, "or you won't be reshaped, and the consequence for you is you're fucked." Paul laughed.

Roberto continued, "Do you know what the theme of the World Economic Forum was last year?"

"I've got a feeling I'm going to find out."

"'The Great Transformation: Shaping New Models.' Last year we're shaping; this year we're reshaping. Doesn't feel like we're making much progress," Kristoff noted.

Roberto scowled at Kristoff. "You're too crass to understand."

"So I'm not a Davos man? I guess I'm just a human being. That has to feed his children. That has to feed *your* children."

Paul interrupted, "Can we review one more time before you drop me off?"

Roberto read from his notes, "Two thousand five hundred people can enter the congress hall itself—about fifteen hundred business leaders from the thousand largest companies in the world."

"There's about ten trillion dollars in revenue walking the halls," Kristoff reminded.

Roberto continued, "There're a couple hundred politicians, about five hundred academics, artists, heads of NGOs, religious figures, and then, of course, the media is everywhere. Then there are the hangers-on who park themselves in the village but can't go into the congress."

"That's us, Roberto and me. We're your handlers between meetings."

"And there's the next generation of leaders, social entrepreneurs, heads of start-ups, young people that WEF predicts will be the future."

"And that, my friends, is where you find the good-looking women." Kristoff clapped his hands.

"What do you mean?" Paul asked.

"Think about it. Who are these gods of Davos—old men along with a few old women like Angela Merkel? How boring. So they realized, to make it interesting, they had to bring in some young, attractive, successful women to hang out with some old, lecherous, wealthy men."

"I think Kristoff is exagger—"

"And they sit around and talk about the WEF themes all day, like 'reshaping.' I say I feel myself reshaping in my pants as we speak."

"Kristoff, we're running out of time."

Roberto and Kristoff continued to fight in the back seat as the car approached the second circle of security. The road into Davos ran along a valley, the snow-covered Alps on either side. As they entered the village proper, Paul noticed wooden towers hidden in the trees and realized there were snipers standing in them. Whole sections of the village were walled off with solid plastic fences. As they drove by, a large gate opened, and Paul saw rows of camouflaged tents with Swiss soldiers holding machine guns and talking on walkie-talkies. "Did you see that? Man, the security here is tight."

"Well just imagine what a target this place is for terrorists. Grab this village, and you own dozens of heads of states, billionaires, business runners of a quarter of the world economy, and a few celebrities to boot. It's a terrorist nirvana," Roberto explained.

Kristoff fumed. "And you have the protestors, who want to overthrow capitalism, who hate globalization, and who hate the reshaping of things into a giant fuck-you. So the world elites need to be protected from both—the terrorists and the proletariat. The elites meet here, eat nice meals, shake hands, and give empty speeches. Then they send their people into war, killing each other. The rich get richer, selling the weapons and cleaning up afterward."

"Whoa, whoa, whoa," Roberto protested. "The whole idea here is peace not war, trade not fighting."

"It's about power and money. There are more troops here than people attending. This tiny Swiss village is sitting on top of a volcano. Don't be deceived."

Paul interrupted, "Well, I just want to thank you guys for helping me relax as I get ready for my first World Economic Forum. Did we pack my bulletproof vest?"

"I'm just busting Roberto's chops." Kristoff chuckled. "Don't worry. You've got your briefing papers, and we've got your back." The limo pulled up in front of Paul's hotel. "OK, your hotel room is just a couple blocks from the congress. Enjoy the village while we settle in outside the walls of the castle and sleep with the sheep."

Paul checked into the hotel, an old-style Swiss chalet. His room was modest. A large window overlooked a small river below that snaked through the center of town. Paul picked up a flyer on the desk in his room describing the village. Davos was the highest city in Europe. Davos was the locale for Thomas Mann's book *The Magic Mountain*. Paul heard a deep thumping sound and looked outside.

A helicopter descended along the slope of a mountain and landed on a heliport next to the river. A few minutes later, it lifted off. Shortly, another helicopter hovered over the mountain pass and swept down to the heliport. Paul was astonished as a stream of helicopters, flying in like chariots, one by one landed, disgorged their passengers, and quickly lifted off the ground. These were the gods of Davos. They landed their corporate jets at a small airport twenty minutes away and helicoptered to Davos itself. They didn't pass through security, and they went directly from the helipad to the Belvedere Hotel—the only grand hotel in Davos—just a few doors down from the congress hall. Its rooms housed the heads of state, CEOs, and billionaires. Its security rivaled that of the White House. Paul felt a little insecure. He was a

Davos initiate, barely invited into the arena. Did he know how to play this game? Would anyone play with him?

Paul observed the frenetic activity outside his window—helicopters, lines of limousines, snipers pacing on tower platforms, soldiers with walkie-talkies, and press followed by cameras everywhere.

His phone chimed. "Hi, Mary."

"Hey. How was your trip? Where are you?"

"I just got into Davos."

"What's it like? Did you start yet?"

"It's OK. Not as beautiful as I thought it might be. Very busy, lots of security. But I just got here."

"OK." Mary paused. "Simon has a problem."

"What's that?"

"His teacher from Juilliard called me." Mary's voice had the intonation of a doctor reporting terminal lab results. "He is not practicing his pieces."

"How can that be? I hear him playing in his room."

"He's playing his own pieces. She says it's something between Jethro Tull and the Pied Piper."

"Ouch." Paul looked out the window as a very large helicopter hovered for a long time before landing. It had US flags on its sides. "At least he's showing some initiative, composing his own work."

"Yes," Mary said, "but unfortunately, he won't be playing *his* work at the spring concert. He'll be playing a Mozart composition. You know he's doing a solo, don't you?"

"No, I didn't. That's great."

"You need to talk to him." Mary's accusatory voice brought Paul back to earth.

"Talk to him about what?"

"About practicing! His teacher threatened to pull the solo from the program. She told me it's the first time a flutist had the solo since she started teaching there. Usually it's a pianist or violinist who gets the solo position."

"Haven't you told him about your conversation with his teacher?"

Paul heard Mary let out a deep breath. "I'm asking *you* to talk to him. He won't listen to me. I'm working too, you know. Just because I'm not in Davos doesn't mean I'm not busy."

"I know—"

"Or that my time isn't important."

"Of course—"

"What little time I have."

Mary provided wealth management services as an independent consultant. She did pretty well until the crash. Paul knew she felt he was insensitive to the demands of her job.

"When does he get home tonight?" Paul asked.

"I don't know. He's got a busy schedule."

"If he doesn't get home until later, it will be in the middle of the night for me."

"Let me look." Paul heard the clicks on Mary's keyboard. "He has calculus tutoring tonight until nine. So you can't call him."

"Maybe I can call him in the morning, your time."

"You know he doesn't get up until—"

"But I have back-to-back meetings here. I'm not sure when I can break out and call him in the afternoon here." Paul scrolled through his calendar.

"He doesn't have time in the morning. He's been late to class twice already this semester. That's the other thing—he won't get up early enough for breakfast and instead eats donuts from the deli."

"I might have a fifteen-minute window at two p.m. here. That's eight a.m. your time."

"Paul, you know Simon's school begins at eight . . . or maybe you don't know."

"Can it wait until Friday? I'll be in transit then and can call from the airport."

"His next lesson is Thursday night." Mary's voice cracked. "Never mind, I'll take care of it."

"What's wrong?"

"Nothing's wrong. What's it like there? Did other people bring their wives?"

"Mary, I don't know, I just got here about an hour ago. I haven't even left my hotel room. All I know is that my boss never took his wife. I've got twenty-six meetings, I have dinners, I have speeches—there'd be no time for you."

"I know, I know." Paul's phone buzzed; a photo of Kristoff's face smiled at him from his screen. Mary's voice quavered. "It's just hard."

"Mary?"

"I'll talk to you later."

"Remember, I have a dinner, and it's a six-hour difference—"

"Whatever. I'll talk to you tomorrow. Or you call me . . . *if* you have a window." The call dropped.

Paul pivoted to Kristoff's call. "Yes?"

"We just got a session with the CEO of Pepsi. But it's in a half hour at the Belvedere. Her EA said a meeting was canceled and she can fit you in. Can you make it?"

"I'll try."

"The briefing paper on Pepsi is in the binder. I put it in there just in case this happened."

"Got it." Paul grabbed the binder, threw on his coat, and ran up the street toward the Belvedere.

Five

Mary stood in front of the bathroom mirror in the master bathroom. The call with Paul in Davos had not gone well, she thought. Showing weakness in front of Paul made it easier for him to dismiss her. He did not appreciate what she did for the family. Mary used cleaner to remove the traces of yesterday's makeup, smeared by her tears.

Mary taped the notes for her morning meeting on the bottom of the mirror. She chaired the parents' graduation committee at Simon's school. She liked to rehearse beforehand so that she appeared prepared and organized.

She stared at the mirror and saw a tired woman. She hadn't slept well the night before. Why worry about a stupid parents' committee meeting? The women on the committee—and it was mostly women— were former sharks on Wall Street or married to sharks on Wall Street or both. The meeting was an opportunity for them to try out their moves again, like a group of older potbellied men playing touch football, dreaming of their high school days, and pushing a little harder than the rules allowed, just to show they still had their mojo. So Mary had to put on her game face.

She needed concealer to hide the dark circles under her eyes. She used her finger to smooth the concealer at the edges so it would not show through the foundation. "Thank you for coming to our progress meeting today, and Happy New Year! Hard to believe, but graduation is only five months away for our seniors!" Mary liked to break the ice with a greeting while subtly making the point that time was running out and they had to make some decisions.

She applied foundation to her face, using a darker shade than normal to highlight the residual tan from Sea Island. She dabbed under her eyes, wanting to conceal the concealer and further lighten the evidence of a sleepless night. "We have three agenda items today—agreeing on an outside speaker, finalizing our musical selections, and reviewing the graduation party arrangements."

Mary looked up from her "cheat sheet." Her face was a flesh tone canvas—no color or texture—indistinguishable from thousands of other women in urban châteaus along the great avenues of Manhattan also getting ready to start their late-morning schedule of workouts and yoga after sending the kids off to school. While not a high-powered trader like her sister, Janet, Mary was a working girl. Running her own business gave her more control over her schedule, but she missed the camaraderie of working in an office with others.

Mary dipped her finger into the jar of highlighter and drew a line from her cheekbones to the edge of her eyes and above her eyebrows. She contoured the hollows of her cheek a shade darker than her skin color and finished with a pink blush on the top of her cheeks, adding a flirty touch to the sensual look she was creating. She looked at her notes. "As you know, this committee has been asked to concur with the selection of the outside speaker for graduation. Just to remind you, there's a three-step process."

Mary stared at her lipstick choices, scattered like pick-up sticks on her makeup tray. "First, the students nominate three speakers. Then the headmaster's office nominates one of the three, or if none of them is deemed acceptable, the headmaster nominates a speaker. The children nominated three speakers deemed inappropriate or unlikely to accept or both, including Kim Kardashian, Mike Tyson, and Seth MacFarlane, voice of Peter Griffin and creator of *Family Guy*."

Mary smiled and picked a red lipstick—too bold for the committee meeting but perfect for her lunch afterward. She rubbed her lips with balm so they would stay soft into the afternoon. "As a result, Headmaster Johnson has nominated Stuart Macintosh, a Trinity alumnus and head of the Yale philosophy department, as this year's speaker. I'm told he's an inspiring speaker, and he steers clear of topics that touch upon religious belief, focusing on"—Mary had to lean forward to read—"the epistemology of things. I sent you his biography last night." Mary smiled at herself in the mirror, her lips brighter than her highlighted cheekbones.

Why did Mary save eye makeup until the end? Because she didn't need much—a little brown eyeliner, accompanied by a light touch of mascara. In the evening, she might try smudged charcoal eyeliner, but it was too much for a lunch meeting, no matter how interesting. "Epistemology is"—she squinted at her notes on the mirror—"the study of knowledge, what justifies belief from opinion." She straightened her shoulders and looked directly in the mirror as if she was giving a speech as opposed to running a committee meeting. "What a great topic to prepare our children for the life ahead of them! I ask for a motion to approve the nomination of Mr. Stuart Macintosh as this year's graduation speaker." Mary was no public speaker.

Her cell phone vibrated on the rim of the sink. It was her sister. She put her on speaker and started to lightly rub bronzer on her neck and chest.

"Hey, sis."

"Did I wake you up from your beauty sleep?"

"I'm getting ready for a school meeting."

"What meeting?"

"The graduation committee."

"Graduation—I can't believe Simon is graduating in another year. My little nephew."

"I know. And we're already planning for his graduation as well as this year's class. His school's so organized, it's frightening. What're you doing?"

"Nothing. You can hear a pin drop here. I'm telling you, the trading floors of Wall Street are like mausoleums."

"Why don't you go home?"

"I can't go home; the phone may ring. Or I might get the tap on the shoulder and the package. Everyone's waiting for the other shoe to drop."

"They'll never fire you."

"I know, I'm the last woman on the floor and I know too many secrets."

"I'm sure you can tell a few stories." Mary gave her hair a final brush.

"Hey, speaking of which, I have a date tonight!"

"That's great. Are you seeing Glenn again?"

Janet laughed. "Give up, Mary. Glenn's a goner. No, it's the guy that I met at the New Year's Eve party. He called me."

"The one you slept with."

"Yes, the lizard," Janet said.

"At the time, you didn't seem that interested in him. What does he do?"

"Well, he is an actor and works at night as a server at parties."

"So you were picked up by a guy serving drinks at a New Year's Eve party?"

"Don't get so nasty, sister," Janet said. "Slim pickings out there. He's really an actor."

"Should I Google him? What has he been in?" Mary caught herself. "I'm just kidding. I'm sure he's good looking, and you're a free woman. Do whatever you want."

"Do you think I'm selling myself short?"

"No."

"With the age difference?"

"What age difference? Don't tell me—does it start with a one?"

"Don't be ridiculous. He's twenty-five. A *mature* twenty-five."

"Nothing wrong with a fifteen-year age difference."

"Men do it all the time," they said in unison and started to laugh.

Mary smoothed her skirt and pulled her cheat sheet off the mirror. "Maybe I should be dating a twenty-five-year-old today; I'm all dressed up."

"Let me see. FaceTime me!"

Mary fumbled with her phone and then held it away from her. "Can you see?"

"Ooooh, very sophisticated for a parents' school committee. Black on brown on black. I like it! Are there good-looking men on your committee?"

Mary put the phone on the sink. "No! I'm dressed for a lunch afterward."

"With whom, my dear?"

Mary put on her earrings. "With a twenty-five-year-old man who wants some financial advice."

"You go, girl! That will teach Paul to leave you alone to play."

"I'm kidding. It's a former client. That's all I have now. Former clients, ever since the crash."

"Maybe you should wear a push-up bra, even though it's under a camisole."

Mary ignored her. "Remember, we have lunch on Thursday. You can tell me all about the actor/lizard friend." Mary noticed the time. "I have to go."

"Love you." Janet dropped off. Mary was running late. She stuffed her notes into her purse and took one last look in the mirror. Mary wore her war paint well. She moved the bottom of her bra, and slivers of her pale breasts appeared beneath the camisole. She smiled—Janet was funny.

Six

The next few days flew by in Davos. The congress itself was pure ceremony, where the powerful played a rich man's version of Kumbaya—billionaires talking to millionaires about the working class. The heads of state, CEOs, and celebrities missed all presentations and panels. Paul missed nearly every session except for the one where he was a panelist along with Will.i.am and a ponytailed billionaire entrepreneur. The real World Economic Forum took place at tables in the strategic partners' lounge or in rooms that even Paul did not know about. The world was carved up in half-hour sessions, with rounds of coffee, thousands of handshakes, and many soon-to-be-broken commitments. For one week, everyone agreed to a common self-interest—being at the center of the universe.

By the end of the week, Paul was exhausted. Kristoff counted more than twenty leads and tens of millions of dollars in opportunities. Paul's panel went well, and people came up afterward to ask questions and exchange business cards.

While Paul attended dinners with clients, Kristoff and Roberto scouted the social scene in Davos. On the last night, Paul joined the festivities. The hottest ticket was the McKinsey party. McKinsey was the world's leading strategy consulting firm, witch doctors to the CEOs of the largest companies. More than a thousand people filled the ballroom, dancing to electronic dance music with Skrillex as DJ. Paul leaned against a wall that vibrated from the music. He had a drink in his hand and was letting the alcohol wash away his stress.

"Hi! Having fun?" An attractive woman appeared next to Paul, swaying to the music in a short black skirt.

"Um, yes, I am. Finally able to relax." Paul smiled at her. She was exotic looking, perhaps Filipino or South American. She had long, straight black hair to her shoulders and large, brown eyes. She continued to sway, but when she spoke to him, she had to lean in to speak over the music.

"You don't remember me, do you?" Her smiling red lips framed her white teeth.

"You look familiar." As Paul shouted into her ear, he could smell her perfume.

"We talked after your panel discussion."

"Wait a second, didn't you run something—"

She laughed. "We all run something if we're here, right?"

"I'm sorry."

"I'm Alejandra."

"Paul—"

"I know who you are. But you don't know me." Her lips touched his ear. "I'll stop teasing you. It's unfair. I'm sure you met a lot of people here. I run WAM—Women against Mutilation. We create media and education programs to influence the culture in countries where the mutilation of women's genitals is practiced."

"I remember now. How did you get involved in something like that?"

"I read an article about it in the *Economist*. I was having a bad time at work, here at McKinsey." She waved her hand around the ballroom. "I was burned out, not enjoying myself, and realized none of it mattered."

"So you just walked away?"

"Yep. It didn't matter to me. I was on the fast-track to partner. Left that. Sold my condo. Put my stuff in storage." She deliberately breathed into his ear. "I broke up with my boyfriend. And still don't have one."

"Do you want to step out to the bar so we can actually talk to each other?"

"Sure." She grinned, and he steadied her on her heels as they walked to the bar. "I haven't had too much to drink," she said, as if reading his mind. "It's just, you don't wear four-inch heels in a village in Kenya. But here . . ." They sat down at the bar. "I'm short, and I need the height." She kissed his cheek and whispered in his ear, "And I need to be able to look you in the eyes."

Paul was taken aback by how forward she was, but it was the last night of the WEF, and she had been drinking. She told him how she grew up with immigrant parents from the Philippines and Venezuela in Los Angeles. Her father was a cook and her mother a cleaning lady, and they did everything to make their children successful. Alejandra went to Stanford and Harvard Business School, ending up at McKinsey. She started WAM and raised millions of dollars. When she wasn't fundraising, she was evangelizing to governments, health officials, and tribal chieftains and their influential wives. She had no personal life and was giving her heart and soul to this cause. She had saved the lives of thousands of women and gave tens of thousands of them the opportunity to lead normal lives.

Paul listened intently; he also noticed her gorgeous legs inching out from her short dress as she rocked on the barstool to the music. The bartender refilled their glasses.

"Sometimes, I get tired of the race." She sipped her wine. "And I wonder, What about me? I'm getting too old to have children. I don't have a relationship."

"You're doing amazing things," Paul said.

"Yeah, but I'm always fighting people to do the right thing or kissing peoples' asses for money." She started to tear up.

Paul wiped the tear off her cheek. "So many people are better off because of you. *Alive* because of you."

Alejandra smiled. "This is too serious, isn't it? We need to have some fun." She finished her glass of wine. "Let me go to the bathroom and touch up, and then let's dance, Paul, and forget about all of it. We're at Davos; we're at the center of the universe."

"Yes, we are," Paul said. "Yes, we are."

When she rejoined him on the dance floor, she looked even more beautiful. For the moment, the music lifted the stress Paul felt the last three days. It invoked more of a primitive time, when men gathered around fires, afraid of the dark and just happy to be alive and fed for another day. Paul and Alejandra leaned into each other, moving with the music. Sweat and laughter filled the ballroom.

Paul watched Alejandra's face as she danced. She was intoxicating. She raised her arms to the sky as Skrillex amped the beat just one cycle more, and she spun like a delighted top. Paul thought about the meetings he had with the powerful. He thought about Mary and his son and his obligations to them. He thought about Alejandra, her beauty, purpose, and sacrifice. He thought of all the women who didn't even know that it was Alejandra who had changed their lives. Paul was overtaken with emotion and love for those people and Alejandra and all the goodness that was in the world.

Alejandra asked where Paul was staying. It was much closer than the apartment she was sharing with two other Davos leaders of tomorrow in the next village. She felt warm against him, and he against her. Paul worshipped her, this angel, this giver of life and hope to many, and he respected what she'd given up, what she was and what she could be. And Paul knew he would sleep with her that night.

The music reached a penetrating screech, and suddenly the ballroom lit stark white, washing away the glow of Alejandra's brown eyes and dark skin and black hair. Fog poured down from the ceiling onto the crowd below. Paul stopped dancing and stared at her. She looked ghostly as she spun, unable to stop. And Paul wondered, *Is there such a thing as goodness, charity, and love, or are some of us better than others in hiding our darkness?*

Seven

Paul slithered out of bed like a snake, picking up a bathrobe on his way to the bathroom. He looked back at Alejandra; the curtains to the window were only partially closed, and the light from outside was spilling over her body, covered by a sheet but for one dark-skinned leg, dangling off the side of the bed. He felt like a voyeur, looking at her sleeping as he closed the bathroom door.

When he returned, Alejandra was awake, lying on the bedcovers in a bathrobe, looking disheveled in a sexy way. She smiled. "I ordered some coffee and rolls. I hope that's OK; I'm a little hung over." She left the bed and gave him a kiss on the cheek on her way to the bathroom. He heard the shower running. Paul looked at her clothes strewn on the floor, then looked at his watch—he had a little time before he had to leave for the airport. But he needed time to shower and pack up. How does he gracefully exit?

The doorbell rang; the coffee and rolls had arrived. Paul sat in bed, propped against a pillow, and sipped his coffee. He looked out the window at the blue skies and tried to remember the previous night's conversation. She ran an NGO focused on helping women. She met him at one of the Davos panels and then at the party. They danced. She didn't want to take the forty-minute trip to the apartment she was sharing with two other Davos pioneers. His hotel was a block away. She asked him no questions about his personal life. He offered no information. They made love quickly but passionately. There was a used condom next to the bed. Paul remembered she was very in charge of what was going to happen. And then they fell asleep.

The bathroom door opened, and Alejandra looked fresh as she joined him in bed. She smiled at him expectantly, and he touched her cheek and said, "That was nice."

She held his hand against her cheek and then kissed his palm. "Yes it was. But I barely remember. Remind me what happened."

"Well, we came back—" She touched his mouth with her finger and then opened the palm of her other hand, which held a fresh condom.

"Remind me what happened again." Alejandra pulled his robe open, and her hand went down his stomach. In no time, she was on top of him, guiding him into her, touching herself as she eased into a dance-like motion. Paul watched her face. Her eyes were closed and faced the ceiling, her expression wavering between a smile and grimace as she rocked back and forth as if still hearing the deep bass of the Skrillex music. After both climaxed, she rolled off and moved next to Paul. "I'm hungry!" She put a croissant on Paul's chest and smiled at him as she bit into it. "I hope you didn't mind, but I needed to feel you inside me again. Last night is still a little hazy, and it's been a while for me. Not a lot of sex in Africa—too hot."

"It must be tough."

"Spending days with women whose genitalia have been mutilated can reduce the female libido, for sure. But let's not talk about that. Let's talk about Paul. Are you married?"

"Now you ask."

"Not a great thing to bring up when you want to fuck someone you're dancing with. And I know you are."

"I'm what?"

"Married."

Alejandra finished her croissant quickly, and Paul brushed the crumbs off his chest and turned on his side toward her. "How did you know I'm married?"

"Because of the puppy look—the big eyes and tongue hanging out, begging for a treat. That's what married men look like when they had too much to drink and are dancing with a pretty girl—or any girl."

"Ok, I get it."

"Single men are like tigers. They don't fool around. They see you, and they want to feed. Their jaws lock on the back of your neck, and they shake you, pull you into the bush, and when they're done, leave you there, bruised and battered. They slink away from you, walking backward, joining their tiger friends in the crowd, snarling at you as if to say, 'You're a meal to me, bitch.'"

"Sounds like you've met some tigers in Africa."

"I've met more in my civilized, Western life." Alejandra ran her hand along Paul's face. "I prefer puppies to tigers, that's all. Especially if I only have one night before I go back to the real jungle."

"Well, I feel very lucky."

"I have a feeling you are a lucky guy, Paul."

"I have to catch a flight soon, so I need to shower and dress. You don't have to leave until you're ready." Paul kissed her.

"What's your next stop—post-Alejandra?"

"Actually, I'm going to see some friends in a little village in England, called Glastonbury. It's near London."

"That sounds nice. What's there? Other than your friends."

"I've never been there, but I'm told it is a New Agey, spiritual place. Full of strange people who act out their fantasies. They can be witches, Druids, elves, or psychics. They even have soul readers!"

"I love that kind of stuff. I believe in magic, you know." Paul loved the way Alejandra's eyes sparkled as she talked. "You and I meeting each other last night—that wasn't an accident; it was magic. My being on a safari and meeting the girl in the village who nearly died from her mutilation. My new boyfriend leaving me to date his boss at work. None of it just happens. Everything has a purpose. Don't you think?"

"I don't know. I've never really thought—"

Alejandra sat up in bed and gave Paul a seductive look that reminded him of when he first saw her. "What do you think I would be in Glastonbury?"

Paul did not want to leave, but he said, "I need to take a quick shower and pack."

"Can I have the rest of your croissant? I'm famished."

"Sure, and stay in bed. I like looking at you in this robe." He touched her hair. "Your black hair against the white robe. Your dark skin."

"Go shower. You'll be late and blame me."

While showering, Paul thought about Mary. She would be asleep now. Paul had checked his cell phone, and she had not called—she was probably pissed off at him. He turned off the shower, threw on his bathrobe, and opened the bathroom door.

"I know what I want to be." Paul was startled, almost forgetting that Alejandra was there. She was sitting in a chair, sipping a coffee. She was fully dressed, looking as if she was ready for another party.

"You're dressed!"

She stood up and walked toward Paul. "I want to be a female magician." She moved Paul toward the bed and sat him down, pulling his bathrobe down around his waist and untying the belt. "I can do magic tricks." She leaned over him and whispered in his ear while touching his lap, "I only brought two condoms with me." Her hair hung around Paul's face, and its smell reminded him of their meeting at the bar. "But I want you to come again so you will always remember me. So now I will do a magic trick." She kissed him lightly on the lips and then his chest. "You do nothing, just lie there." Alejandra kneeled. She glanced up at him, smiled, and then pushed him gently down on the bed. "You are the magician's assistant, like the girl in the box about to be sawed in half." She moved her head toward his stomach. "You're trembling in anticipation at what Alejandra the Magnificent is about to do!"

Paul felt her head below his stomach, and her teeth traced a line across his body like a saw. Paul lay on his back, facing the ceiling, and he closed his eyes. It was dark as if he was in a box, and he forgot about everything except what he was feeling in that moment. He felt as if he would explode, jumping out of the box as it shattered. His senses left him for a moment, and he could not see or feel or hear anything but the faint sensation of a man and woman touching. And then the explosion and the box shattered into pieces around him.

He was floating in space, with nothing supporting him. No wires, no illusions, it was Paul floating as Paul. Time stood still. He heard a faint thump of a door. He hesitated, not wanting to open his eyes, but he did. He was lying on the bed staring at the ceiling. He raised his head, looking for Alejandra. She was gone. The magic show was over.

Eight

Edward had picked up Paul at the train station near Glastonbury, and they were nearing the village proper. "Davos sounds like fun. Meeting all those important people. Are you ready to rejoin the common folk?" Edward teased.

"As long as I don't have to present any PowerPoints."

"Maybe after you've had a few pints." The car turned the corner and pulled into the driveway of the bed-and-breakfast. "Here we are— Turnips, the finest shelter in Glastonbury." Edward saw Paul staring at the hill rising behind their house. "And that's the Tor."

The Tor rose more than five hundred feet above the village of Glastonbury and the surrounding countryside. A tower, the remains of a medieval church, stood on top. The Tor beckoned to Paul on this early spring evening, an energetic gravity that pulled him in. Normally, Paul barely acknowledged anything around him as he raced from one meeting to another, but now he stood transfixed and had no idea why. It looked ominous in the dusk light, as if it were lying in wait. Paul felt a tinge of fear, almost expecting the Tor to move toward him like a giant earth creature erupting out of the ground.

Edward interrupted Paul's reverie. "Let me take you to your room. Jeanne should be back from her errands shortly." Paul followed Edward into the bed-and-breakfast, but his eyes were drawn toward the Tor, which seemed to be staring back at him.

"I'd like to learn more about the Tor. What's so special about it?"

"We have books for the guests," Edward said as he opened the door and followed Paul into the living room. He ran his fingers across a row of books and pulled one out. "Here's a good primer on Glastonbury. There's a whole chapter about the Tor. Why don't you freshen up and then come down for a cocktail?"

Paul went upstairs to his room. He knew his in-box was piling up following all the business meetings he had in Davos. After washing up, he settled on the bed with his computer but noticed the book about Glastonbury. He could see the Tor from his window. He shut his computer and opened the book to the chapter on the Tor. People had been gathering at the Tor for millennia. The Tor was also referred to as the Isle of Avalon. It was believed to be the entrance to Annwn, or Avalon, the land of the fairies. In Arthurian legend, it was the home of the Lady of Avalon and the other goddesses and high priests. They supported King Arthur, but as Christianity suppressed pagan beliefs, the Lady of Avalon escaped with her followers to the Otherworld.

Paul noticed it was time to go downstairs. Should he call Mary before? It had been twenty-four hours. Perhaps he should wait until after dinner, so he had more time. He looked out the window of his room. It was now so dark; you couldn't see anything. Streetlamps marked the road leading to the Tor.

Edward shouted from downstairs, "Paul, the pub is doing an all-hands alert. We're missing in action." Paul took a minute before descending to the living room. Jeanne was back and gave him a big hug. "Edward left without us. Hurry. We have to catch up."

Jeanne led Paul through the village. It was night, and the shops were closed. But some display windows were partially lit, and Paul glimpsed inside the shop windows—witch paraphernalia, goddess gowns, Native American headdresses, crystal rocks—it was a spiritual window-shopping experience. Paul peeked into each window quickly as they tried to catch up to Edward. "What's this?" Paul had stopped in front of a shop dedicated to fairies. Small ceramic fairies hovered above life-size mannequins wearing revealing dresses and wings on their back in forest settings.

"It's a fairy store," Jeanne explained.

"I remember a movie about fairies—"

"You must be parched," Edward's voice boomed as he stuck his head out from the doorway of the pub just ahead, holding two pints in his hands.

Jeanne shook her head, grabbed Paul's hand, and pulled him toward the pub. "Come on. We better get there before he drinks both of them."

A large fireplace greeted them as they entered the Rifleman Arms. There was a good crowd, and their voices competed for airtime at high decibels. They found an open table, and Edward started telling stories that Jeanne had heard many times before.

Edward told the story of a guest who came for a week and dove into every sort of treatment, from soul reading to Reiki to ear candling. As the days passed, his eyes became brighter, his hair more disheveled, his words less coherent. He asked for his room to be cleaned several times a day. He asked for lunch and dinner to be served despite the fact that Turnips only served breakfast. They were counting the days before he was scheduled to leave.

One night, Edward and Jeanne retired before this guest returned. As they were falling asleep, the sound of a man moaning carried up to their bedroom window. "What the hell," Edward said as he reached for his robe and cricket bat.

"Be careful, Edward," Jeanne mumbled, half asleep. "You don't know what's down there."

"I have a pretty good idea," Edward grumbled. He descended the stairs, cricket bat in hand, and found the guest in the back garden. He lay on his back, moaning to the sky. "What are you doing, man?" Edward demanded. "It's very late, and you're disturbing us and the other guests."

The man patted the ground next to him. "Join me. Look into the sky, and tell me what you see."

"You're mad," said Edward.

"Please."

Edward reluctantly lowered his substantial body to the ground and lay next to him. The man started moaning louder. He clutched Edward's hand. "Do you have a drum?"

"Why?"

"We need to play for the Druids."

"That's it." Edward struggled to his feet. "Let me explain the mystical ways of Turnips. You are a guest. You do not disturb your neighbors at all hours of the night, you do not ask for meals that are not served. Read the sign." Edward pointed to the large sign at the corner of their property. "'Bed-and-Breakfast.' So there's your bed." Edward angrily motioned toward the window of a room upstairs. "And breakfast is served in the morning, after which, I would ask that you kindly leave us and take your pilgrimage elsewhere."

Edward finished his story with his laugh, which grew into a chorus as others in the restaurant laughed as well, not knowing why. Jeanne just smiled and shook her head.

The trio headed back to the bed-and-breakfast. Edward wanted to visit another pub for a nightcap, but Jeanne steered him home. As Paul neared Turnips, he sensed the Tor's presence in front of him in the black night.

Jeanne put Edward to bed and rejoined Paul to say good night. "I'm so glad you came!"

"I wish I had more time here. I have to come back," Paul said. "I really didn't see much in the dark."

"You should have stayed at least one more day."

"I was barely able to squeeze this in."

"Perhaps, if you wake up early tomorrow morning, you could take a walk to the top of the Tor. The entrance to the path is very near here. You'll see signs for it." Jeanne pulled a jacket and umbrella from the closet. "Here's Edward's jacket and a brolly. Climb to the top and back, have breakfast with us, and you can still make your flight."

"I might be too tired for that," Paul said.

"Just a thought," Jeanne said with a twinkle in her eye. She watched Paul climb the stairs to his room and turned out the lights when he closed his door. She knew he would wake up early tomorrow. First-time visitors had trouble sleeping in Glastonbury.

The combination of the intensity of Davos and the heavy food and wine at the pub exhausted Paul, and he fell asleep immediately. He woke up a few hours later. Every half hour, he checked the time. He felt wide awake. Finally, at six o'clock in the morning, he decided he would visit the Tor as Jeanne recommended. The fresh air and walk would be a healthy prelude to his flight back to New York.

He put on Edward's oversized coat, which could have wrapped around him twice, and left Turnips, following the signs to the Tor. A gate marked the entrance to the path up the hill. The trail wound upward in a serpentine fashion. It was dawn, foggy, and overcast. As he climbed, he could see the tower ruin at the top of the hill. Sometimes it looked like a pile of stones on a faraway hill; other times, it loomed menacingly above his head, its arched windows peering down at him. He passed a man sitting on a bench, dressed in white, his eyes closed and hands resting on his knees.

Paul shivered. He was not sure if it was the cold morning air or an inexplicable excitement. He reached the top of the hill and stepped into the tower. The roof of the tower was gone, and the early morning light glided down its walls like syrup. Entrances faced east and west, and his eyes followed the light coming from the east, to a small plateau of grass. A dozen women sat in lotus position on blankets, waiting for the sunrise. The world was silent and beautiful.

He looked at his watch. It was time to head back. On his descent, he stopped at the bench, now empty; the man dressed in white was gone. Paul had an urge to sit down, if only for a moment. He imitated the position of the man before him, closing his eyes and putting his hands facing up on his knees. He could hear his heart beat. He thought he could hear the mist rising from the grass around him. He heard the chanting of the women on the top of the hill. Paul lost himself in this quiet cacophony. Then he heard the voice: *Go see the soul reader.* The idea of an uncontrolled voice in his head terrified him. He shook, and for a moment, he thought he would get sick. And then it passed. He opened his eyes. Paul was very late and hurried down the hill toward Turnips.

"Where have you been?" bellowed Edward. "You've missed the opportunity for a genuine English breakfast by the master chef!"

"Sorry, I went to the top of the Tor. It took longer than I thought it would." Paul ran upstairs to quickly pack.

"Did you see any Druids? Any drum beating?" Edward shouted from the hallway.

"No, there were some women sitting on the top of the hill. They were doing some sort of meditation." Paul lugged his bag down the stairs.

"Did they have their clothes on?"

Jeanne came out of the kitchen. "Shame on you, Edward." She slapped Edward's arm, then looked at Paul. "Well? Did they have their clothes on?"

"Yes, of course."

Edward reached for his jacket in the hallway closet, muttering, "Oh, well, then I didn't miss anything."

"Jeanne, I must go, or I will miss my flight. Thank you so much for having me. I enjoyed the dinner and the Tor this morning. I have to come back."

Edward was already loading his bag in the car, yelling through the open back door. "Come on, let's get you home before you end up sleeping on top of the Tor, chanting with the Druids. Mary wouldn't like that."

Edward drove Paul at high speed to the nearby Bristol airport and got him there with barely enough time. Paul settled into his seat, breathing hard, and typed an email on his phone:

Jeanne and Edward,
Thx so much for a wonderful time. I'll be back for my soul reading. What's her name/website?

All the best,
Paul

Jeanne immediately responded,

You're most welcome—we loved having you. I hope you enjoyed your walk up the Tor—not great weather, but sounds like you heard something up there. Christine Lachaud is the soul reader—Google her and you will see her website. You and Mary should think about taking a retreat with Christine. I think it would be life changing.

Stay well and keep in touch with Glastonbury!

Best,
Jeanne

Nine

Paul arrived home from Glastonbury after being away for a week. When he entered the apartment, Mary greeted him. "How was the trip?"

"It was good," Paul said as he threw his bag on the bed. "I really enjoyed the stop-off in Glastonbury and seeing Edward and Jeanne."

"That's right. I forgot you visited them. By the way, I haven't had a chance to shop for food, so it looks like we are having Thai takeout tonight, if that's all right."

"Sure. I'm late for a conference call, though, so I need about an hour before I can eat," Paul said.

"I'm glad you can fit us into your schedule," Mary muttered as Paul closed the door to his office.

Paul listened to his team update him on the progress on his latest project about the emergence of smart devices. It was an intelligent device connected through a network to content sitting on a PC or in a cloud somewhere. Rumors were flying about a new phone that Apple was launching, and lots of Ascendant's clients were trying to figure out what they should be doing. Paul had created a simple graphic—a triangle with the words "device," "network," and "content" at each corner.

He called the concept "trivergence." The idea was that these smart wireless devices will proliferate, starting with smartphones but soon attached to everyone and everything in the world. It would become the "internet of things"—a trillion smart, connected devices. Devices and sensors would be in everything—cars, appliances, clothing, pets, perhaps people. Paul thought trivergence was a significant business opportunity. So did his client. He half-listened as the team argued about deadlines and deliverables. Jack, the team leader, was giving him an update: "We have a least two more weeks of field work before we can even think about writing the report."

Paul's attention drifted to his laptop, where Jeanne's email was open. He clicked on the link to the soul reader's website:

A soul reading contains your own universal wisdom. It brings you the answers and insights into how things work for you in daily life, in the way you think, and on a heart and soul level too. When you understand your Self, life becomes easy.

A fight broke out on the call. "The earliest I can complete the interviews is the end of this week. I can't even get people to return my phone calls."

"That's not good enough," said another team member.

Paul looked at a photo of the soul reader—Christine Lachaud. She had blonde, curly hair; large green eyes; and a smile revealing beautiful white teeth. She looked unusual, but in an attractive, not scary way.

Paul navigated the website while listening to his team continue the debate. He clicked on her email contact.

Jack appealed, "Paul, you need to jump in here. If we can't complete the research, you won't be able to make the presentation in Barcelona at the end of the month. What do you want to do?"

That's right, Paul thought, *I have to be in Barcelona in a few weeks. Maybe I can return via London and visit Glastonbury again.*

"Paul, are you there?"

"Yes," Paul replied. "I'm comfortable that we know our story line at this point. You guys have enough material to do a first draft. Send it to me, and I'll take it from there. We'll incorporate any additional research at the very end."

Cynthia, the marketing director, jumped in. "Remember, I need lead time with internal PR to get approval for anything we're issuing as a press release or public presentation. Can we talk about the overall theme now? Because I'd like to start to socialize the idea with our friendlies in the press."

Paul had started an email to Christine:

Christine,

My name is Paul Moore, and I live in New York City. I am a friend of Jeanne and Edward Clarke. Jeanne had encouraged me to visit Glastonbury, which I did yesterday. Jeanne also encouraged me to have a soul reading with you.

Paul reluctantly came back to the call. "OK, give the team the date when we need to finalize the material for approval, and we will work back from there."

Mary walked into the office and put a plate of pineapple chicken and rice under his nose. Paul muted the call. "Thanks, I'm just finishing. Will be out in a minute." Mary didn't look convinced as she left the office, closing the door behind her. "Let's think about the theme. I don't like 'internet of things.' What are these things? And how does it relate to trivergence?"

"I agree. Suggestions?" Cynthia asked.

Paul had a revelation. "This might work. Or maybe it's crazy. Why don't we call these devices 'tridgets.' They aren't just any devices; they're triverged devices, with the properties we discussed. Over the next twenty years, the world will make a trillion tridgets, with huge implications for technology and every other industry—health care, transportation, retail, you name it."

"A trillion tridgets," Cynthia said. "I like the sound of it. We'll have to explain it, of course. It sounds like widgets or gadgets, but I think people will get it."

Paul was eager to get off the phone. If he could make it to the dining table before Mary and Simon finished eating, he could get partial credit.

"We're good to go," Jim said.

Paul signed off the call and returned to his note to Christine:

I'm not very religious and pretty agnostic about spiritual things in general, so this is all new to me. But I'd like to have a reading.

In my business, I travel to Europe often and may be passing through London the last week in May. Is there any chance that you're available at that time? I would be taking a train that Tuesday morning from London.

Please let me know if it can be arranged, and I look forward to meeting you.

Best regards,

Paul

Paul looked at his remaining emails—they could wait. He took his half-eaten plate of food into the dining room, but no one was there. Mary was sitting in the TV room, sipping a glass of wine and watching the news. Simon's bedroom door was closed as usual. He reheated his plate of food, poured himself a glass of wine, and joined Mary on the couch. "What did I miss?"

"Simon got a C on his Latin test. You should talk to him. He didn't want to go to school this morning."

"OK. How's work?" Paul knew work was a safer topic than Simon.

"Not great. All my clients are pissed. They lost a lot in the crash. They blame me, withdraw their money, and give it to another advisor who will put it in another fund that got killed in the crash. But they feel better because they did something."

"Isn't it a zero-sum game? Why don't you just get new clients who are pissed at their old advisors? That would make up for the ones you lost."

"That's not how it works." Mary shook her head and sighed as if she were talking to a child. Paul thought it *was* how it works, but he chose not to push that button.

"I'm feeling tired. I think I'll take a shower and call it a night. It's three a.m. my time."

"I'll join you shortly," Mary said. "I'm tired too. Say good night to Simon. He needs a little support right now."

When Paul knocked on Simon's door, he heard his son say, "Come in." As Paul opened the door, he saw Simon close his laptop and sit up. Paul flopped on a beanbag chair as Simon said, "What's up? How was your trip?"

"Good. I went to this conference and was on a panel with Will.i.am."

"Really!" Simon looked impressed. "That's rad. Did he perform?"

"No. We talked about technology and how it was changing the music industry."

Simon nodded, then changed the subject: "I'm thinking I might want to major in theology when I go to college."

"Really? Where is this coming from?"

"First, I come from a family of ministers—"

"One minister," Paul corrected.

"Second, I can put to use the Latin I've studied for five years."

"If you get your grades up."

"Mom told you?"

"Yes."

"So much for our little secret," Simon hissed.

"We don't keep secrets in our family."

Simon laughed. "Oh, really? You spend too much time on the road, Dad. The secrets are piling up here."

Paul yawned. "We need to get to bed; otherwise, I'd grill you until you tell me all your secrets. For now, promise me this—you'll get some Latin tutoring, and you'll practice the music you will be performing at Juilliard, not Jethro Tull, OK?"

"It's a deal."

Paul got up and ran his hand through Simon's hair. "And you'll get a haircut this week; it's really thick."

Simon pushed his hand away. "Dad, my hair's fine. Get out of here—I have to study."

"I forgot to mention—I also went to Glastonbury to see Edward and Jeanne."

"Really? Is that where they have the music festival?"

"Yes. How do you know about that?"

"I saw it on a YouTube video of Jethro Tull performing at the Glastonbury festival years ago," Simon said. "What's it like?"

"It was interesting. I was there for less than twenty-four hours."

"Cool." Simon opened up his laptop. "I'll look it up."

Paul yawned and absentmindedly patted Simon on the head one last time, saying under his breath, "I might go there again." He reached the door of the bedroom.

"Good night, Dad."

Paul shut Simon's door behind him. He finished his email, took a shower, and crawled into bed. He turned out the lights. In the darkness, he thought back to his morning climb on the Tor. It seemed like ages ago. He remembered sitting on the bench and becoming aware of everything. Now lying in bed, he became aware of his body—its warmth, the fresh smell of his skin, and his damp hair against the pillow. He heard Mary quietly slip into bed beside him. He wrapped his arm around her and became aroused as he gently caressed her.

Mary rolled toward him. They embraced and made love—quickly but gently. Both satisfied, they lay on their backs in the darkness. "Well, that was a pleasant surprise," Mary whispered. "I thought you were tired."

"I am," Paul said. "But you felt so warm when you crawled into bed."

"You never answered my question: How were Jeanne and Edward?"

"They're good. It was too brief a visit, though," Paul said. "I didn't even get to see Glastonbury. I was thinking of going back to spend a day or two there and maybe see the soul reader that Jeanne mentioned. Would you like to come? Jeanne said it could change our lives."

"Are you kidding me?" Mary shook her head. "With work and the issues with Simon at school and getting the summer house ready, no way." She rubbed Paul's chest playfully. "Let me know when you're going to St. Bart's, and I'll come."

Paul smiled. "I understand. I might stop by the next time I get to London."

"What does a soul reader do?"

"I don't know. I guess she's like a fortune-teller?"

Mary sat up in bed. "I think it's strange that you're going to this little village to see someone, and you don't even know what she does."

"I don't know why I'm drawn to the place again. Jeanne said the soul reader changed people's lives. One was a businessman like me."

Mary reached for her phone. "What's her name?"

"Who?"

"The soul reader. I want to look her up."

Paul hesitated. "Her first name is Christine. I just know her website."

"What's that?"

"Don't worry about it." Paul patted her arm.

"I'm not worried." Mary smiled. "What is it? Why won't you tell me?"

Paul muttered the web address and rolled over, facing away from Mary.

Mary's eyes widened. "Paul, she's a dead ringer for Jenny. What the hell."

"Really? I didn't notice."

Years ago, Mary discovered Paul was having an affair with a waitress/aspiring actress, Jenny. Jenny offered a ditzy package of curly, blonde hair and an *artiste* sensibility. Paul offered Jenny a respite from sharing a studio with another starving artist in the backwaters of Brooklyn next to the Gowanus Canal. When Mary found Paul's hidden email account that documented their hotel rendezvous, she was struck by how often Jenny referred to using the minibar—her favorites included minibottles of Stolichnaya Vodka, honey-roasted nuts, and jelly beans. If not for Paul's betrayal, Mary would have enjoyed reading their email exchange. Paul's soft-core fantasy riffs were answered by Jenny's *New York Times* book review–like assessment of the hotel room and its minibar. Mary sometimes wondered if they even shared the same room. And how did Jenny maintain her skinny fucking figure despite the allure of the minibars? Did she do cleanses in between their trysts?

Marriage therapy did not help. Mary carried forward no illusions about Paul's ability to be monogamous; instead, she chose to question her own. Maybe he and Edward were planning a weekend of horse racing and pubs, and he didn't want to tell her. Or maybe he found a foxy little witch in Glastonbury. This could very well be the next Jenny.

Her voice rose. "How could you not notice? The hair, the eyes . . . I'm not comfortable with this."

"It's a completely different situation." Paul hoped they could exit this conversation before they fell back into the circular discussions that made marriage therapy sessions so painful. "The resemblance between Jenny and Christine is a coincidence, pure and simple. I didn't even know what she looked like when I asked Jeanne for her contact information."

"You know how uncomfortable I am when you are on the road. I have no idea what you are doing, who you are seeing. And now you're seeing this soul reader that looks like someone you had an affair with?"

"Call Jeanne. She'll vouch for her."

"I don't know Jeanne that well. Besides, I'm not dragging a stranger into our marital problems." Paul put his arm around her and pressed against her back. She liked feeling him against her. "I'm just uncomfortable. You can understand why, can't you?"

Paul felt her relax. Mary knew this discussion was just beginning, but she also was tired.

Paul murmured, "I understand. Let's get some sleep. We can talk about this tomorrow." Despite the tense conversation, they fell asleep holding each other as if desperately wanting to believe there was something to hold on to.

Paul's last thought was the email he received earlier that evening:

Paul,

It was good to hear from you, and of course I know Jeanne and Edward well. I would be pleased to give you a soul reading on May 28. Is 11:00 a.m. too early?

If that date and time works, I will send you some materials for preparation. Nothing too hard, just some exercises that will ensure we have a productive session.

Blessings,

Christine

Ten

Paul's car neared his terminal at JFK when his phone rang. It was Susan, his marketing manager, and she sounded panicked. "Paul, I have some bad news. We did a trademark search for 'tridget.'"

"Yeah?"

"We discovered there's an entertainer—a dwarf—who also uses the name Tridget as part of her act."

Paul was nonplussed. "So what? She's using it for a different purpose. We're not talking about an internet of a trillion dwarfs; we're talking about wireless devices! I think we're OK."

"But, Paul," Susan said, "this woman is a porn star."

Paul's head started spinning—time for damage control. The study and press releases were done. He was speaking tomorrow at a conference in Barcelona. "Well, that's a little . . . embarrassing. But none of our clients are going to accuse us of leveraging a dwarf porn star brand!" This was a serious issue, but Paul couldn't help but smile.

Susan continued, "I agree, but think about it—because it is a new name for something, a new idea, people will Google it. And when they do, they will see a page full of links to that porn star—websites and pictures. Paul, it isn't pretty. Even if we optimize the placement of our site, her stuff will overwhelm it."

Paul's car was pulling up to the terminal, and he was already running late for the flight. "Susan, let me think about it, but I don't think I've a choice. It's in our presentation; we're locked and loaded. I think we'll be OK. Let's do the release tomorrow morning, European time, and hope no one decides to make fun of the name. Is the *Financial Times* still interested in an interview?"

"Yes," Susan said unenthusiastically. "We scheduled something right after your speech. He's doing a broader story but may give us a quote regarding the trillion tridgets idea. Paul?"

"Yeah?"

"I'm sorry we fucked up."

*   *   *

Paul made his flight. He had millions of miles on American, so they held the plane at the gate. In his seat on the plane, he looked out the window, waiting for the Ambien to kick in. Fields of clouds hovered in the sky, pink in the dusk light. This potentially public fiasco could be a career killer. Why didn't marketing check the tridget name before now? Was Susan's boss, Cynthia, playing him? When will she find out? Does she already know? Twenty-five years invested in a career brought down by a dwarf with large breasts. Paul ordered a double scotch. Nothing he could do in the air except hope the plane would never land. He reached for his computer, looking for a distraction.

Christine had emailed Paul instructions in preparation for the soul reading. "No drugs or alcohol for a couple of days before the reading." (*Already broke that rule*, he thought.) "Imagine lying on a blue orb, and silently repeat, 'I open my heart and listen to what it says.'"

Paul reclined his seat, closed his eyes, tried to imagine an orb, and decided it looked like a spherical marshmallow. *I open my heart and listen to what it says.* Paul's mind raced. He could not forget this recent crisis. The blue orb he imagined now had a trampy dwarf bouncing on it, laughing at him. He opened his eyes.

Did he really have time for the stopover in Glastonbury? Maybe he should cancel the appointment with Christine. Her instructions said she would tune into his soul even before he arrives. What if Christine could see the porn star sitting on the orb—what would she think of that? Paul closed his eyes again. He found it impossible to visualize a dwarf-less orb. What was the mantra he was supposed to repeat? Gradually, the Ambien kicked in. Everything—the orb, the dwarf, and the mantra—disappeared, and he escaped into a deep sleep.

Eleven

"Hello?" Paul answered groggily. He turned around to look at the clock on the bedside table—two o'clock in the morning.

"We dodged a bullet!"

"Susan?" Paul was staying at the Savoy Hotel in London.

"Sorry to wake you, Paul, but I thought you'd want to know. The *Financial Times* article just went online, and no mention of 'tridget.' You have three great quotes." Susan started reading from the article excitedly. Paul was too sleepy to feel any emotion other than relief. The presentation in Barcelona went very well, and none of the online press coverage used the *tridget* term. The *FT* interview was the last potential shoe to drop. But he still had to navigate the internal political minefield. A number of his Ascendant colleagues learned about Tridget the porn star, and he was being bombarded with filthy links and jokes. Not good. Enemies like Cynthia could exploit this. "Should I check in tomorrow? You sound tired."

"Sure." Then Paul remembered. "Actually, I've got a full-day client commitment tomorrow. Text me if we have to talk, OK?"

"I don't know how you do it."

"Do what?"

"Keep your cool. Give a great pitch, knowing the sky could fall on you any second. I guess that's why you make the big bucks."

"It's all an act. I almost pissed my pants today."

Susan laughed for the first time. "I'll try to forget you said that."

"I will too. Good night." Susan could not have called at a worse time. He had been visualizing the blue orb and kept trying to push Tridget off it—to no avail. He repeated the mantra "I open my heart and listen to what it says" over and over—until he fell asleep. Paul's last image was himself, barely a speck, sinking into very large blue orb. Until Susan's call woke him.

The Soul Reading

Twelve

The train pulled into the station near Glastonbury. Edward was there to greet him again. "You're so kind to pick me up. I could've taken a taxi," Paul said.

"Nonsense. We're full service. Besides which, it got me out of cleaning the kitchen after breakfast!" Edward loaded his bag in the boot. As they drove toward the village, Edward became more serious. "Jeanne asked that I drop you off in front of Christine's house for the reading. I'll take your bag back to the bed-and-breakfast. Here are the keys to your room and the front door. Jeanne says that you'll want some time for yourself after. In fact"—Edward slowed down the car and pointed—"there's a very old, small chapel down that alley that she recommended you visit afterward. She said it's quiet and you can be alone. It's only steps from Christine's house."

"OK." Edward's serious tone surprised Paul.

"Now we'd love to have dinner with you tonight, but you may just want to be on your own or stay in your room—feel perfectly free to do what makes you comfortable. We understand fully. We'll be downstairs, and if you don't appear by six or so, we'll assume that you won't be joining us."

Paul grew nervous. "I came here to see you guys. What am I going to do all day?"

"I'm only telling you what Jeanne said. She's sent a number of people to see Christine." Edward meandered through the village, pointing out other places Paul might visit. The car came to a stop in front of a townhouse. Paul realized that for once, he didn't have his game face on; in fact, he must have looked worried, because as Paul got out of the car, Edward smiled warmly and said, "She doesn't bite." When Paul shut the door, Edgar added, "Her dog does." Then he drove off, turning the corner with a slight squeal of the tires.

Paul stood in front of the townhouse. It seemed like only yesterday since his last visit to Glastonbury. And now he was standing at the front door of a soul reader in the middle of the village because a voice told him he should do it.

Paul grew dizzy and started to hyperventilate. Yesterday, he gave a presentation to thousands and kept his cool. Now he couldn't catch his breath.

What was happening to him? Paul was seeking something, though he didn't know what. But he believed a soul reader might. It was that simple and that bizarre.

A small garden fronted the townhouse. Thin rods sprung from the ground, holding glass renderings of butterflies, angels, and stars. Heart-shaped stones littered the ground. It was a peaceful setting.

Paul looked at the red door and its brass knocker in the shape of an angel. It was eleven o'clock. He knocked.

Thirteen

He could hear a dog barking on the other side of the door, but no one answered. He stepped back and peered at the windows of the three-story townhouse. Large pieces of blue and white crystals sat on the ground-level windowsill like a row of pigeons. A wooden statue of a woman looked down from the second floor, her hands extended, palms facing upward, as if reaching for Paul. In the third-floor window, glass angels dangled from delicate silver chains. They shimmered in the sunlight, an array of colors. Paul wondered if Christine ran a shop where she sold these items. Was that part of her business? She does a soul reading and then tries to sell trinkets to make more money? *I hate to shop*, Paul thought to himself. He looked at his watch—11:03.

Should he knock again? Maybe she wasn't there and he should just walk away. He could tell Jeanne and Edward that Christine didn't answer. Maybe seeing her was a dumb idea. He felt silly.

Paul jumped when the door opened. She stood in the doorway. Christine was a tall, striking figure with blonde, curly—Medusa-like— hair. Her skin was pale and translucent. She was perfectly made up, black eyelashes, bright-red lips, and silver jewelry hanging everywhere.

She wore a loose tunic blouse with tights. Paul was drawn to her green eyes, which were staring intently at him. Paul hesitated and then reached out to shake her hand. She held his hand in both of hers and smiled. "You made it. Please, come in. If you don't mind, could you leave your shoes at the door?" Paul removed them. "I'm so happy to meet you. You found my place all right?"

Paul tried to be casual. "Actually, I came here from the train station. Edward dropped me off. He was kind enough to take my bags to the bed-and-breakfast."

"Excellent. Edward and Jeanne are delightful people, aren't they? Come, the room where I do my work is upstairs."

Paul followed her and entered a small room at the top of the stairs. They sat down across from each other. Paul looked around. The walls were covered with pictures and sculptures of Mother Mary. A massage table was in the middle of the room. To Paul, it looked as ominous as the trolley in an operating room. He realized Christine was staring intently at him, smiling.

"I've never done anything like this before," Paul confessed. "I mean, I'm not really sure what to expect. I've always been skeptical about anything religious or spiritual—I'm not really sure why I'm here."

Christine said, "That's not unusual. Many people come here and have no idea why. They're drawn here. Relax, and know that you are here for a reason."

But Paul couldn't relax. Usually he knew exactly what was going on and what he should be doing. This situation was different. Why did he even care? He would probably be embarrassed by the whole thing and move on. No one would see what happened. No one even had to know about it. He was sitting with a strange woman in her house. What could she possibly do to him?

There were shelves full of heart-shaped stones, geometric symbols, and figurines. He didn't notice any price tags. "You've got a lot of interesting things here," Paul said. "And hanging in the windows, scattered in the garden."

Christine laughed. "Yes, too many things! My clients send me mementos. They know I draw energy from Mother Mary and her angels. And that I love heart-shaped stones. I can't throw them out. They support my energy." *OK*, Paul thought, *so she isn't a retailer.*

"I tried to do the meditation that you sent me," Paul said. "But two nights ago, I was on a plane, and it was hard to concentrate. And last night I fell right to sleep."

"That's OK," Christine said. "The meditation helps open you up— like a flower to sunshine."

"What do you need to know about me?" Paul asked. "Has Jeanne told you anything?"

She shook her head, smiling as if talking to a child with too many questions. "No, I haven't talked to Jeanne for months. What I need to know about you I've already sensed or will discover during the reading." Could Christine read his mind? "Let me explain what's going to happen. You'll lie facedown on the table, and I'll cover you with a blanket. I'll say a brief prayer and give you an image to visualize and a mantra to repeat in your mind silently. Then I'll gently make small circles on your back and head and tell you what I see there. At some point, I'll also use the water from the basin—it's sacred water from the Chalice Well. I put a little bit on your clothing and your head. At all times, you should feel comfortable. I'll be talking and telling you what I see. When I'm silent, I haven't gone anywhere; I'm just looking and listening. You may not understand everything that you're hearing, and you'll forget some of what's been said. That's normal. I record the entire session and send you a copy. You can and should listen to the reading. Listening repeatedly will reinforce the messages and further open up your heart and soul. Do you understand? Are you comfortable?"

Paul was trying to follow her words, but he was really only hearing her voice. It was mesmerizing. It was as if her voice jumped from her lips into his head without crossing the air between them. "What do you talk about—the future?"

Christine smiled and motioned toward the massage table. "It's better for us to begin before we run out of time." Christine seemed highly confident about what was about to happen even if he wasn't. Nonetheless, as he lay on the table and she covered him with a blanket, he began to relax. "For the treatment today, I want to focus on your soul and its needs. I can hear it speaking to me already." She put her hand on the small of his back.

Paul closed his eyes and listened to her voice as she said a prayer to Mother Mary and her angels. She made small circles on his back with her hand, sometimes pausing as if contemplating what was there. He listened to her words, drifting in and out. Her presence became overwhelmingly intimate, as if she were the blood in his veins and the breath in his lungs, a strange but beautiful feeling.

She spoke, "In the first chakra, I see darkness and a candle burning. The flame is nearly out. It's your soul. You must nurture yourself or you will become sick. For too long, you have not listened to yourself." The images she described were like a vivid dream. He could see and feel what she was saying.

"In the second chakra, I see a dark house with shuttered windows. A dusty attic with closed boxes scattered on its floor. The air is stifling." Paul saw himself bending over one of the boxes in the attic, trying to pull off the tape. It was very dusty and hard to breathe. Paul finally let go, floating in her spell. His eyes filled with tears. He was bobbing in a dark sea, barely able to keep his head above water. "Now I see you are crying, which is good. It's OK to cry." Paul's nervousness gave into a profound sadness as he watched his life fly by like a silent movie. All the effort, all the success, all the excess took a toll on the part of him that had no voice—until now.

"In the third chakra, I see nature bringing you back to life." Christine dipped her hands in the basin next to the bed and gently rubbed the water on his forehead and his back. "This water will help you nourish your inner self." Paul was barely following Christine's words. What was a chakra? Where did she say the water came from? "I see a garden or a place with trees where you can listen to yourself. Ancient wisdom . . . turtles . . . and a raven. Maybe snakes . . ." she almost hissed.

Christine paused for minutes at a time. "Your partner will sense your change, and it will change her . . . not in the same way—differently. Your son is an old soul and is a window into yourself."

Christine moved her hands to Paul's chest. "In your heart chakra, I see betrayal. Early in your life, your friends betrayed you. There's a lack of trust as a result . . . in your own feelings. This is important.

"I see Mother Mary coming toward you. She holds your hands and looks into your eyes. You cannot look away. She tells you she will fill your heart and soul with her great feminine energy. 'I am everywhere,' she says to you. 'I'm in nature. I'm in strangers you will meet. I am in the white morning mist that cleanses you, restores you.'"

Her voice and energy activated feelings in Paul that had been asleep for most of his adult life. Unlike his unsuccessful attempts to visualize lying on an orb, Paul now saw everything Christine described. It was as if she found an old eight-millimeter movie projector in his attic and turned it on after many years. Agnostic Paul stood in front of Mother Mary, and his sadness gave way to a great joy, like a shaft of light emerging from the horizon during a sunrise. The experience was powerful, wrapping him in a whirlpool of profound memories— being born, falling in and out of love with his first wife, falling in love with Mary, the birth of Simon, and the soul reading. Christine whispered a prayer to herself, and the soul reading ended.

"Take your time. When you are ready, sit up slowly," she said. Paul didn't want to move. But he became self-conscious, knowing he'd shared so much with a stranger. She had no idea what she had done, what she touched upon. If she could bottle it, she would own the world, he thought. He opened his eyes and slowly sat up. Christine was sitting on the couch, looking at him. "How do you feel?"

"I'm cold, actually." He shivered.

Christine put a blanket around his shoulders. "There was a lot of bad energy in you. Feel my hands." Paul held her hands, and they were hot as if she had a severe fever. "That's normal. There was a lot of stuff in there." Paul did not want to let go of those magic hands.

Paul was, atypically, at a loss for words. "That was very nice." Christine laughed gently. Paul felt he had just lost his spiritual virginity. "I feel good, very good. But I also feel sad."

"Why sad?"

"All those years wasted." Paul felt his eyes water. "I've been racing toward something. I don't even know why. Neglecting everyone around me, including myself."

"Not wasted," Christine said. "You have a family, you've accomplished many things with your work, and you found your way to this place. Embrace your life; don't feel like it's been a waste." Christine watched Paul struggle to keep his composure. "You're feeling very tender right now, and you must take care of yourself." She handed him a sheet. "Here are some instructions on what to do after the reading. The key thing is to take your time. It's a beautiful day. Relax outside. Be with nature. Don't think too hard about the reading. It won't leave you. Let it settle. Drink a lot of water. Avoid confrontation or violent movies or TV shows. Treat yourself with care for the next few days."

Paul hung on to her every word, this soul reader he had never heard of, who he almost walked away from, who he still did not understand. Did she understand the effect of the reading? It was the equivalent of a heart transplant, but the donor was the real Paul, and the organ was the soul. He was not prepared to face the world. He needed more time with her.

Christine continued, "I'll send you a copy of the reading in a couple days. Listen to it every day, if possible, for a while. It will reinforce the changes you will experience. Do you keep a journal?"

"No."

"I want you to start. Buy one today here in Glastonbury. Write down what you are thinking and feeling. Write every day. I saw a book in the soul reading—with your name on it."

Paul nodded. "And what do we do next?" It surprised him that he was suggesting a "next."

Christine did not look surprised. "Let's see. I think I should talk to you by phone at least once before July. Then I'm gone for two months—I'm writing a book—and won't be having any sessions or phone calls."

Paul really did not want to leave. Her presence wrapped around him like a warm blanket. Christine sensed his anxiety. "You have a lot to work with. It'll take time. Let it sink in, and you'll feel the change. But now I must break, as I have another session to prepare for."

They walked downstairs, and Christine opened the front door. "Are you OK?" Paul nodded but wasn't sure. Christine gave him a hug. She pulled back and stared intently into his eyes, as if willing him to feel safe. "Relax today, and don't think about anything. Just let it be. Your life is changing for the better." Paul was reluctant to leave, but he did. Christine closed the door behind him.

Paul was overwhelmed by the light and noise as he left her house. She lived near a traffic circle, and the cars and people were streaming by. He remembered the chapel that Edward had pointed out a few doors down from Christine's house, and he stumbled there, seeking refuge.

A little sign read "St. Edward's Chapel" and pointed down a narrow cobblestone sidewalk. A wooden door opened to a grass courtyard lined with small buildings that looked like living quarters and an archway that led to a chapel, whose wide doors were open. No one was there. A small altar sat in the center of the room. Chairs and benches were scattered across the floor, and Paul sat down on one. His eyes adjusted to the darkness. The chapel was tiny, capable of holding a few dozen people at best. Paul felt protected, alone with himself. Jeanne was right; this was a safe place to be following the soul reading. He gazed at the few lit candles. It felt like no one had been here in a while. Paul saw a shadow on the wall, and he realized someone was coming from behind. An old man, probably the caretaker, walked up and placed a box of matches on the sill. As he strolled back out, he smiled and glanced back at the matches, as if suggesting that Paul light the candles. Which was what Paul did. It seemed crazy, but Paul lit every candle on every sill of the windows that lined the walls. He remembered Christine's comment about his candle nearly dying out. He wanted all the candles lit. Then Paul sat in silence for what seemed like an eternity. His impromptu ritual reinforced everything she had said. He enjoyed the beauty of the chapel brought to life by dozens of candles that he lit. In the light, he saw the medieval painting on the wall behind the altar. Mother Mary stared at him, with a hint of a smile, holding her child. The child had the face of an older man. *She was everywhere.*

Paul felt compelled to pray, drawing on childhood memories of church. But as an agnostic, he was not sure who to pray to about what. He was overwhelmed with gratitude. *Thank you, soul reader.* The thought of the reading brought tears to his eyes. It was as if he had consumed her words, and now they were working their way through his body like a spiritual virus.

Finally, he felt comfortable enough to leave the safety of the chapel. The caretaker stood outside, smiling at Paul. For the first of what would be many times, the people of Glastonbury were there to take care of him. Paul mouthed a silent thank-you and returned to the street.

As he walked up the high street, he noticed a café called the Blue Note. It had a New Age feeling to it. Colored glass balls hung from the ceiling over odd-shaped, freestanding tables and chairs. A couple of girls stood behind the counter. They wore long flowing dresses, over-sized pieces of jewelry, and spectacular tattoos and piercings in every possible place. Paul walked up to the counter and looked at the black-board on the wall with the day's specials. "Do you have a menu?" Paul asked. He was hungry and thirsty.

"Surely," one of the girls said. She looked like Pocahontas with her hair braided down to her waist, red and black paint streaks on her face. She handed Paul the menu. He stared at it, finding it hard to concen-trate. "I think you should have some soup."

"I'm sorry?" Paul said.

"You look cold. A soup would warm you up. We have a great potato leek with brown bread," she said.

"I *am* feeling cold. Soup might be a good idea." *Does everyone read people's minds here?* thought Paul.

She pointed. "Sit over by the window, and I'll bring it over to you." Paul watched the people walk by the café window—amid the hippies and seekers and townies, there was no one like Paul there. Yet he felt strangely comfortable, maybe the most comfortable he had been in years. "Is this your first visit to Glastonbury?" Pocahontas slid the soup in front of him as he was staring out the window. He looked down at his suit and tie. She laughed. "We don't have many customers dressed in blue pinstriped suits."

"I came from a meeting in London this morning and didn't have time to change," Paul said apologetically.

Pocahontas laughed again, this time touching his shoulder like Christine did. Her laugh was infectious. "That's OK. You don't actually stick out. I mean, who really fits in? Look at me. Maybe we need more of your type here. You can start the pinstriped Druids movement."

Paul laughed with her.

"Well, welcome." She looked at the steaming soup. "Now have that soup before it turns cold. Cold soup won't warm you." She moved to another table, leaving Paul to enjoy his soup. She was right. It was the perfect choice. In fact, he started feeling deliciously dreamy and almost broke out laughing. He looked at the remaining soup. He wondered if they spice it with marijuana.

Pocahontas returned. "Here's a weekly newsletter that talks about all the things you can do in Glastonbury."

"Thank you!" Paul said.

"It's such a beautiful day." She paused as if reflecting on something. "Do you have some time after lunch?"

"All the time in the world," Paul blurted, surprising himself that he was ignoring the work that was piling up on his computer. It was the first time he even thought about work since the reading.

"I think . . . you should go to the Chalice Well from here." She pulled a map from a wall of brochures and postcards and drew on it. "It's a ten-minute walk from here. When you get there, drink the water. Lots of it." She nodded as if agreeing with herself. "They say it has healing properties. You'll be a new man."

Paul was pleasantly confused. He was a very private person who never elicited advice from strangers. But in Glastonbury, it was different. The people around him understood what he was seeking and would help him—as if they were angels looking out for him. Even stranger, he wanted to accept their help. Paul enjoyed the rest of the soup as he looked at the other patrons. The locals were easy to spot. They wore Glastonbury costumes—Druid, Wiccan, fairy, and goddess fashionistas. And they smiled. The village did have pockets of burned-out hippies, lost souls seeking answers in alcohol and drugs. They reminded him of the crowd in the pub when he visited Glastonbury for the first time. The tourists looked like normal people; they came to see the famous landmarks.

Paul thought about Christine. What was her gig? She wasn't selling trinkets as he had thought. She received them as gifts. She certainly wasn't doing a hard sell in terms of follow-up sessions. Usually, if Paul would spend a few minutes with someone and ask a few questions, he would be able to figure out exactly what they did and why. Not this time. He looked at the newsletter cover—the *Glastonbury Times*. He opened it up. The first thing he saw was an article titled "By Giving, You Receive." The author's photograph was next to the title. It was Christine. What a coincidence!

A large latte slid into his field of vision. "This will give you a little energy for your walk to the well." Pocahontas grinned.

"You're reading my mind." It was true: Paul was thinking it was time for a coffee.

She winked. "Or your tummy."

Paul was not sure if she was joking or not; in Glastonbury, it was hard to tell if something was real, a fantasy, or a joke. "This newsletter you gave me. There's an article here by a Christine Lachaud. Do you know her?" She smiled but shook her head no. "I ask because I just saw her this morning for a soul reading."

She laughed, leaned down, and looked into Paul's eyes. "Well, isn't that something."

"What a coincidence, don't you think? I see her this morning, and she has an article in this week's paper—the same paper you gave to me!"

"It's called synchronicity." Another patron called for Pocahontas, so she touched Paul's hand as if to say goodbye and hurried away.

Paul sipped his latte. He thought about the soul reading and that feeling of joy that overcame him. He was feeling it again. He looked at the bottom of his empty coffee cup. It was the best latte he had ever tasted. The best potato soup he had ever had. The best waitress who had ever served him.

He looked at the circle on the map. Paul was going to the Chalice Well.

Fourteen

Paul left the Blue Note Café. The hot soup and latte warmed his body and took the edge off the crisp air. He walked up the high street, following the route Pocahontas drew on the map. In the daylight, Paul was taken aback by the rows of colorful shops. Bright pastel signs hung from storefronts, calling out to pilgrims and tourists alike, like a New Age Times Square. The Witchcraft Ltd. beckoned with full-size mannequins dressed in black gowns wearing tall pointed caps. Like Saks Fifth Avenue stores at Christmas, each window was a scene. But unlike Saks, these scenes conjured dark images of witches at work—dropping dried insects and roots into a boiling cauldron with simulated steam rising from the strange brew. Spiders hanging from webs looked over the shoulders of witches who scowled at the passersby. The mannequins' eyes were opened wide, circled with black mascara and splashes of rouge on their cheeks, and Paul could feel them looking at him, tempting him to walk inside. It should have been funny, or at least silly, but the soul reading lowered Paul's defenses, and he felt their dark energy in a disturbing way. He remembered Christine warning him to steer clear of disturbing television or movies after the reading. He hurried past the shop.

As Paul turned the corner onto the main stretch of the high street, the names and logos of shops were everywhere. Signs hanging from awnings swung in the brisk spring breeze. Paul watched them bob and weave. The total effect was a wonderful emergence of color and strangeness, like the Munchkins coming out to greet Dorothy. Paul's senses switched from black and white to color, lit by the residual energy of the soul reading. Christine had said it was everywhere—and it was. Each storefront was more colorful than the one before it—Natural Earthling; the Majick Box; In the Mists of Avalon; Star Child; Speaking Tree; Man, Myth, and Magic; the Witchcraft Emporium; Enchanted Flowers; and Hemp of Avalon.

Bookstalls poured out into the streets. But the books were not from the *New York Times* bestseller list. Their covers conjured visions from an unseen world of fairies, Druids, goddesses, and angels.

Even the restaurant names had a mystical branding—the Psychic Piglet, the Green Moon, Monkey's Mind, and Rainbow's End Café.

At the end of the high street, Paul passed a shop called Nature/Roots. Christine mentioned getting back to nature and his roots. *I'm not a shopper*, he thought. He walked in anyway. The shop was dark and smelled of incense. His eyes adjusted, and he saw tables covered with every sort of trinket—many could have been in Christine's house. He realized he was the only person in the shop, which made him uncomfortable. A woman watched him from behind a counter. He hated shopping and felt uncomfortable around salespeople. He turned to leave.

"Can I help you with something?" The woman's voice was soft and nonthreatening. Paul hesitated, nearly out the door. Normally, Paul would mutter under his breath, "No thank you," and run out the door—but he turned back and looked at her for a moment. She was a short, heavyset woman in a red dress, cut low so her large breasts poured out, though obscured by a black gauze scarf that wrapped around her shoulders and draped down her arms. A spray of white flowers covered her left breast. Heavy bracelets on her wrists completed the effect and jangled when she gestured with her hands. Paul realized he had been staring at her without saying anything. "Well, I don't know," he stammered. "I-I mean you seem to have everything here." He looked around the shop, not knowing where to start.

She laughed. "I'm afraid I'm a better collector than shopkeeper. That's what my husband says, anyway. I tell him, How am I to know what people are looking for? We never know, do we?" Before Paul could respond, she moved from behind the counter. She was deceptively quick, and before he knew it, she was very close to him. "What brings you to Glastonbury?" she asked.

Paul said, "I have friends who live—" He realized she was looking at what he was wearing. "I'm passing by on a business trip. Had a breakfast meeting in London this morning. They invited me." He decided to change the subject. "Someone suggested I go to the Chalice Well."

"What a beautiful place." She walked over to a table covered with little cloth bags. She held one, then another, then another, feeling the bags and turning them in her hand as if she was sampling apples at a fruit stand. She found a bag she liked and placed it in his hand, folding his fingers around it. "Take this. It's a special root. Find some dark moist ground in the gardens, and bury it. Then sprinkle some water on it from the well." She noticed Paul's confused look. "Don't worry; it's a ritual," she said. "It will anchor your root chakra."

They walked to the checkout counter. The glint of a red stone sitting on a pile of stones in a basket caught his attention. He picked it up. It was in the shape of a heart. "I was just at a house that was full of heart-shaped stones," he said out loud to himself.

"Glastonbury is the heart chakra of the world," the shopkeeper said. *Chakra again*, Paul thought. Christine had used the word in the soul reading. He needed to Google it later. "You'll see hearts all over the village—on signs and clothing, in artwork and jewelry, everywhere!"

She added the red stone heart to his bag. "Take this stone with you. Rinse it in water from the Lion's Head fountain. It is the sacred Chalice Well water." She rang up the purchases. "That will be four pounds." She handed him the bag.

"You know a lot about this stuff," Paul said.

"That's because I'm a witch." Paul nearly dropped the bag. She laughed. "Don't worry. These rituals will help you. Trust me." Paul, for reasons he didn't understand, did trust her. "Now do me a favor," she said as she pulled a flower from the spray clipped to her dress. "Take this flower with you. Place it at the well. Bless yourself and me. Good for both of us," she said as she touched her heart and his. "Will you do that?"

"I will, and thank you." Paul actually thought it was unlikely he would do anything she suggested. He did not yet understand where he was, listening to would-be witches suggest weird rituals. Too woo-woo for Paul's taste. He looked down, trying not to grin as he left the shop. When he looked up, he saw a sign across the street with an arrow and the words "Chalice Well Gardens."

Paul passed Turnips on his way. He would have liked to change into something more comfortable but hurried by instead. Jeanne was right; it wasn't time to see them just yet.

He approached the entrance to the Chalice Well Gardens. As he entered, he saw a sign:

The Chalice Well has been in continual use for at least two thousand years, having never failed, even during droughts. It is thought to have healing powers, flowing at a constant fifty-degree temperature, even in the middle of winter.

Paul watched as people passed by—a man in a wheelchair, a pale woman wearing a red bandana, a hippie carrying a large walking stick but holding it parallel to the ground. Paul felt conspicuous in his blue pinstriped suit by comparison. He continued reading:

> For pagans and goddesses, the well was a symbol of the female deity (with the male symbolized by the Tor). The reddish hue of the water was symbolic of divine feminine energy.

Paul looked up. He could not see the Tor from where he was, but he sensed its presence yet again.

The garden climbed on a slight incline to the Chalice Well. Well water ran down the hill through various constructions like a mystic waterslide ride. Paul started at the bottom, where a pond formed, surrounded by gardens and benches. A cascading set of seven bowls fed the pool. The bowls were in the shape of the female vulva, representing the energy of the divine feminine.

Paul walked up the incline through an archway into a natural room. A small waterfall ran down the far wall. Its water was stained red. Large stone slabs jutted from the wall, forming natural shelves and cubbyholes that held candles, fruit, flowers, and other gifts.

A man holding onto the arm of his female companion walked in a shallow pool at the bottom of the waterfall. He struggled to step out of the pool and, with the help of his companion, eased his way into a wheelchair.

The woman in the red bandanna reappeared. She stood at the bottom of the waterfall, placed a candle on a stone shelf, and lit it. She removed her bandanna and put her head under the water. She turned, water dripping from her head, her clothing half soaked; looked at Paul; and smiled. When he made eye contact with people in New York, his instincts were to look away. But in this healing garden, Paul stared back and even smiled.

He looked at the sign in front of the pool—"The Healing Pool." He removed his shoes and socks, rolled up his blue pinstriped pants, and stepped into the pool. The water was cold and shot through his feet and into his body. He closed his eyes. When he opened them again, there were a half-dozen people with him in the pool, some standing still like egrets in a pond, others moving like turtles. He wondered if they thought he was as crazy as he looked, standing in the middle of the pool in rolled-up suit pants?

Paul climbed the stairs to the next garden room, which featured the Lion's Head fountain the witch in the shop referred to. Water poured out of the mouth of a terra cotta lion's head into a stone basin, over a set of drinking glasses. People approached the fountain one by one. A girl filled a jug with water and hurried off. Paul walked up to the stone basin and held the red heart stone under the water. It sparkled in the sun. He drank a glass of the red water. And another. Suddenly, he was very thirsty.

He continued up the hill to a wrought-iron gate, partially opened. On the top of the gate were the words "The Chalice Well." Beyond the gate was the wellhead—the source of the sacred water feeding the fountains and pools below—encircled by a stone bench where visitors sat silent. Paul placed the witch's white flower on the wellhead among the other mementos, as she requested. He sat down and closed his eyes. *Bless the shopkeeper.* He touched his heart, surprised at his own action but more surprised by how peaceful he felt. When he opened his eyes, he saw someone had placed candles on either side of the flower. *Angels are everywhere.*

Paul wandered farther up the hill and found an empty chair on a knoll. Now he could see Tor in the distance, covered with tourists. They were tiny silhouettes, climbing up and down Tor like an army of ants. Paul was tired. He thought about the day. What did it all mean? He tried to remember what Christine said. He wanted to hear her reading again.

Typical of the English weather, the sun had been playing hide-and-seek all day as clouds passed by. But at that moment, it broke out, and

Paul felt its warmth. He leaned back and closed his eyes. A peace came over him. The warmth of the sun was like a blanket protecting him. At that moment, he realized that today was not about acting on what Christine said or even absorbing it. It was about rest. That's what she said. Paul dozed off for a while.

Voices nearby woke Paul from a dead sleep, and he jumped to his feet. How long had he slept? He felt the cloth bag in his suit pocket and remembered the witch's instructions—*bury it*. In front of him was a tree trunk, rising out of the ground, curling through space, and falling back into the ground, in the shape of a misshapen rainbow. He found a bare patch of earth underneath the trunk and pushed the root deep into the ground. He filled a glass at the Lion's Head fountain and returned to water the buried root. He stood up and looked around one last time, surprised he was listening to witches and soul readers yet feeling exceptionally calm and connected in this exceptional place. The Chalice Well Gardens were nearly deserted, its colors darkening in the late daylight.

He returned to Turnips and slipped upstairs to shower and change. Paul checked his email, but he could not focus—none of it looked important. He thought about calling Mary but had no idea what to say to her. It was 6:30. He felt obligated to join Edward and Jeanne for dinner, despite what Edward had said to him that morning. It would be impolite to stay in his room. He dressed and came down. Jeanne greeted him with a hug, bursting with curiosity. "Well? How was it?"

"Wonderful," Paul said softly. "I've you to thank for this."

Edward appeared, armed with glasses and a bottle of wine. "I want the dirt. Did you take your clothes off? Did she take her clothes off? I mean, did she read every inch of your body? Any horse tips? Come on, out with it."

"Edward!" Jeanne protested. "Leave Paul alone. Of course they didn't undress. This is a serious matter."

"All right, well, what happened?" Edward asked.

"It was a special experience. I can't really describe it. I feel changed in some way I don't fully understand."

Jeanne smiled. "Beautiful. I thought you might feel that way."

"What did you do afterward?" Edward asked.

"I went to the chapel that Jeanne recommended. Visited the Chalice Well. Actually, met a witch in a little shop. The whole day was special."

"Did you meet Christine's nasty dog?" Edward asked.

Paul laughed. "No, I didn't. I heard it barking though."

"I'm surprised the village hasn't collected it for the pound."

"Edward!" Jeanne said. "If Christine heard you talk that way, she'd be upset."

"Maybe she can hear us now," Edward whispered. "She put a little bug in Paul's head."

"Something happened, that's for sure." Paul nodded. "But I don't understand it." The room got uncomfortably quiet.

Edward cleared his throat. "Right. Well, let's go to dinner."

The dinner flew by. Jeanne and Edward realized Paul was in no condition to talk about the day. They talked about friends, children, and politics, entertaining themselves and Paul. It was an early night, and Paul retired, armed, once again, with a jacket and umbrella in case he wanted to have a morning stroll to the top of the Tor.

He crawled into bed. He could feel the energy from the Tor, similar to his last visit. It was pouring through the wall of his room. But this time, he looked forward to it, and without another thought, he fell asleep.

He was drifting down a brown water river. It was a warm tropical day. The river was in a jungle. He floated on his back, enjoying the cool water and the sun beating on his body. He let the lazy current take him as the river meandered through the underbrush. A tree had fallen across the river, barely leaving room for him to float underneath. As he neared the tree, he noticed a large lizard sleeping on the middle of its trunk. It was bright green with dark skin around its eyes and on its feet and tail. He floated closer. It was big. Suddenly, it opened its eyelids, revealing large bloodshot eyes. It saw Paul as the current pulled him closer to the tree. It snarled, revealing rows of teeth shaped like arrowheads. It turned its head toward him. The current moved faster. He was at the tree. He threw up his hands in defense.

Paul woke up, breathing heavily, drenched in sweat, his hands in the air. He looked at the clock. It was six o'clock in the morning and time for a walk.

Fifteen

Paul quickly dressed and left Turnips. The world outside was dark and cold at that hour. Paul walked briskly toward the Tor, eager to get there. As he climbed the footpath, the tower once again stood in front of him. He saw a hint of light peeking over the hilltop and realized he was going to see the sunrise. As he stopped to pull out his phone to take pictures, the faint light turned a dark red, flowing over the top of the hill like hot lava. *Click.* The sun emerged next to the tower, shooting red light through its windows in the shape of a burning spear. A large bird flew along the length of the spear, black on red. *Click.*

He came to the landing with the bench and sat down. He gazed at the horizon. A sea of fog slowly lifted, rooftop by rooftop, from the village below. Glastonbury slowly took shape. Church spires and ancient towers loomed over a carpet of red tile roofs. All the while, Christine's words streamed through Paul's mind like a psychic tickertape: *And when you feel her energy, you will begin to know yourself. Thoughts will drop into your mind like raindrops falling from the sky.* Paul closed his eyes, and words and images came into his head.

I see a room with no windows and boxes covered with dust. I see you opening those boxes and finding yourself inside. The image of the room was a familiar one, but he wasn't sure where he saw it before.

Your soul is a candle. It is flickering, nearly extinguished. You must nurture its light, or you will become sick. He saw an image of himself as a teenager, sitting in the Quaker meetinghouse, determined to find that "inner light."

Your son is an old soul, and you can learn from one another. He saw Simon walking the dog along Riverside Park, staring at the moonlight, which rested on the still Hudson River.

I see you using nature to open your heart and soul. I see a tree, a place in nature, a place blessed with the earth mother energy. It will happen. Paul thought about their weekend home on Long Island. Perhaps he should start a vegetable garden.

Paul was lost in thought when the caw of the raven nearly caused him to fall off the bench. It had landed on the back of the bench, opposite from where he was sitting. Its left eye stared at him, and it opened its wings as if to caution him to remain still. Paul was going nowhere. *I see you with the raven.* Paul had never seen a raven so close before. Now Christine's words came to life right in front of him. *The raven connects everything.* The raven fidgeted as if it could hear her words and slowly launched into the air and glided down the slope of the Tor into the village below.

Paul felt raindrops as the fickle English weather conjured up a brief shower. He had forgotten Edward's umbrella. The water poured down his face and into his shirt. He looked at his watch. He had to go. Hurrying down the steps, he almost fell several times on the slippery steps. But he didn't worry about the steps or the rain or being late. He felt as if he could dance his way home.

Edward greeted him outside by the car, tapping his watch. "OK, you missed my breakfast again, and you may miss your flight. Grab your bag, and let's go."

Paul hugged Jeanne, and she, in turn, held him by the shoulders and looked at him intently. "Wow, I can feel the energy. What happened up there?"

"I don't know. I felt something. I saw an orb surrounding the sun and took pictures. I'll send them to you. Had all kinds of thoughts. Things from the past. The soul reading."

Jeanne laughed as Paul realized he was babbling. "Well, whatever happened, you look great. I'm so happy that you came back to Glastonbury."

"I'll be back," Paul said.

"I know you will," Jeanne said. "You're always welcome here."

"You may be back today if we don't leave now for the airport," Edward exclaimed. Paul scrambled into the car, and they took off for the airport. Edward traveled at warp speed, and most of the trip was silent. Paul didn't want to distract him while he was doing an excellent Formula One race imitation.

"So you're happy you came?" Edward asked.

"Absolutely," Paul said. "I feel different."

"Well, let me tell you something," Edward said, uncharacteristically serious, "you know that I'm skeptical about all this Glastonbury hocus-pocus. But I've seen what Christine has done, and her effect on people. We've had guests see her, and return, and return, and their lives change. Not all the time, but many times. Looks like she rattled your cage."

"She is taking off for the summer, so I'm not sure what I'm going to do," Paul said nervously. "I feel a little lost. I'm telling you, Edward, it was a very unusual experience this morning."

"Lost your spiritual virginity, but now what?" Edward started laughing. "I'd have a go with Mary—maybe she'll feel the energy." Edward brought the car to a screeching stop at the curb of the terminal, and Paul ran for his flight.

As he settled in his seat and opened his computer, Paul remembered Christine's suggestion that he keep a journal. Should he work on his emails or start a journal?

He created a Word document and named it the "Glastonbury Journal." He began his first entry, writing as if he were a character in a story about Glastonbury. He wrote for hours, enjoying the process as he relived every moment in Glastonbury, even embellishing a little. And he enjoyed it. Sitting on the plane, disconnected from family and work, he escaped into a world where magic was real and lives changed overnight.

Sixteen

The raven flew above Tor, preparing to roost in the nearby woods for the night. The lights in the village below were turning off one by one in a predictable pattern. The raven watched a handful of people gather around a fire burning next to the St. Michael's Tower. More pilgrims climbed up the path to the top of Tor, using flashlights to guide their way.

The second floor of Turnips remained lit. Edward had gone to bed early, feeling winded from his gardening. He decided not to end his day at the pub—he didn't have the energy. Jeanne lay next to him, reading a book. She was thinking about Paul's visit. His aura had changed after the reading and yet again after his visit to Tor in the morning. She knew he was going through a wonderful change. "Edward," she whispered, "do you think I should call Mary? Paul really seems to have taken it all in, and I don't want Mary to be frightened by it. I think they'll both benefit greatly. It'll be better for Paul and therefore better for Mary. What do you think?"

"Let it go." Edward turned to her. "Let's be English about this. It's their business. Don't even think about it."

"I'm just thinking a call. I do feel responsible," she said.

"You're not responsible," Edward boomed. "It was meant to be. Isn't that what your goddess friends say? Paul was meant to come here, have the soul reading, climb the Tor." He paused and then whispered, "Darling, you have to believe it will all work out." Edward rolled back onto his back and began to laugh. "See? I do listen when you get together with your friends to reshape this universe of ours."

Jeanne laughed. "I'm impressed. Maybe you *do* hear some of what I say, even if you don't believe a word of it. In this case, though, you're probably right. I'll stay out of it." She went back to her book.

Edward thought about Jeanne and how lucky he was. He didn't need the savants of Glastonbury to tell him that he was blessed. She was an angel. Inexplicably, he had a strange feeling that he could lose her at any moment, and he panicked. He reached for her, and they held hands in silence.

Then the sound of a beating drum began. "Oh, for Christ's sake, not another ceremony," Edward complained. "It's really not fair to the rest of us who want to sleep early."

"I forgot," Jeanne said. "Tonight is the celebration of King Arthur's return to the Isle of Avalon."

"Well, I wish King Arthur had found a resting place in bloody Wales, where he really lived, if he lived at all."

Jeanne smiled to herself, listening to the booming drumbeat. No doubt Tor was covered with women in their goddess garbs, beating the drum, banging tambourines, and waving lit torches. King Arthur is said to have returned to the Isle of Avalon in a white barge following his final battle, where he killed his son, Mordor, but was mortally wounded. The goddesses cared for him in his last days, though here the legends proliferate. One says that King Arthur died and is buried beyond the veil in Avalon. Another says he died and was returned to Glastonbury, where he was buried at the abbey. And one legend says he is still alive and will return from Avalon to lead his people again. Jeanne felt grateful she was living so close to the place of legends. Every ritual, every celebration, reminded Jeanne she was human and alive and sharing this earth with others, past and present. *It's so easy to forget that*, she thought to herself as she drifted off to sleep.

Seventeen

Deep in thought, Paul was barely aware that he was sitting on an American flight with hundreds of strangers thirty thousand feet above the ocean. They were on a journey unthinkable a hundred years ago. Back then, the Boeing 777, imagined but fantastical, lived behind the veil of Avalon, the world of past and future. It hovered above the isle like a futuristic Excalibur, waiting for its time to fly.

Sitting in the plane, Paul continued writing:

> I am over the Atlantic right now. Just four days ago, I was flying over the Atlantic to Barcelona—and all I could think about was the soul reading. Am I nuts? Am I grasping at straws? Now I think something is waking up inside of me. And I have no idea what to do next, for maybe the first time in my life.
>
> I am afraid. How will I reintegrate to my home and family? What will work be like?
>
> The journey begins.

Paul closed his computer. Christine was right—writing a journal was a good idea. He could barely stay in his seat; he had so much energy. He looked out the window of the plane. He saw it as if for the first time, despite hundreds of flights and millions of miles in the air. His seat overlooked the wing, which spanned more than two hundred feet end to end. He saw a row of landing lights repeating to the end of the wingspan like footlights on a stage. He looked at the engine, appearing close enough to touch. A smooth silver skin held the engine together, occasionally disturbed by a vent and topped with a bulging spherical shape that looked like a white whale. Inside the engine, twenty-two thousand moving parts, fed by jet fuel, shaped a freezing (–80°F) airstream into the power of one hundred and twenty thousand horses, straining in their harnesses to move the plane forward. It was a modern witch's brew. The flight was a miracle. What was once not real was real. And what was real was now more real to him. The plane began to descend, like the barge carrying King Arthur to his home in Avalon.

As Paul's plane was landing, the raven perched quietly on the tower. A bell rang, signaling the arrival of King Arthur's barge, gently docking at the base of the isle. The goddesses descended Tor in the pitch black of night, their ritual complete.

The plane touched the ground, and it slowed quickly, helped by the unimaginable reverse of direction of its equine hordes—a quarter of a million horses in all—gasping at the end of their journey, bringing the plane's speed to a crawl. The plane taxied on the tarmac and pulled up to the gate. A bell rang. Paul unbuckled his seat belt and rose to leave the plane.

He was home.

Eighteen

Paul stared at his phone as his limousine pulled away from the JFK terminal. The emails poured onto the screen like a digital waterfall. He concentrated on the most important messages. The chief marketing officer had already sent an email about the naming fiasco and smelled blood. She copied the entire executive committee in an email openly critical of what happened. His secretary already booked three related calls for later that day. Things were escalating quickly, but it all could be fixed if he got to the right people in time. He looked up from his phone as the car pulled up to his apartment building, and the doorman smiled at him through the window as he reached for the door. He had taken his eye off the ball while in Glastonbury and dug himself into a hole. And what would he say to Mary about the soul reader?

As Paul was riding the elevator to his floor, Mary was in their apartment, on the phone with her sister. "So I'm telling Paul I'm shutting down the business. It's been dead lately. Why spend the money on an office and assistant?"

"No shit, sister," Janet said. "And it's getting worse. Nothing's happening. I'll be lucky if I keep my job. There's hasn't been any business since the crash."

"I'm hoping Paul understands," mused Mary. "Sometimes I think that's the only thing he likes about me. If I don't work, what'll we talk about?"

Janet said, "Tell him you're tired of taking care of everything at home on top of running your own business. Besides, he makes plenty of money."

"Right? Simon's going into his senior year, and he'll need to do all the application stuff, the auditions, the trips to schools. It'll be a nightmare. That'll be a full-time job alone," said Mary.

"I'd hire a consultant for college applications. The guys here use them for their kids. Do you want me to look into it?"

"I'm not telling Paul I'm hiring a consultant for Simon," Mary said. "At least not at the same time that I'm telling him I'm closing my business."

"Sis, I hate to say this, but you could tell Paul you're taking Simon on a year-long trip around the world, and he'd say, 'Let me know when you're coming back.' He's clueless."

Her sister's tough love was funny sometimes. It was not as if Janet figured out relationships with men. She cut through them like a buzz saw in the lumberyard shed. But she was sexy, so men just waited in line, waiting their turn, like lemmings in heat as she tore through the latest guy. Mary laughed. "I don't think I should be taking relationship advice from you."

"Just calling it the way I see it," Janet said.

Mary heard the door slam shut. "I think Paul just got home. I'll call you later."

"Good luck, sis. And remember—*he doesn't care.*"

Nineteen

"I'm home." Paul peeked into the kitchen. "How are things? Do you have some time now? I'd like to talk to you about something."

Mary frowned. "Thanks for calling me last night." Mary got angry whenever he didn't call her at least once a day on the road. "It's all I ask," she would say. Paul ignored her tone and motioned toward the living room.

They sat down on the couch. "I was in Glastonbury yesterday."

"I'm aware. How are Edward and Jeanne?" she asked.

"They're wonderful."

"And how was Glastonbury? Did you see more of it?"

Paul smiled. "I did. There's a special feeling about the place, an energy that really touched me. While I was there, I saw that soul reader I mentioned."

"And? How did it go?" Mary asked.

Paul hesitated, unprepared for what to say next. "Well, she read my soul. I know it sounds strange, but it was a small, flickering light in danger of going out. She said I could get sick. She suggested for me to listen to my soul, to feed it. To open my heart. Things like that." Paul's eyes were moist, and he finished with a whisper: "I've closed myself off from myself and everything around me."

"Are you OK? What happened next?"

"She told me to rest and to visit a place called the Chalice Well. This morning, very early, I walked to the top of the Tor, a hill in Glastonbury, and had a strange experience. I heard voices and saw things that she had talked about. It was a wave of images and memories pouring into my head. I could hear her voice. I felt changed. The Tor was beautiful with this strange light and orbs and people standing there . . ." Paul looked away, seeing the images again.

Mary persisted. "This soul reader. What did she look like in person? How old is she?"

"She's attractive," Paul admitted. "Maybe forty years old. She's French. Her eyes glowed."

"What was she wearing?" Mary asked.

"I don't know. A blouse and yoga pants?" Paul's expression darkened, tiring of the questioning.

"Did she mention me?" Mary's voice rose.

"She did, actually," Paul said. "She said that you would not follow this path directly but will be influenced by it in your own way." Paul smiled at the thought.

"Hmm . . . What is she charging for all of this?"

"Ninety-five pounds so far," Paul said. "She's sending me a recording of the reading. I'll talk to her in a week or two by phone. Perhaps go over for a retreat in the fall."

"Are you kidding me?" Mary reached for her phone and tapped the screen. "I want a copy of the recording."

"I won't give you that," Paul insisted. "She specifically asked that I not share it with anyone."

"Including your wife? This is such bullshit." Mary started to cry. "It's bad enough that you're constantly traveling and don't call me."

She showed Paul her phone with a picture of Christine. "Now you're seeing some attractive soul reader who's telling you things you won't share with me!"

Paul reached out. "I know this is strange, but I feel like this'll be good for our relationship. The details of the reading are private, that's all. Please understand." Mary hesitated. Paul held her in his arms and looked into her eyes. "I'm fine. I'm better than fine—I'm happy, and I love you."

She cried softly on his shoulder. "It's just so strange." She looked up at his face, and he smiled at her and wiped her tears away. "You're not the Paul I know." She put her head on his shoulder again. "But . . . I guess we can see how this goes."

"Thank you," Paul said. He needed to start making some calls for work, but he felt her arms tighten around him. They held each other without speaking for a few minutes. The apartment was still. Paul felt Mary relax finally.

It had been years, Mary thought, *since we held each other this way. If I could freeze a moment, it would be this one.* Mary would keep to her word—she would see how things developed. But if she saw anything she didn't like, she would call Jeanne and tell her off and make sure Paul never talks to the soul reader again.

The rest of the day flew by. Paul worked through the torrent of emails regarding the tridget crisis. Now he was receiving emails from his staff asking why he didn't reply to the accusations from marketing. He clicked through the emails but couldn't concentrate enough to sort it all out. He decided to walk the dog and get some fresh air. While he was gone, Simon returned home from his flute lessons and disappeared into his room, barely saying hello to Mary. Paul stopped outside his door when he returned. "Good night, Simon."

"Good night, Dad," came Simon's muffled voice.

Paul was too tired to try to talk his way into Simon's room. "Let's catch up at breakfast tomorrow."

"For sure."

Mary sat in the den with a glass of wine, watching TV. "Honey, I'm going to bed," Paul said. "I'm hitting a wall, and the jet lag is catching up to me." He kissed Mary on her head. "It's great to be back." Usually, Paul would spend another hour or more on his computer checking his email before going to sleep, but this time, he went straight to bed.

Also, Paul normally took an Ambien after a big trip; otherwise, he would have a sleepless night. Paul was proud of his ability to regulate his life rhythms, using a combination of caffeine, alcohol, and Ambien—he was a living on/off light switch with a dimmer. Today he hadn't used anything, and he felt in perfect balance. As he turned out the bedroom light, his computer rang, signaling yet another email, but he didn't even hear it. Had he looked, he would have seen the incoming email was from the CEO about the tridget fiasco. But Paul was already asleep, dreaming about his newly found world, flying above the Tor and the dark Glastonbury vale.

Mary turned off the TV. The apartment was silent. She rested her head on the back of the couch and thought about her conversation with Paul. She never had the chance to tell Paul her secret—that she was closing her business. It didn't seem like the right time. Maybe she would tell him tomorrow.

Mary thought about the soul reader and looked at her picture again, reminding her that Christine was a double for Jenny, Paul's former lover. It was clear to Mary—Paul had fallen in love again.

Mary lay on the couch with her eyes closed and thought about Jenny, the minibar mistress, and listened to the drumbeat of distrust pounding back into her as she drifted into an unsettled sleep.

The outlines of a dark hotel room emerged in front of her. The curtains to the room were closed, but a faint light from the bottom of the curtains poured along the floor, suggesting that it was the middle of the day. Like a camera moving on a dolly close to the floor, her eyes followed the light toward a large bed. At the foot of the bed was a pair of high heels. She saw a black camisole and short skirt draped on a chair and a push-up bra next to it on the floor. As she made her way to the bed, there was a crumpled pile of sheer pantyhose and a red string thong next to it. A lamp on a nightstand lit a short glass with a touch of scotch left at the bottom. Next to it was a half-full champagne flute, bubbles still rising to the surface. There was a silhouette of a sleeping man—not Paul—lying in the bed uncovered to his waist, his chest rising and falling. A woman slept next to him with her head on his chest, her arm draped casually across his stomach. The woman opened her eyes. Mary was staring at herself.

Mary awoke in a jolt, almost knocking over her glass of wine. Mary had another secret—one she could never tell Paul: her affair with Kevin. Kevin had been her client. When they first met, they hit it off immediately. He was married with a family and lived by Central Park on the East Side. They had more lunch meetings than either could justify; they could not disguise their mutual sexual attraction. At one lunch, he proposed they have an affair. He was clear about the ground rules: they were not going to fall in love. Mary surprised herself at how quickly she agreed to his proposition. He caught her at a vulnerable moment—Paul's recent promotion led to more travel, and Simon was reaching an age where he began becoming closed off to his mother.

They both were comfortable with the routine. She would dress provocatively, he would describe a fantasy to her at lunch, and they would work themselves into a sexual frenzy, seeking relief as soon as they got inside the hotel room. Kevin liked her to play out fantasies that neither had in their marriages.

Mary closed her eyes again, overwhelmed with sadness. Tears ran down her cheeks. She and Paul had too many secrets. Maybe she would tell Paul in the morning. It was time to fix their marriage.

And he wasn't seeing that soul reader again.

Twenty

Mary smelled coffee and opened her eyes. A mug sat on the table next to her. She looked up and saw Paul dressing. "What time is it?"

Paul sat next to her. "It's six thirty. I made you some coffee."

"Why are you up so early?"

"I couldn't sleep. I'm going to walk through the park on my way to work. Go back to sleep."

After Paul left, Mary could not sleep. She sat up and sipped the warm coffee. She had a half hour before starting her routine. She reached for her laptop and started scrolling through the news, trying to forget about her secret.

What triggered that dream about Kevin? She last saw him two days ago, after the parents' committee meeting at Simon's school. Kevin had a bad week at work and was rougher with her than usual—maybe that's why she had the dream. Still, it worked for both of them, and she liked the commitment to a lack of commitment. Knowing the rules took the emotion out of it. She sipped her coffee.

Synchronicity

Twenty-One

WHAT THE HELL!!

What are you going to do about this?????

Steve

The CEO's email churned Paul's stomach as he sat in his office in Ascendant's headquarters in Midtown Manhattan. His trip to Glastonbury gave his enemies time to build an active campaign against him. What was he thinking? Yes, the tridget issue seemed silly, but the head of marketing turned it into a question of business judgment. He scrolled through the emails—time for a counterattack.

Paul crafted an email that laid out all the facts—a dozen media mentions of tridget with no one picking up on the porn story, dozens of leads, and millions of dollars in the pipeline generated by the idea—and he finished by thanking marketing for their support. The email went to everyone. The tone was understated, as if asking what all the ruckus was about. He also sent an email to Steve offering to call him to provide more details if he was concerned.

Paul's email dropped into the mailboxes of the corporate leadership. Like birds sensing a tsunami, his enemies had an uneasy feeling they should fly away before it was too late as they opened their mail. His case was compelling; while left unsaid, everyone knew marketing had dropped the ball—they should have checked out the "tridget" name. A storm was brewing.

Steve was having lunch with one of the company's most important clients when Paul sent the email. The client mentioned he had read an article about Ascendant's proposition that tridgets represent a trillion-dollar opportunity in the upcoming decade. The client wanted to hear more—it was exactly the kind of thinking he was looking for from Ascendant. The timing could not be better.

Responses to his email poured into his mailbox. His allies supported his case. Others couched their support with questions, hedging their bets until they heard the CEO's response. Cynthia, the head of marketing, was strangely silent, as were her allies. Paul continued to scroll down his mail list looking for the CEO's response, the one that really mattered. No response yet. Paul looked out the window. His computer chimed, indicating another email—perhaps this was the CEO. Paul had goose bumps—it was from Christine, and his soul reading audio was attached. He left his office and hurried a few blocks to Central Park and found a bench next to a pond. He put on his earbuds, leaned back, closed his eyes, and touched the play button. The spring sun warmed his face, reminding him of when he sat at the Chalice Well Gardens and the sun came out from behind the clouds. The soul reading began, and her voice warmed his heart as well.

I see a dark house with shuttered windows. A dusty attic with closed boxes scattered on its floor. The air is stifling. He replayed her words over and over. Hearing the soul reader's voice with his eyes closed, he visualized the place she saw. At first, it was a black room. He turned on a light, a single naked bulb hanging from the rafters. Dusty boxes lay everywhere, in some cases stacked three or four deep. The attic was nondescript, though vaguely familiar. Then he noticed the wooden cross lying on its side, at least eight feet long, and flinched in recognition—he was looking at his parents' attic. His father, Earl, built that cross for an Easter pageant. He remembered the three of them—his father, mother, and himself—struggling to lift the cross up the stairs to the attic. His mother, Helen, wanted to use it for firewood. Paul smiled. *Really, Mom? You're married to a minister, for God's sake.* "No harm having a cross in the attic," Dad would say. "It's like having a lightning rod, in case God gets angry." Maybe his father was right, but the cross did not save his wife. Cancer struck her anyway.

Earl never forgave God for taking his wife away. Maybe he chopped the cross into wood after all. He certainly took an ax to everything in his life that reminded him of Helen. He thought that either God was a sadist or Helen was a sinner.

The soul reading ended. Paul still visualized the attic as if it were a vivid dream, panning across the piles of dusty boxes. He opened his eyes, jumped up from the bench, and walked quickly through the park, knowing where he had to go.

Twenty-Two

Edward paused outside his church at the end of the high street in Glastonbury. A black raven sat on the steeple of the church, staring at Edward as if he were an intruder. Edward found the sight of the raven to be disturbing. Was the devil sniffing around for a new home? The fact is that the church was on its last legs. There were four remaining members, including Edward. It was only a matter of time; nonetheless, he picked up a pebble and threw it at the black interloper. The raven raised its wings as if to threaten its attacker and then rose above the church in a tight circle. Edward felt something on his shoulder. It felt like a large raindrop, but it was a parting gift from his adversary. Edward used his handkerchief to clean off the dropping and hurried inside for protection.

Edward began to dust the pews, starting with the back row. He rationalized his quixotic dedication to the church as a way of honoring his father's memory. His father was the senior elder of the church for many years. By the time he passed away, the congregation size was already dwindling, and he worried as much about its future.

Edward eased into a pew to rest for a moment. A wood altar stood a few steps above the pews. A yellowed altar cloth covered it, leaving the needle legs exposed. A simple wooden cross hung on the wall behind it. It expressed the rustic legacy of its Protestant roots.

Edward remembered sitting in the Sunday-morning service with his family more than thirty years ago. He had been infatuated with Jeanne. They were both home from boarding school for the summer. As youngsters, they played together, but she had ignored him the whole summer, focusing on older boys instead. The summer was coming to an end, and they had not exchanged a word. Edward fidgeted during the pastor's sermon. His voice droned like the sound of black beetles flying through the air. Edward closed his eyes and prayed. He prayed—pimple-faced, clumsily dressed, unathletic, unposh, and undeserving soul that he was— that God grant him a miracle. Give Edward a chance, and he would take it from there. He crinkled his forehead as if the force of pulling all the muscles in his face together into a contorted mask would compel God to hear his prayer. And that's when Edward had a vision of horses racing and realized that going to the races would be the way to her heart.

Sunday-afternoon racing in Bath attracted families from all over Somerset, and Edward learned that Jeanne planned to go with her friends. At the race, he watched Jeanne from afar. She walked with her girlfriends, teetering in her high heels. She wore a yellow fascinator in the shape of a giant rose, firmly attached with a white clip. The group glided through the grounds like a flock of starlings until they settled near a row of older boys, home from college, dressed sharply in colorful blazers, some in derby hats. The boys assumed a pose of disinterest. They leaned against the rail, looking at their race sheets. The time was now. Edward walked directly behind her, ignoring the glares from her friends. He looked to the sky for a sign. Then her fascinator, detached by the force of a sudden strong gust of wind, fell to the ground in front of his feet. Edward reached down and picked up her headpiece. Jeanne turned to look for it but instead saw Edward in front of her and broke into a smile. He shyly offered it to her. "Edward, you rescued my fascinator." She laughed. "I'm such a bumbler. I'm really not meant to dress like this. I haven't got a clue what I'm doing," Jeanne said while trying to reattach the fascinator. Edward barely heard her. "Could you help me?" She held the fascinator out to him.

"What?"

"Would you help attach it? I must confess, I've never done it. My mother does it for me." The scene overwhelmed Edward's senses. Her gentle, thin fingers brushed his hand as he took the fascinator. She turned her head to the side, revealing her neck, inviting him to step closer, and he could smell her fragrance. He gingerly touched her hair, which was pulled into a bun. He opened the clasp and slid it deep into her hair, praying he would not scrape her head.

Suddenly, a clanging noise rang out. The doors to the starting gate opened. Jeanne clutched Edward's arm. Horses stormed out of the gates, bumping into each other, seeking an early advantage. Edward became aware he was standing next to the girl he loved. Her hand remained on his arm, and her grip seemed stronger than necessary. Within a couple minutes, the horses took the final turn in the mile-long race. The crowd roared. A smaller horse was in the lead, but a larger horse came on strong. Would it catch the leader? Both jockeys used the whip liberally. It was down to the wire, and the crowd enjoyed the tension. Jeanne removed her hand from his arm and clapped in excitement. The larger horse closed the gap and won by a nose. The crowd applauded both horses as they passed the grandstand.

"The winner looks like the loser." Jeanne laughed, pointing at the horses as they walked by them at the rail.

"What do you mean?" Edward asked.

"Well, it's walking slowly. It and the jockey are covered with mud. The second-place horse is clean and trotting pretty quickly, don't you think?"

"That's because the second horse led the race until the very end, so there were no horses kicking dirt in front of it. The second horse was behind most of the field for at least the first six furlongs," Edward explained.

Jeanne listened intently. "That's interesting. It must be tough to be behind the other horses."

Edward warmed up. "Actually, they have different gaits as well."

"What do you mean?"

"Well, the losing horse was a sprinter, a speed horse. Even after the race, he's more comfortable at a faster pace. The winning horse was a closer. Closers tend to trail the field, but they are more consistent and have more stamina by the end of the race. In this case, the sprinter took the lead, but the closer was far too close at the final turn for the sprinter to have a chance. You could see the sprinter was tired. The closer was the favorite. It's got better bloodlines, and the handicap weights were equal, which was a huge advantage for the closer, who's better built to carry the weight. I would have bet on the winner."

Jeanne frowned. "My little accident kept you from making a winning bet?"

Edward shook his head. "Not at all. I'm glad you had the accident—I mean, I'm glad I could help. There'll be another race."

Jeanne looked at the tote board. "Actually, wasn't that the last race?"

Edward realized she was right. "Um, yes, it was. There'll be another race some other day."

"You're right. But I am in your debt." Jeanne patted his arm.

The crowd headed toward the exits, and a girl appeared next to Jeanne, looking at Edward warily. "Oh," Jeanne said, noticing her friend. "Edward, meet Louisa. She is a schoolmate of mine who is staying with us for the weekend. This is Edward; we were playmates at a very early age. But we've lost touch since boarding school." Edward's face was red, and he could barely acknowledge Jeanne's friend. Jeanne smiled gently. "And he rescued me today." She leaned forward and kissed Edward on the cheek. "There. Goodbye, Edward."

"Goodbye" was all Edward could say before she turned and hurried away, arm in arm with her friend, laughing and whispering in her ear.

Edward snapped out of his daydream. He was still sitting in the pew, dust cloth in hand, savoring the memory. It felt like it happened yesterday. God answered his prayer and gave him a soul mate. He struggled to keep the church alive, but he also felt that, so long as the church stood open, his love was secure.

Edward and Jeanne had few secrets between each other, but this was one of them. Jeanne could never know that God swept into their lives, manipulating her heart, serving her like a luscious dessert to someone undeserving. "She could have done better" was what Edward always said to anyone who would listen.

If people heard of his secret deal with God, it would undercut his ability to question the spiritual charlatans living in Glastonbury or the naïve seekers passing through Turnips. If he were to admit to a role for God, where would he draw the line? Glastonbury stretches the boundaries of belief until they almost have no meaning—as if there were no end to the world.

Jeanne kept her own secrets. How does one re-engage with a childhood friend after realizing, as a young woman, that she always loved him? Loosening her fascinator, when she noticed Edward behind her, hoping it would land at his feet. Wondering why he did not compliment how she looked when she posed for him, leaning on the rail, fascinator and all. Acting interested in his version of the race. Not telling him that she had picked the winner of the last race—and the winner of her heart—on that day.

Twenty-Three

"I'm thinking of visiting my father this weekend," Paul said excitedly, poking his head into the kitchen. Mary stopped putting groceries away in their kitchen.

"Really?"

"I haven't seen him since Easter. He'd like the company."

"I'm sure he would," Mary said unconvincingly. She put the vegetables on the chopping board.

"You're welcome to come with me."

Mary shook her head. "I'll stay with Simon. He has class tomorrow, and then we'll take the train to Quogue. You have some father/son time," Mary muttered under her breath as she started chopping. "If that's possible with Earl."

"Where's our phantom boy?"

"He has a study group tonight, remember? I'm making pasta with some chopped veggies, something light for the two of us."

"Sounds good. He's so busy," Paul said.

"Depending on his mood, that's not necessarily a bad thing. Doesn't give him time to get into trouble."

Paul picked a carrot off the board, risking losing a finger as Mary chopped. "They say they reconnect in their twenties."

Mary pushed Paul's hand away. "It's funny. I always wanted to savor every moment of Simon's life. But the last year or so, sometimes I wish we could hit the fast-forward button. It's a horrible thought."

"Well, you're the one that has to deal with it. I know it isn't easy." He patted Mary on her rear on his way out of the kitchen. "I've got to check on some emails before we eat."

Mary continued sautéing the vegetables in a pan as she thought about the new Paul. It was like having a strange man in her kitchen just now. Maybe this strange man could be her new lover. When Paul tapped her rear, she thought of Kevin for an instant and blushed. She decided not to tell Paul about her affair with Kevin—bad idea. Should she end it? She could never erase her guilt, but she could stop adding to it.

She put on a pot of water to boil. After Helen's death, Paul's father lost any vestige of joy in his already Calvinist temperament. When they were together, Paul wanted to talk about his mother, trying to hold onto his memories. Earl refused to play that game. So why was Paul going?

Paul took a quick glance at his email—still no reply from Steve. His father replied to his note: *Sure, come on down. I'm not doing anything.* Paul hesitated. *Maybe this is a bad idea*, he thought. But the soul reading directed him homeward.

Twenty-Four

Earl sat in an upholstered chair in his sunken living room. The pole lamp provided him light as he read the Bible. His thin features came in and out of the shadows created by the golden light. The scene glowed like a chiaroscuro composition by a Dutch master. Earl read the Bible each night with a forty-ounce bottle of Olde English 800 beer next to him. This habit started after Helen's death. He always kept to the one bottle, though, never reaching for a second.

"Do you mind if I put on the TV, Dad?"

"Not at all," Earl said, not looking up from the Bible. "It's not like I haven't read this before." Earl retired as minister a few years ago, but he still taught adult Sunday school. He liked the distraction, and the church let him stay in the parsonage, where Paul had lived for most of his childhood. Paul surfed the channels until he stumbled across a colorized version of *Singin' in the Rain*. Earl looked at the TV. "Helen loved that movie." He smiled for a moment before catching himself.

Paul remembered his parents sitting on the couch watching old movies on TNT. Helen would hold his father's hand on her lap. When she got excited during a scene, he would pat her with his other hand as if to get her to calm down, always with a smile on his face. Now his father's head was buried in his Bible.

"Too many commercials during these movies." Paul muted the TV. His father did not look up. "Dad, do you remember if there's anything of mine stored in the attic? Papers or things that you or Mom might have saved from my childhood?"

"Your mother might've saved a few things. I'm not sure. But we lost a lot of your things when the basement flooded about ten years ago."

Paul was disappointed. Normally, he would have shrugged it off and retreated into his email or the TV, but he was on a quest. "Let me take a look."

Earl looked quizzically at his son. "Sure, go ahead. It's a mess— mainly Christmas decorations, old clothes, and such. Your mother liked to save things. She threw some things out right before . . ." Earl's voice trailed off. "One of these days, I'll clean it all out."

Paul climbed the unsteady pull-down stairs to the attic. His eyes adjusted to the dim light the single bulb hanging from its ceiling provided. Dusty boxes lined the floor. Paul carefully walked in between rafters. After a few minutes of scanning the area, the only things he found were old containers, suitcases, and garbage bags full of musty clothing. He wasn't even sure what he was looking for.

"Find anything?" his father asked from the hallway.

"Not yet."

"I think it all went in the flood. I'm going to bed, OK? See you in the morning."

Paul considered coming downstairs to say good night, but then his eye was drawn to a small cardboard box, crumpled as if someone had stepped on it. "Sure, Dad." He brushed away a layer of dust and saw the words "Paul's Stuff." The box smelled of mildew. He lifted it carefully, afraid it would disintegrate along with its contents.

When he returned to the stairs, he noticed for the first time that the far wall of the attic was bare—the cross was gone. He thought of asking his father about it, but he could guess its fate. It served no purpose there; instead, it might be feeding the fire that was burning his father up.

Paul sat alone at the kitchen table. The box looked pathetic, like someone had tossed it out but it missed the dumpster and was left to the elements. He opened the box like a grave robber looking for treasures. He found a pile of them bound with a brittle rubber band—letters written on a blue paper stationary. Paul held them close to his face and could smell a hint of a lavender perfume remaining after all these years. What a find. In Paul's hyperkinetic, digitally charged world, handwritten letters on perfumed paper were the equivalent of finding a box of ancient runes. He felt warmth from deep inside, a small flame. *Your light is flickering and nearly out. Open the windows of the attic, and let the light in.* Paul's first wife, Samantha, wrote these letters in college during summer break nearly thirty years ago.

> It wouldn't be an exaggeration for me to say that I think about you constantly. I'm at the beach watching waves disappear into each other. I've been trying my damnedest to send good feelings down to Harrisburg for a while. Maybe we could try an experiment in which, at a specific date and time, I concentrate on a particular thought, which you then try to pick up on (and vice versa). Think I'm crazy? I've done it before. How about Saturday, June 15, at dusk, as the date for our attempt at psychic intercourse? It's the day that Franklin discovered electricity. (I thought it fitting!)

Paul and Samantha shared a passionate love affair in their junior year in college. After a few weeks of torrid infatuation, they parted ways for the summer, both returning home—central Pennsylvania and Boston, respectively. Paul had forgotten that Samantha believed in another world full of goddesses and ghosts and superpowers.

I hesitate and have hesitated in revealing such things for fear of imposing the idea of dependency upon the love that we share. If I were to wish for anything to be created from our mutual feelings, it would be that we would be able to bring out the best in each other rather than be restricting ourselves. I "commit" myself by saying that I love you now under these circumstances and will love you in the future under whatever different circumstances may arise.

The memories of their years together poured into his soul like the water flowing from the Chalice Well, filling him with memories of a forgotten world—quite different from the one that he and Mary inhabit.

He opened another envelope, which contained a photograph of Samantha. In the picture, she wore a red bandanna and smiled as she pruned a rose bush. Paul closed the box and brought it into his childhood bedroom. It was late. He lay awake, feeling a deep sadness. What went wrong? Paul had chased money and women when they moved to New York City, and within a few years, their marriage was over. The letters reminded him she was an old and beautiful soul; surely, their failed relationship must have cast a long shadow in her life. Not for Paul—he raced ahead, never looking back. It had been twenty-five years since he'd talked to her. His last thought before he fell asleep was that he didn't even know if she was alive or where she was living.

Paul woke at three o'clock in the morning, his body popping into the air as if propelled by an electric shock. A voice inside his head said, *Find Samantha and ask for her forgiveness.* The letters brought back the feeling of guilt he thought he buried deep inside, and now it howled like a trapped animal trying to get free. How would he find her?

He pulled his computer out of his bag and turned it on. He started to type. He felt like a knight on a quest. But unlike a medieval quest that took years, Paul rode his digital horse through the Google search box in seconds. He multiplexed himself into thousands of digital knights, rushing over the horizon at the speed of light, reappearing every few seconds from a trip around the world while Paul waited patiently in his bedroom in Harrisburg. The riders knocked on the doors of millions of villagers and read through terabytes of scrolls and galloped on a grid of a trillion connections. Having a perfect map of the world in bits and bytes, they dropped down through continents to towns to streets to sidewalks to the front doors of homesteads. While a medieval knight measured time by the change of the seasons, Paul measured his quest in milliseconds. And he found her in a small town in New York's Hudson Valley. Samantha ran a café, was married, and had a daughter. Now that he found her, Paul closed his laptop and fell back to sleep; he knew what he had to do.

The familiar aroma of coffee filled the small Moore home and woke Paul from a dead sleep. He heard his father putting dishes away. The television news blared in the background, reflecting the ineffectiveness of Earl's hearing aid. Paul entered the kitchen, hoping to cut off his father before he started to make breakfast, but it was too late. Bacon was sizzling in the forty-year-old black iron pan, and the eggs were already whipped and ready to pour. Add the smell of the warm cinnamon buns, and Paul's mouth watered with nostalgic memories of a Pennsylvania Dutch breakfast.

"I told you not to do this, Dad. We could go out for breakfast," Paul protested unconvincingly.

"Sit down." He pushed a chair out from the kitchen table and put a cup of coffee in front of Paul as he sat down. "You have a long drive ahead of you." Paul watched his father finish cooking breakfast. His erect posture and steady hands belied the fact that he would turn eighty-seven that year.

As Paul put the news on mute, Earl joined him at the table. "You know, Simon asked me the other day why I didn't become a minister like you."

His father tried to hide a grin. "What did you say?"

"I told him each generation tends to rebel against the previous one. I told him how I became a Quaker when I was his age. He and I had never talked about it before."

"Ah, yes, the inner light." Earl jabbed at his plate. "The Quakers thought all the answers were inside you." Paul nodded nervously. Earl looked up. "And how did that work out, Paul?" His eyes were cold even though he smiled.

"What do you mean?"

"Did you find all those answers you were looking for?" Earl stood up and took his dishes to the sink. Paul pushed his chair back. "Sit down. I got it." His father disappeared and returned. Paul knew what was coming next. Earl slammed his well-worn Bible on the table in front of Paul and took away his dishes. "The answers are in here. You tell your son that." Paul remained silent, not wanting to get into a fight with his father before leaving. He stared at the Bible in front of him and regretted bringing up the topic. He unmuted the TV while his father finished putting the dishes away. There were so many questions he had for his father. Did he miss Helen like Paul missed her? Does he regret devoting his life to the ministry? What does he think of Paul? "Are you leaving soon?" Earl stood in front of him drying his hands on a towel.

"Uh, yes. I have to get to Quogue for a dinner tonight."

"Did you find anything in the attic last night?" Earl lifted his Bible and wiped the table before putting it back in front of Paul.

"I did." Paul smiled. "I found a box of my stuff. It had some letters from Samantha. It reminded me what a free spirit she was."

"She was a little out there. Mary has her head on her shoulders. Better choice." Paul opened his mouth but thought better of it. "Take the box with you."

Earl had a strange expression on his face. "I gotta take a shit. Can't control it like I used to. You have to go." They both hesitated and then gave each other a short hug. Earl thumped Paul's back as if he was trying to knock all those crazy ideas of him. Then he turned away and walked down the hall to the bathroom.

Every time Paul left his childhood home, he wondered if it would be the last time one of his parents would still be living there. Paul looked at the Bible on the table and felt a surge of energy go through him like a fever. He saw the image of the raven's eye staring at him while he sat on the bench on the Tor. He opened the Bible. His father's handwritten notes filled the margins. He leafed through the book. Notations—in all colors and sizes—were scattered everywhere. The comments stained the thin Bible paper pages like a verbal action painting. Every comment ended with question marks followed by exclamation points and surprisingly few with periods.

He put his bag and box in the car and pulled out of the driveway. As he put the car in drive, he looked at the box on the passenger seat. He had written Samantha's phone on a Post-it and attached it to the lid this morning.

Twenty-Five

"Hello?" It was her voice.

"Samantha, this is Paul." Paul was sitting in his car at a 7-Eleven, sipping a cup of coffee. "It's been too long."

"Yes, it has."

"I just left my father's house. Last night, I found some old letters from you in the attic. So I looked you up online."

"What a surprise." Paul noticed she did not say a *nice* surprise.

"I see you left the city. You're in Hudson Valley?"

"Yes. Where are you living? Still New York?"

"Yes."

"I figured."

"Why do you say that?"

"Oh, I don't know. You were always . . . a city bug."

"Sure. I see you're married?"

"Yes. After our divorce, I thought I'd never marry again. What's the point? But I met someone, and one thing led to another. Now I have a daughter getting ready to go to college." Paul listened to Samantha tell a funny story about her daughter. Her laugh was as memorable as the day he met her.

"How about you? Are you married? Kids?"

"I've a son, Simon. Same age. Same thing. Looking at colleges."

"What's he like?"

"He's a bit like me. Sometimes he drifts off into his own reality, caught up in his ideas about the world."

Samantha laughed. "Oh boy, better pull him back before it's too late. He won't know what world he's in. I always thought that about you—running away from the present, floating into the future, forgetting the past."

"Really?"

"Oh, sure. Like you're a hot air balloon. You were like me. You needed to be staked to the ground, to the here and now."

"Well, I certainly believe the hot air part."

"Sorry." In the awkward silence, Paul thought about what he should say next.

"Paul, I don't want to cut this short, but I have to pick up my daughter."

"Oh, sure. I understand," Paul said trying not to sound disappointed.

"It's interesting to catch up . . . after all these years," Samantha said softly.

"Samantha, one more thing," Paul said. "I've been going through some changes lately. Midlife crisis—I don't know. Your letters reminded me how special you were. I know I didn't treat you well. I was unfaithful. It was my fault—our divorce—and you didn't deserve that. I wanted to ask your forgiveness for what I did."

The silence was agonizing. "So that's why you called?" The tone of her voice grew sharper.

"Yes."

"What's happening? Your shrink is telling you to get over your guilt by asking for forgiveness?"

"Not really a shrink—"

"I'm not sure why I should forgive you. You have no idea how difficult it was for me to trust anyone, to trust my own judgment. Your behavior was despicable."

"I know . . ."

"And now you expect everything to be OK? Making this call out of the blue? Reminding me of a bad time in my life? No! It's not OK! I'm sorry I picked up the phone. Goodbye."

It began to rain. Paul stared at the front windshield as it collected a film of water. Large raindrops snapped against the glass like pebbles dropping out of the sky. Paul reluctantly started the car. He watched the wipers in a futile battle with the downpour. Finding the box in the attic, reading her letters, locating her online: breadcrumbs scattered along the path leading him to her. It seemed so right but came out wrong. Everything was not OK. Paul looked at himself in the rearview mirror. A single tear ran down Paul's cheek. The man he saw did not deserve forgiveness.

His phone rang, and he impulsively answered it before seeing who was calling. "Paul, this is Cynthia. I'm so glad I was able to get you on the phone. Do you have a minute?"

Paul regretted answering. His nemesis had been trying to get to him all week, and he ignored her messages. "I promise to make this quick. The executive committee meeting is coming up this week, and Steve is featuring you front and center. He thought you could use a version of the presentation that went so well at Mobile World Congress— maybe customize it a little?"

"That's exactly what I was going to do."

"OK, great. I'll let Steve know. He might want to see the deck before the meeting?"

"Sure, I'll get something for you on Monday."

"Thanks." Cynthia hesitated. "Paul, there's something else."

"What's up?" So far, the conversation was going too smoothly. What was she up to?

"I just wanted to say that I'm sorry I went after you on the tridget thing. I went too far. And my group was just as culpable because we didn't catch it." There was a long pause. "Paul, are you there?"

"Yeah, I'm here. Look, I didn't appreciate how happy you seemed to be, finding me in a jam. When things go wrong, let's fix them. When things go well, let's celebrate. We can play hardball with each other, but then everybody gets hurt."

"Look . . . Steve sent me an email last night. It had an email thread between you and Steve, which I don't think I was supposed to see. He said that I fucked up the tridget thing and should be fired, but you told him we all fucked up. You could've slit my throat. But you didn't. And I appreciate that."

Paul was pleasantly surprised. "Look, you and I have had some tough times, no doubt. But life is way too short. It's a shared responsibility, right?"

Cynthia was quiet for a moment. "I almost feel like I can trust you."

"You can," Paul said, wondering why he was being so open.

"I know everyone thinks I'm the slippery one, but I feel like no one is watching my back. Steve gives me no feedback. I'm the only woman on the management team. Then I see this email. This stupid little email that you sent made me cry. That's how sick I am." Cynthia paused. "So I'm sorry I tried to fuck with you. Anyway, I just wanted to get it off my chest. So we're OK for the meeting this week?"

"We are. We're OK."

"Thanks."

"Enjoy your weekend."

Paul drove until the Manhattan skyline appeared on the horizon, like a modern castle—another two hours before he gets to Quogue. He wasn't sure why Cynthia opened up to him in such a personal way.

The phone rang again, and Paul did not recognize the number. "Hello?"

"Paul?" Samantha's voice was a welcome surprise.

"Samantha?" Paul pulled his car over to the shoulder of the road.

"I wanted to call you back. I just dropped my daughter off, and I was thinking about her and us . . . how young we were when we married. Not much older than my daughter." She was silent for a moment. "Don't feel bad. I'm fine. We were too young; we didn't know what we were doing. And I do appreciate your calling me. It sounds like you're getting to a good place. I always worried about you, even after we divorced. I thought you lived life wearing a blind-fold but always racing somewhere. I wondered when you took the blindfold off, would you be where you wanted to be? I knew I wasn't meant to be there."

"I wish I could snap my fingers, go back in time, and undo the bad things I've done," Paul said.

Samantha laughed. "Well, you know I always believed in time travel."

"Oh yeah. I was reminded when I read your letters last night."

"I'm sure I wrote about my dreams as well."

Now Paul laughed. "Sure did. It was uncanny how you remem-bered your dreams."

"I had a dream about you this week. Don't get a big ego; I have lots of dreams. This one was vivid. You stood on a hill, watching the sunrise. A light drizzle started. You smiled with your arms spread wide, as if the rain were washing away all of life's burdens." Her voice cracked with emotion. "It was magical. I was happy for you."

"I'm sorry, Samantha."

She whispered, "Paul?"

"Yes?"

"I forgive you . . . I do. Take care of yourself."

She hung up. Paul closed his eyes and let her words slide deep inside his soul. Joy overcame regret, and forgiveness prevailed.

He drove off. He wished he could snap his fingers and be home.

Twenty-Six

"She really loved you, didn't she?" Mary was reading one of Samantha's letters in their living room in Quogue. "She's quite poetic. 'Standing on the beach, I look to the horizon, watching the spray from the migrating whales, light reflecting off the waves. Any sign of life? Yes, perhaps . . . Looking for my Paul.' Aww, it's so corny and sweet."

After returning from a dinner party, Paul told Mary what happened in Harrisburg. Mary listened quietly, asking no questions. She asked to see the letters and propped herself on a pillow at one end of the long couch as Paul did the same at the other end, their feet touching in the middle.

"I forgot how spacy she was," Paul said. "She believed she had telepathic skills."

"I wish we had the letters you wrote back to her," Mary teased. "Or maybe they were postcards. *Dear Samantha, I really don't have time to swim to a Massachusetts beach right now. I'm too busy. But I look forward to seeing you, and thank you for your letter.*"

"C'mon. Give me a little credit. I was more of a romantic back then."

"That was before you moved to New York and fell into the rat race. And then you married a New York bitch who thinks magic is finding a parking spot."

"You're not a New York bitch."

"Well, I'm not a dreamer like this one." Mary read, "'Sometimes, I feel like I can close my eyes and transport myself to you, ending up in your arms. I really believe we can, once we open ourselves up to the universe.' Hmm . . . she obviously did not major in physics." Mary sipped her wine. "I wish we had been more romantic, don't you? No letters, no dreamy poetry." Mary reached for another letter.

Paul knew she was only half-kidding. "Look, Samantha and I got divorced shortly after tying the knot. You and I have been married for almost twenty years. Something's working, right?"

As she pulled the letter from the envelope, a photo dropped out. "Oh, here's her picture." Mary held the picture in front of her. Samantha wore a tank top and cutoff shorts and was leaning over in a garden, picking flowers; one of them she had placed in her hair, held in place with a red bandanna. She smiled at the camera. Mary read the note on the back of the photo: "'Paul, I haven't figured out how to beam myself to you, so this picture will have to do. All my love, Samantha.' She's pretty; long legs. Was she taller than you?"

"About the same height."

"Am I too short for you? Did you want a taller woman?"

"Of course not. You're perfect." Mary's jealousy drew Paul closer to her. He reached for her feet to rub them.

Mary put the photo down and pulled her bathrobe tighter around her. "Paul . . . this is all wonderful, don't get me wrong. I think it was a really brave and thoughtful thing to do—I mean that. But I'm a little jealous. She's very pretty."

"That photo is thirty years old."

"I know, but you loved her, didn't you? I just don't want you to talk to her again, OK? I'd feel uncomfortable."

"Don't you want to meet her someday?"

"No, I don't! Who needs an ex-wife in the picture? Just promise me."

Paul moved toward Mary on the couch. "I promise you."

Mary's eyes glistened. She whispered, "Thank you." Paul slowly moved on top of Mary, and she eased toward him until they were flat on the couch. "And she does have longer legs than I do."

Paul kissed her gently. He reached under her bathrobe and moved his hand down her stomach slowly, the bathrobe's belt coming loose. "Oh, I don't know about that. Let me measure yours."

Twenty-Seven

Later that night, Mary was asleep in their bed, but Paul was still awake and restless. He got up and returned to Samantha's letters, reading them over and over again. Her words, her voice, the lavender scent—they all pulled him back in time. *I guess Samantha was right*, Paul thought. *Time travel is possible.*

As Paul bundled all her letters together to put away, he noticed another letter inside the box. He carefully removed it from his personal time capsule as if it were a rare document. Yellow with age, the envelope was blank but sealed. He tore open the brittle envelope and removed a folded letter. "Dear Paul," the letter began. It was Paul's handwriting.

> You are four years older now. I hope you don't consider seventeen-year-old Paul's philosophy to be childish. As I write, I realize that I don't know who you are—who I will be.

Paul realized that he wrote this letter in his junior year in high school. He barely remembered even writing it. It was also clear that his younger self intended it to be opened when he graduated from college.

The letter was full of youthful angst:

Even now, I have the foresight to realize my limited vision of myself.
I want to prove myself instantly—today—even though I can see how
impossible that is.

Does the world know you are living? Do you consider the question of a spiritual reality, and are you still a Quaker? Are you "tied down"? I am. I know the world has enveloped me until I cannot move and am no longer free. But someday, I hope to be free.

Paul was uncomfortable; he realized these words echoed inside him for many years, like a forgotten prisoner, locked deep in the dungeon, pounding at the door, wondering if anyone was outside. Paul had gone into the world, propelled by the spring-loaded pinball launcher, and the noise of the bumpers and scorekeeping drowned out the sound of the imprisoned young voice.

"My god!" Paul said to the empty room as he finished reading the three-page letter. "Simon could have written this letter." He realized he had written this at the same age as Simon, just as he was preparing to go to college.

Paul put the letter down and rubbed his forehead, trying to absorb it all. He could learn so much from his son, and vice versa. The letter revealed to Paul that his son was his mirror.

Too excited to sleep but too tired to think, Paul lay down on the couch with a pillow and blanket. He turned out the lights and put in his earphones.

Twenty-Eight

"How do you pronounce it?" Steve asked. Paul's boss sounded tired and irritated. Paul was reviewing a pitch deck with Steve and others on the executive team. It was Steve who insisted on having the call on Sunday morning. They were still on the title slide, which was a picture of an opened ancient book, its yellowed pages curling at the edges. Underneath the picture was the presentation title—"Digital Domesday and the Naming of Everything."

"*Doom*sday," Paul said.

"But it's spelled *domesday*."

"It's the medieval English pronunciation."

"But we're not in medieval England."

"But the book is. It was created in 1086. I'm using the Domesday Book as a metaphor for what is happening today. William the Conqueror realized that conquering England was not enough. He had to understand what he conquered. So he commissioned the most comprehensive survey of its time in Europe. Surveyors captured information about everything—land, people, cows, sheep, hides, gold, and homes—everything that could be named and recorded. It was called the Great Naming. And it turns out that this information continues to be used today. Not just by historians, but even by barristers in modern court cases. It is an early demonstration of the power of naming everything that existed."

"But why is it called *domesday*?" Steve asked.

"We really don't know the significance of the title. Some scholars think it refers to the word *duum* and is a reference to the Last Judgment. In this case, it referred not to the end of the world but to the fact that whatever was recorded in the book was truth. It was final. Really didn't matter what reality was; what mattered was what was in the Domesday Book."

"Sounds pretty gloomy to me." Paul didn't recognize the voice.

Steve barked, "Sorry, I was on mute and on a three-minute riff before I realized no one could hear me. How's this whole conversation going to make money for our clients and therefore make money for us?"

Paul continued, "I explain the concept in the introduction of the presentation—very quickly. It's a little storytelling to open the conversation. Then I will move to today's digital world, where we are on the verge of naming everything again. Only this time, it will be digital. Everything will have a digital presence and be connected—people, homes, land, cars, and every object. We are moving to a digital equivalent to William's Domesday. It is real time and always connected and will enable a host of things. It won't just be for William the Conqueror; it will be for every William, Tom, Dick, and Harry in the world. And then I click to the next slide." The slide shows dozens of dots with blinking dashed lines connecting them to each other. Paul read the slide title, "Digital Domesday—the Internet of Things," and then said, "And then I segue into trivergence and tridgets and how all of this will work. How companies can take advantage of the trivergent world to make money, to help customers, and so on."

The conference call was silent for a minute. Everyone was wait-ing to hear Steve's verdict. "Damn this mute button," Steve sputtered, coming back onto the call. "It kind of makes sense. A little conceptual, though. It's a downer though, talking about doomsday. Can we pro-nounce it the way it's spelled—*dome*sday?"

The anonymous voice jumped back into the discussion. "*Domes-day* is good. Reminds me of *Mad Max Beyond Thunderdome*. Not that upbeat a movie, but at least it is action oriented." Paul wanted to kill the person talking. It was probably someone from marketing. He looked out the window of his home office. Mary was sitting by the pool, having a coffee and reading the Sunday *New York Times*. He promised her that this would be a short call and that he would join her after. He was wrong.

"Is that the one with Mel Gibson?" Steve and the marketing min-ion were getting them dangerously offtrack.

"Folks, hold on. We cannot make up a new pronunciation. We'll come across as ignorant. That is not how the English pronounce it," Paul protested.

Steve persisted, "Look, this is an American client. They'll be like me. I never heard of this thing before. They'll have no idea how to pronounce it. Who gives a shit what the Brits think?" Silence. "Sorry, James. I didn't mean that."

"No offense taken, boss," said Paul's European lead, who bit his Oxford-educated tongue.

"Cynthia, what do you think? We almost had a disaster with this tridget name. We got away with it, but barely. Now we're referring to the end of the world on our first slide."

"Well"—Paul involuntarily cringed hearing Cynthia's voice—"actually, Steve, Paul used the domesday analogy with the *Financial Times*, and the reporter really liked it. He said he was going to use it. He even asked where he could find a photo of it. And *Harvard Business*

Review liked it. They haven't committed to an article yet, but I think we have a real good shot."

The disembodied voice came back: "How did Paul pronounce the name with the reporters—*domes*day or *dooms*day?"

"*Dooms*day," Cynthia said sharply. "Fred, we need to move on. I agree with Paul—if we use it, and I think we should, we have to pronounce it correctly." Now Paul placed the voice. Fred worked for Cynthia in marketing and probably wished he could sink into a corner right now.

Steve's voice relaxed. "OK, OK, I get it. When Paul and marketing agree, I know I'd better back off. Listen, I paged through the rest of the deck, and it looks good. I really like the number at the end—one million dollars. Just for a feasibility study? Do you think they'll bite, Paul?"

"Our internal source says it is already in the budget. If the meeting goes well, they want to start next week. Number one strategic priority, he says."

"Damn. This stuff is really heating up." Steve's voice rose. "But if we get into the meeting and, after five minutes, the client is as confused as I am, I will tell you that I told you so. All right?"

"All right, boss." Paul watched as Mary stared up at the back of the house, looking for him in the window. She picked up another section of the *Times*.

"Hey, is the client's CEO Jewish? He may be put off by this Last Judgment thing."

"I will check, but I don't think so. And I'll make it very clear that the Domesday Book is not about the Last Judgment." Paul rubbed his forehead and wished he could refill his coffee cup.

"Or maybe he's a Mad Max fan!"

"Steve, we can't—"

"I'm just busting your chops, Paul. I don't know where you come up with this high-concept bullshit, but it sells, and that's what matters.

I have a tee time coming up, so it's been fun. Paul, I need to talk to you one-on-one for a minute. I'll call you on your cell."

"Great, thanks." Steve hung up. There was an awkward pause. Was anyone going to say anything? No. The series of bleeps indicated that everyone was dropping off. Before Paul had a chance to run to the kitchen for another coffee or call out to Mary that he was on his way out, his cell phone rang. "Paul, I wanted to touch base for a minute. I'm fine with the pitch, OK?"

"Good." Paul was relieved.

"Do I need to read this Domesday Book before the meeting?"

Paul wondered if he was kidding. "You really can't read it. It lists everything that existed in England in 1086. It's very long and tedious."

"Could somebody just put together a little write-up about it?"

"Absolutely. I'll send it out later today."

"Wait until I tell my golf foursome about the Domesday Book. One of them is an expat from England, runs the US division of Barclays. I'm going to play with his head. Distract him. He's prissy."

Paul sipped the last bit of cold coffee in his cup. He watched Mary heading back into the house. "Sounds like fun."

"The reason I called—the rumor is you're going to Italy for a month? Renting a house?"

"Yes, it's something I promised my family for a few years now, and we finally booked it."

"Are you taking a month off?"

"Not really. I'll spend about two weeks shuttling to different client meetings and conferences before my real vacation."

"You're my go-to guy, and we're onto something really hot right now. I'm just worried that we could lose momentum."

"I'm going to do a lot of client pitches in Europe."

"There's more money in the US for this stuff, don't you think?"

"All our offices are begging for visits right now. Europe will be dead later in the summer, and I'll be in the US then, where people never take a vacation."

"Paul, I'm very supportive of your spending time with the family. Italy's great. It's just . . . we've talked about this. You kick ass. People like you and me, we're in a race. It's not how fast you are on the track; it's how short your pit stops are. Do you understand?"

"Well, I'm not sure Mary would like the pit stop analogy—"

"Here's my point—you are nearing the finish line. No promises. No guarantees. But someone will need to take over for me. Not this year, not next year. But the time will come. Do you have what it takes to win the race?"

"Are you suggesting that I not take a vacation?"

Steve's voice turned cold. "Now you're putting words in my mouth. Don't fuck with me, Paul. Take a vacation. Take a pit stop. But make it quick." Steve hung up.

"Thanks, Steve," Paul muttered to himself. He looked outside. Mary was nowhere to be seen. The newspaper was on the ground beside her empty lounge chair. A breeze grabbed a section of the paper and scattered the pages across the patio into the pool. Paul guessed it was the book review section based on the size of the pages. His eyes adjusted to the outdoor light. It was a beautiful day in Quogue.

"Paul?" Mary's voice came from the bottom of the stairs. "Is your *short* call over?"

"Yes, I'm sorry. It took longer than I thought."

"I'm going for a walk."

Paul walked out of the office and saw Mary at the foot of the stairs, glaring at him. "Let's go out by the pool," Paul offered. "It's a beautiful day, and I need another cup of coffee."

"OK, so long as you don't ignore me."

They returned to the pool and sat down. Paul gestured toward the papers floating in the pool. "Did I miss anything in the book review?"

"Nothing special. One 'New Agey' book about meditation and mindfulness that you might appreciate in your new mind-set."

"Really?"

"It sounded like the latest psychic fad to me, but maybe I'm not mindful enough. Are you going to show Simon your letter today?"

"I think so, yeah. Do you think it's a good idea? Will he be spooked?"

"He'll probably be angry. No kid wants to think he is exactly the same as his father at the same age. But it's just so unbelievable, you have to show him." Mary looked up at Simon's bedroom window. "Assuming he gets up sometime today." Mary leaned toward Paul. "Paul, how are you feeling? It's been a couple of weeks since seeing that woman in Glastonbury. Are you OK?"

"Sure, I'm good."

"I saw you out in the yard early this morning before your call. You looked like you were in a daze."

"I like the early morning; I can think clearly then. So I was walking along the woods in the back, and I thought it's funny that we don't have a place to sit there. I'd like to put something there so I can maybe meditate in the morning."

"Better than staring at a computer, I guess," Mary said under her breath. They sipped their coffee.

"I've been thinking. In the soul reading, Christine talks about connecting to nature and tending to my garden. You know the old garden behind the garage? I was thinking we should plant some vegetables there," Paul said excitedly.

Mary looked concerned and reached for Paul's hand. "Are you kidding?"

Paul looked hurt. "No, I think it would—"

Mary held his hand and said, "Paul, we plant vegetables there every year."

"Really? I've never been back there."

"Where do you think the fresh tomatoes come from?"

Paul looked down at Mary's hand and suddenly felt very tired. "I don't know. I guess I thought you bought them at the farm stand." They held hands in silence; the only sound was the cawing of a bird circling above.

Twenty-Nine

The raven floated above the ruins of the Glastonbury abbey. The grounds of the abbey dominated Glastonbury like a smaller version of Central Park in Manhattan. A six-foot wall divided the abbey from the rest of the village, forming an imperfect rectangle of a green lawn, interrupted by the remains of medieval buildings. In the late afternoon sun, the ruins of the abbey cast long shadows on the grounds.

The raven circled lazily along the perimeter, watching the activity below. At the west entrance to the abbey, tourists passed through a museum and gift shop on their way to the grounds. Just to the right of the entrance was the Abbot's Kitchen—an octagonal building with a round roof and a large chimney. Next to it was a small café and a dozen tables where visitors could have a snack. The raven watched a couple sit at a table with a food tray.

"Cheese sandwich. Not exactly a Sunday pub brunch," Edward muttered as he eyed his sandwich, which was tightly wrapped in white paper.

"Edward, it's such a beautiful day to be in the abbey. Away from that smelly pub," Jeanne said. "Look at that sky. Not a cloud. I'm so glad you agreed to come with me."

"Coerced, you mean—just because I drank too much last night. Now this is my punishment."

"I hardly think it's a punishment to be spending the afternoon with your beautiful wife in this gorgeous setting."

Edward winced as he bit into his sandwich. "Of course it isn't." He stared at his bottled water. "I miss our Sunday tradition, that's all."

"Maybe we need a new tradition—dry Sundays!" Jeanne scanned the people passing by as she picked at her salad. "Look at that girl. She's dressed like a medieval kitchen maid. Isn't that cute? She must be a guide."

Edward nearly spit out the water he was drinking. "I feel like a bloody tourist in my own town."

"We're so lucky, Edward! We live in a place that people come to see from around the world." Jeanne waved at the girl as she passed by, a few German tourists in tow.

"The whole thing's a farce. Do you know what kitchen maids looked like back then? Their clothing stunk and was covered with grease and soot. They had wooden teeth, bad breath, hairy legs, hairy . . . everything. Lecherous monks chased them around the table."

"Sounds like you were there in a past life." Jeanne winked. "I'm sure praying in the chapel." Jeanne watched the tour guide and then leaned forward and whispered, "I think she's cute. Probably from university. Maybe she's a history student."

Edward ignored Jeanne. "And by the way, they would be drinking *ale* back then, because the water was not reliable. This pathetic café serves nothing stronger than Coke!"

"But now the water *is* reliable." Jeanne tapped Edward's water bottle with her own as if they were toasting something. "Do you think she's too young for Trevor?"

"I'd have to examine her teeth." Edward put his half-eaten sandwich on the wrapping paper on the tray, dismayed that he was still hungry. "Inedible, this sandwich." He thought he could smell the aroma of roast pork drifting from one of the pubs on the high street on the other side of the wall. But it was probably his imagination.

Jeanne sighed. "I do miss our dear boy. Why does he have to live in America?"

"So he can get a job?"

"I know, but what if he meets an American girl and settles down there? We'll never see him again."

Edward held her hand. "He'll be back. He's a momma's boy. Let's take a picture of the kitchen wench and tell Trevor that we found his wife—she was hiding in Abbot's Kitchen."

* * *

The tour guide smiled at them, nonplussed that they stared at her. She felt silly in her costume, but it was good money on the weekends. And on beautiful days like today, it was fun telling the story of the abbey to tourists—even if they only understood a portion of what she was saying. She was finishing her tour at the entrance to the abbey park and noticed the large raven sitting on top of the gate. Amid the bright sunlight that turned the stone entrance from brown to tan, the black raven stood out, and she shuddered slightly as a gust of wind caused the raven to spread his wings and rebalance himself on top of the gate.

The raven often perched on the entrance gate. It lived in the woods north of the Tor but came to the village to forage for food. "Above the entrance, you can see the large black raven," the guide said. "His predecessors are often referred to in history and literature. Celtic gods of darkness and death often took the forms of ravens. No doubt ravens have observed the history of this part of the world going back to Stonehenge, and some believe they pass those memories down through the generations." The guide was improvising, inspired by the raven and bored with the usual script. "Ravens are very intelligent birds. Scientists believe they are one of the only species other than human beings who have the ability to communicate about objects or events that are distant in space or time."

"Are they dangerous?"

The guide looked down at the little boy asking the question. She smiled and placed her hand on the boy's head. "No, not really dangerous. But they are omnivorous."

"What does that mean?"

The girl hesitated. "Well, it means they eat anything." The boy's mother scowled at the guide, putting her arm around the boy. She quickly added, "But I've never seen a raven attack anyone at Glastonbury." She smiled at the mother and son while thinking, *Relax, bitch. I'm just making pocket money while going to school.* "This ends our tour for today . . ."

*   *   *

The raven perched above the gate, perfectly balanced in the soft afternoon breeze, plugged into the memories of past ravens. One memory far outweighed any other—the dissolution of the abbey. The raven heard the sounds of Henry VIII's henchman laughing as they walked under the entrance, still drunk from too much ale at a midday visit to the pub. They had work to do. It was 1539, and they were dissolving England's richest abbey. Pilgrims pulled at the tunics of the soldiers but let go as the men touched the handles of their swords with a menacing look. The monks ran frantically back and forth, screaming, praying, and crying. Two foot soldiers stood in front of the cathedral. The sergeant glared at them. "Where's the abbot?"

"He's saying his last prayers inside."

The sergeant slapped the soldier on the side of his helmet. "You fool. He could escape!" They ran inside and found Abbot Thomas Whiting lying face down in front of the altar, his small figure obscured by the black smoke pouring from massive candles lining the walls of the nave. The effect caused them to pause for a moment.

*   *   *

Whiting was praying for forgiveness. He signed the Act of Supremacy, which denounced the pope and recognized the king's sovereignty. He wanted to save his beloved abbey, monks, and, yes, himself. But he lost it all anyway. Thomas More's greed was insatiable. Within months, the abbot was imprisoned in the Tower of London. Then the orders for his execution were signed by the king, and he returned, in irons, to Glastonbury. Now his face pressed the cold stone floor of his beloved abbey for the last time. He smelled the dirty, unbathed soldiers standing around him as he lay, shaking on the floor. They pulled him to his feet. Tears streamed down his face as he whispered Hail Marys. The past decade of fear weighed his body down as the soldiers pulled him out of the cathedral. They lashed him to a mule cart and proceeded up the high street toward the Tor. A company of drunken soldiers accompanied him. Monks who protested too loudly and came too close were brutally clubbed and left groaning in the street. Half the village lined the streets, jeering and spitting at the abbot, supporting their king. Some villagers peeked through their shuttered windows, fingering rosaries and wailing to their Roman pope, who was nowhere to be found. Another group followed the procession quietly, feeling sorry for an abbot who, by all accounts, was honest and cared about his flock. The medieval raven left its perch at the abbey entrance and flew above as the crowds surged up the slope of the Tor. Soldiers tossed a thick rope over one of the buttresses of St. Michael's Tower, creating an ad hoc gallows. The abbot was brought to his feet on the cart, the mule passively chewing on the grass, and the noose was placed around his neck. The crowd jostled for a view. Their noise rang so loud and shrill, it even gave pause to the raven circling far above the fray.

The sergeant read the letter condemning Abbot Whiting to death. The crowd grew quiet, craning over each other, lifting children onto shoulders. The voice of the sergeant competed with the even louder voice of Abbot Whiting insistently reciting blessings from the liturgy in Latin. Suddenly, the abbot stopped speaking. He saw the glint of a steel hook on a pike, held by a tall man whose head was covered with a black coarse wool hood. He pressed the cold steel against the abbot's warm body, loosening its limbs from each other.

Abbot Whiting looked up at the sky and noticed the black raven sitting on the buttress supporting the hanging rope. The raven stared at him. He felt the memory of this moment being sucked into the raven's eye to be shared across the centuries. The crowd sensed the moment was at hand and renewed its roar. The raven left the buttress, reacting to the noise. The rope snapped tight around the abbot's neck as the mule moved forward to eat a piece of fruit offered by a soldier, and the cart abandoned the abbot. Wild cheers could be heard in the village below as the abbot's loyal monks cried on their knees or ran away in horror.

Whiting's body was quartered, and parts of it were nailed on town gates and public squares through Somerset County as a warning that even the most powerful of God's men paid a horrible price for treason.

The raven remembered the abbot every time he returned to the Glastonbury abbey gate. It always perched next to the stone spike that the abbot's head was impaled on following the quartering. The raven remembered his head was a source of sustenance until the rotting flesh became indigestible. It sensed the existence of the head as if it were a phantom limb, but the spike was empty—it could not feast on a memory, and it was time to eat.

Edward's phone rang. "Hello? Thomas, where are you? Lucky you! And have you eaten?" Edward beamed as he talked to his older son,

Thomas, who had remained in Glastonbury, married a local girl, and was Edward's business and drinking partner. Jeanne half-listened, still enjoying the scenery. "I had this ghastly cheese sandwich at the abbey café, washing it down with spring water. Yes, ghastly. I couldn't even finish mine." Jeanne shook her head at Edward. "Well, let me see." Edward put his hand over the phone. "He wants to know if we would join him for one drink. They miss us."

Jeanne frowned. "No, Edward. We agreed to have an alcohol-free afternoon outdoors."

"And we did, so now let's have a beer." Edward listened. "My dear, your daughter-in-law says she is looking for someone to share a glass of wine with. Do you want to talk to her?" Edward winked, knowing Jeanne loved to gossip with Thomas's wife.

"Oh, OK." Jeanne threw up her hands as if helpless. "Let's stop by the pub on the way home. But just one drink and then home."

"God be praised, my son. Your mother has blessed a visit to the pub. We will be there in just a minute." Edward leaned back in his chair as if thanking the heavens. "My darling, aren't we so lucky to have such wonderful boys?"

"Of course we are, and strangely, they know when to call their father to invite him to the pub—right after you visit the loo."

"Yes, well . . ." Edward sensed a trap.

"I'm sure you didn't text Thomas asking him to call you."

"My darling, how could you think such—?"

"Don't you ever cheat on me, Edward! You cannot tell a lie."

"I just texted him asking what he was doing—"

"What am I going to do with you?"

"Love me forever, my darling, and have a drink with me. You caught me again! I confess!" Edward threw up his hands as if he were being arrested, brushing his half-eaten sandwich and its wrapper onto the ground.

JOURNEY   159

As he bent over to pick it up, Jeanne saw a shadow come across the table and instinctively shielded his head. "Edward!" Edward saw something out of the corner of his eye. In that instant, they shared the fear of being attacked. He looked up and saw the raven. It brushed against Edward's head on its way to the half-eaten sandwich. In an instant, it was in the air, its shadow moving toward the far end of the abbey grounds.

The color came back to Edward's face. Jeanne gasped. "Oh my god, did you see that? Edward, he almost picked off your head. You could have been hurt."

Jeanne's expression reminded Edward how deeply she loved him and he loved her. "It stole my sandwich!"

"Edward, that bird was large. I think it was a raven."

Edward smiled. "Clearly a sign it's time to escape these natural dangers and move into the safety of a pub."

Jeanne playfully touched his head as they both rose. "You have a one-track mind. Let's go."

They walked arm and arm underneath the abbey entrance. Edward was already embellishing the tale he would tell in the pub after the third pint—how he battled the abbey raven for his cheese sandwich and lived to tell the story. His phone rang. "Yes, Thomas, we are coming. And do we have a story to tell."

Thirty

Paul knocked on Simon's door for the third time. "I'm coming, I'm coming," Simon said behind the door.

The door opened a crack, and Simon peered cautiously from his still-dark room. "What?"

"You're going to sleep the whole day away! C'mon, it's almost lunchtime. Plus, I have something I want to show you."

Simon frowned. "Listen, Dad, I'd love to help out, but I have a full day of school work. I really can't do anything else."

"It's not work. Just something I want to show you. Come downstairs. I'll make you some eggs."

"Give me a minute." Simon closed the door.

"OK, but don't go back to bed. I'm starting to cook now. Five minutes."

Simon appeared in the kitchen fifteen minutes later. He sat down to eat. His father and mother sat across from him, looking expectantly. "What?" Simon grew nervous, thinking of his drug stash hidden above one of the beams in the basement.

Paul pushed an envelope toward him. "This is a letter I wrote to myself when I was your age. I found it when I visited my dad this week. I had sealed it. The idea was for me to open it when I graduated from college. It's me talking to myself when I'm older. Mom and I thought you should read it."

Simon put his fork down and pulled the letter out of the envelope. He began to read. Paul and Mary looked at each other. He turned the pages, then returned to the beginning again.

"What do you think?" Paul asked.

Simon looked up at his father. "I think the acorn doesn't fall far from the tree." And he smiled. "The way it's written, the questions, it's almost like I could have written this."

"That's why we thought you should see it," Mary offered.

"Dad? Maybe we should take Snuffy for a walk and talk about this letter." Mary looked hurt. "Sorry, Mom. It's a father-son conversation."

Mary stood on the porch, watching Paul and Simon walk down the street, with a leashed Snuffy trying to navigate between the two, as if herding them toward each other. Mary wished she could hear what Simon was saying. They both were smiling, sometimes pausing in the middle of the street, and then they would resume walking. As they neared the corner of the road, they paused again and hugged. Snuffy tried to fit between them, but they were too close. She sat on her haunches and watched them, her tail scraping the road like a windshield wiper. Mary was jealous but still happy that Paul and Simon had found something in common.

As they disappeared around the corner, Mary's phone buzzed. She looked down—it was a text from Kevin. She told him not to text on weekends. "Plans changed. No travel. Lunch tomorrow?"

Thirty-One

"Maybe I should write a letter like yours. I'm the same age you were." Simon waited patiently as Snuffy circled, ready to do her business.

"What questions would you ask yourself?" Paul asked.

"When will I have a 'ship?'"

"We have a boat already. The damn thing never starts up."

"*Relationship*, I mean. You talk about your girlfriend in your letter. I don't have one. All the bad girls in my class want to be friends. They won't hook up."

Paul picked up Snuffy's deposit in a bag and twisted it. "Be patient. Crumbs on the water."

"What does that mean?"

"Talk to a lot of girls. Friends can become girlfriends or introduce you to a future girlfriend. There's nothing better than a female wingman."

Simon walked in silence, an indication he was absorbing Paul's advice. "You know what surprised me about the letter?"

"Tell me."

Simon stopped and looked at his father. "How little you knew about your future. Your girlfriend, religion, job—you had no idea what would happen in your life." Simon spoke earnestly and looked at his father as if he felt sorry for him.

"No person knows what will happen to him or her. That's what makes life exciting—the unknown."

Snuffy buried her nose in a bush, and Simon yanked on her leash. "I see the unknown."

"What do you mean?"

"If I wrote a letter like yours, I would say that I can see the unknown, but I can't tell anyone because they'll think I'm crazy."

"Give me an example," Paul said, trying not to act concerned.

"You know when you went to Glastonbury a while ago?"

"Yes."

"I looked up pictures of Glastonbury on the web, and it was crazy. I've seen the Tor and the tower on top. I've looked down on that hill and the village at night."

"In your dreams?"

"Yes. But it was very real, Dad. And the question I have for my letter is what does all this mean? Am I crazy?"

Paul patted his son on his shoulder. "Probably déjà vu. When you saw the picture, you thought you had seen it before."

"But it wasn't the same as the picture on the screen."

"What do you mean?" Paul asked, stopping as they entered their driveway.

"The picture of the Tor on the website was taken on a bright afternoon. In my dream, I saw the Tor at sunrise, and an orb floated above the tower." Simon grinned. "Now you're going to think I'm crazy, right?"

Paul kneeled, taking off the dog's collar, not wanting to look at Simon. "Not at all. But you do have a healthy imagination."

The two of them watched Snuffy run to the back door, her tail wagging in hope of a reward for a job well done.

Thirty-Two

Will he even recognize me? Mary thought as she combed her hair in front of the hallway mirror. She had little makeup on—nothing around the eyes—and a pale-pink lip gloss. She was dressed in a spring tent dress, which ballooned in the center down to her knees, suggesting a kind of modesty. Even when she was sitting, it covered her knees. The bright spring colors of the dress were girlish, but she was no ingenue. And she wore her wedding ring.

Her phone rang. It was her sister, and she chose not to answer. She shared everything with her sister except for the affair, but she was about to break it off. The apartment was deathly quiet. She was alone. Paul left that morning for a business trip, and Simon left for school hours ago. There was no one to share the burden of her terrible secret—even its ending. She was pale as a ghost. Instinctively, she reached for a brush and added a little color to each cheek. It was not a funeral, just an ending. She left the apartment quickly, already late.

Kevin rose from the table with a big smile on his face as he watched Mary enter the restaurant. "I'm so glad we could meet on such short notice," he said, kissing her on the cheek. The waiter held her chair, and

Mary sat down. The restaurant was half full, but it never got too packed. It was a French bistro hideaway. It stepped down from the street into a small space with a dozen tables and a small bar with four stools. Its location was conveniently between their apartments, but not on a street that either visited otherwise. It was next to the small European-style hotel they used after lunch. During all their rendezvous, they never ran into someone they knew. If they did, they would say it was a business lunch. Kevin was initially Mary's client, after all.

"What is this you're wearing? What happened to my hot lover in the black stockings that disappear into that wonderland underneath the tight skirt?" Kevin had already finished half a glass of wine and started to pour one for Mary.

"I'm fine, Kevin. I'll stick with water," Mary said, ignoring his question. The waiter recited the specials. They lunched here so often, even the specials were repetitious, and they tended to order the same dishes. They liked to feed each other tastes of what each had ordered. It was one of several rituals, which, along with the effect of the wine, ensured they were sexually ravenous by the time they reached the hotel room.

"Stand up." Mary stood. "Turn around." Mary caught herself following his script and quickly sat down.

"Kevin, I wanted to talk to you—"

"So why this outfit? You're turning into an Annie Hall persona on me? Late-blooming hippie? A slower, more innocent reveal to turn me on? I love this."

"I'm not trying to turn you on. I want to have a conversation."

"Wait a second—please tell me you're wearing cotton panties under this dress. If you are, so help me god, I'm going to bend you over this table right now, pull that dress over your head, and fuck you so hard. My god!" Kevin raised his voice above a whisper.

"Kevin!" Mary noticed a few people looking over at their table. "That's enough."

Kevin started pouring her a glass of wine, ignoring her request. "You've such an imagination—wasted on Paul, really. You know what? I don't want any lunch; I just want to fuck you right now. We should leave."

"Kevin, I think we should stop seeing each other." Mary listened to her own words as if they were coming from another person. The words lay on the table, staining the conversation like a spilled glass of red wine.

"What?"

"What we've been doing . . . it's not right. We have to stop. Now, today."

"Did Paul find out? You didn't tell him, did you? This has got to stay quiet."

"No, Paul doesn't know. I never want him to know. This is our secret. We had our moments, and I feel ashamed to admit that, but this ends now." Mary was surprised she sounded so calm.

"Mary, Mary, Mary. This"—Kevin gestured at the two of them—"this is perfection. We see each other. We enjoy each other's company. We have sexual adventures. Then we go home and live a safe, boring, but necessary life. Don't screw this up."

"But, Kevin, this is wrong."

"What is? To enjoy ourselves without breaking up our families? To live on the edge once in a while? To take risks without really risking everything?"

"Something's changed. I don't feel right anymore. I never felt right, really. And we are lucky we haven't been found out. It would destroy our families."

"So that's it? You're done?"

"Yes. I just wanted to tell you in person. I thought I owed you that. I'm sorry, Kevin." Mary held back tears. "I have to go."

Kevin reached across the table, trying to hold her hands. "Don't go. This is a big mistake. I'm not done with you yet."

Mary paused. "Excuse me? I'm not some toy."

"Oh, but you are. I wound you up, and you let go of everything, didn't you? The job, the school, the family—all of it left you for a moment as you moaned and begged me to fuck you. You loved every moment. Like I said, I'm not done with you."

"I think we've said enough." Mary felt the eyes of other diners on their table. "This is getting embarrassing."

"*Now* you're embarrassed? *Now?*" Kevin leaned forward, whispering so hard, she could feel his breath. "You wanted this, Mary. This is on *you.*"

Mary glared at Kevin. "I didn't come here to be insulted by you. I'm leaving."

"You'll regret it."

"You won't tell anyone. It would ruin your marriage, and you can't afford it. In the end, you just care about the money."

"I care about putting my head between your legs and hearing you beg—"

"I won't listen—"

"You'll listen to me. Here's the truth—you enjoyed this fantasy more than I did. And you'll regret cutting this off. I won't. You were fun, but you're a little pathetic, a little needy."

"You're just trying to hurt me, and that's sick. Look, we fell into this, but it was a mistake. I want to fix my marriage."

"You'll change your mind. And when you do, you'll beg me to come back."

"I thought we were going to have an adult conversation today," Mary whispered, holding back tears, shaking in anger.

"We just did." Kevin rose from the table, reached in his pocket, threw a hundred-dollar bill on the table, and stormed out of the restaurant.

Mary got up slowly. She had to leave before she began to cry. She couldn't bear to look around her, so she brushed the front of her dress, straightening it out, and slowly walked toward the door.

"Good afternoon, ma'am," said the maître d'. He opened the door and smiled, as if he overheard nothing.

She stepped outside and felt the wave of heat coming off the afternoon sidewalks. She reached the corner of Broadway and Eighty-Fifth Street, where the southerly wind caught her dress, lifting it for a moment until she pushed it down against her legs. Overcome with despair, she pressed her forehead against a store window, hoping that passersby might not notice a woman crying uncontrollably.

An eight-foot-high poster of a Victoria's Secret model filled the window display above Mary's slumping profile. It was a headshot of a deeply tanned, blue-eyed, blonde woman. Her rich, wavy hair, wind-blown by an unseen fan, was filled with yellow sand. Sand speckles painted her bronze cheeks like decorative sparkles for a party. Her bright white teeth and full lips conveyed happiness. Her eyes seemed flat by comparison, staring into the camera. Whether purposeful or not, her eyes conveyed emptiness as they watched Mary, who rocked back and forth like a mourner wailing at a funeral.

New Yorkers flew by and, looking up from their phones, observed a woman crying. Her body obscured the Victoria's Secret slogan at the bottom of the poster, which said, "You Can Have It All."

Thirty-Three

"That was an absolute kick-ass pitch!" Steve shouted, toasting Paul and Cynthia at the hotel bar in Chicago. The acoustics of the bar amplified every noise. Paul's ears rang as the patrons shouted over each other. The three of them finished a dinner with their team, and Steve insisted on a nightcap in the hotel bar. "And domesday worked! It's all they talked about. Trivergence, the digital domesday." Steve bowed and waved his hand. "Paul, I stand in awe of your ability to tell a story."

"I knew we'd nail it when the client said he was a history major," Cynthia agreed.

"Christ, are you kidding me? He asked more questions about the Domesday Book than he asked about our fees. A million to get started—no problem."

"And then when he asked about getting the slide so he could use it in his exec meeting—" Cynthia laughed.

"I was going to say, sure you can have it—for a hundred thousand dollars!" Steve and Cynthia clinked their glasses, enjoying the joke. Paul sat on the barstool quietly, enjoying the conversation and nursing his one drink for the evening. The cacophony of sound suggested the crowd in the bar had been drinking all night like Steve and Cynthia. Paul found that late-night hotel bars had two scenarios—deserted except for a scatter of loser alcoholics or really lonely travelers or packed full of adventure-seeking men and women ready to slip into a dangerous vacuum of judgment. Paul agreed to a nightcap with Steve, even though it often led to trouble. He checked his phone. Mary had not called; she was probably asleep by now.

Steve checked his phone as well. "Shit, I have to call my wife; she's pissed. My son is headed to rehab again." For a moment, Steve looked upset, but then his face brightened. "Hey, I forgot to tell you my story about golfing yesterday." Paul eased back on the barstool. "So I tell the Brit about the Domesday Book, and we're going back and forth. It's obvious he's thinking, 'How the fuck does Steve know anything about English history? He's a stupid American!' We get to the seventeenth hole, which is a par three with water in front of it. And we're all square on the match. He's unsure about his club. We're talking about my visiting England soon and how he'd host me at his club and so on. I know he really doesn't want to spend time with me. So he's getting ready to swing, and I say, 'That would be great, and maybe I can see the Domesday Book while I'm there.' I pronounce it *domes*day, not *dooms*day. Well, he swings and hits it fat. It drops in the water short of the green. Match over. He just glares at me. 'It's pronounced *dooms*day, Steve.' And he storms off the tee. I was fucking with his head. That alone makes the whole thing worth it. And now a new client." Another clinking of glasses. "Cynthia, thanks for your help. You guys were right, I was wrong."

Cynthia looked startled. "Well, thanks—"

Steve winked. "I'm just practicing my call with my wife. 'You were right, I was wrong.'" He looked around the bar. "Some interesting ladies in this bar. I wish I could stay." Steve looked at Cynthia. "You didn't hear that politically incorrect statement, did you?"

Cynthia smiled. "Some nice-looking men too," and she winked at Paul.

Steve observed Cynthia and Paul for a moment. "Well, you kids stay out of trouble." He staggered out.

Cynthia motioned to the bartender. "I might have another. It's great to be able to celebrate something for a change."

"I'm still working on this glass of wine, but I'll keep you company," he said. The bartender appeared. "She'll have another Macallan."

"You were really good today," Cynthia said.

"Well, thanks."

"I mean it," Cynthia insisted. "It wasn't just the pitch and the story and all that. You're authentic. The client believed what you were saying."

"I believe what I'm saying. The world's going to be connected."

Cynthia put her hand on Paul's arm. "You've changed, haven't you?" She looked at him as if trying to read his mind. "In a subtle way. It's how you come across—I'd believe anything you say."

"You're kind." Paul changed the subject. "Cynthia, do you wonder sometimes if you're doing what you're meant to be doing?"

"What do you mean?"

"When you were a girl growing up, what did you want to do?"

Cynthia sipped her scotch. "I wanted my father to love me. I wanted to be the prettiest, smartest, best-behaved girl in the world—someone he could be proud of."

"And what happened?"

"Well, I never lived up to that standard. I tried. I think he knew I tried. He supported me going to school and working and thought it was great that I was dressing in nice clothes and making money. He worked in a factory—no college education. But he never told me what he really thought."

"You speak in the past tense? Did he pass away?"

"Yes, heart attack. I wasn't there. I was traveling." Cynthia's eyes moistened.

"And your mother? Is she still alive?"

"Yes."

"And what does she do?"

"She misses him. She focused on him, not me. We're not that close. Sometimes it felt like we competed for his attention."

"You feel a lot of pressure in your job, don't you?"

"Yes." Cynthia took another sip of her drink. Cynthia always dressed modestly. But tonight, as she leaned toward him, he noticed the top buttons of her blouse were undone. A half bra supported her small breasts, lacy blue, matching her blue silk blouse. "I feel a lot of pressure, even though my father is dead and my mother doesn't care. What a life!" She smiled and tapped his shoulder affectionately. "Why are you asking me all these personal questions?"

"I'm just curious. It seemed like you wanted to talk."

"You're getting better and better, Paul. You know how to get a woman to talk about herself and open up. Even a hardened bitch like me."

"I think I'm opening up. Becoming more empathetic, maybe? I don't know. I think it's getting very late, and I need to go to bed." He stood up from the barstool. "But I like getting to know you a little better. Don't be afraid to show more of yourself; it's attractive."

"You say that to all the girls." Cynthia almost fell as she reached for her purse under the bar. Paul steadied her by holding her elbow. She stood close to him for a moment. "You've changed, haven't you?"

"What do you mean?"

"You're not just bullshitting me. You mean it."

"It's what I feel. I'm just telling you."

"Keep telling me. It feels good. And thank you for this special evening." Cynthia touched his cheek with her hand and smiled. "You are a good man." She turned and walked away.

Paul remained at the bar, observing everyone around him. They were drunk and loud, frantically trying to reassure each other they were having fun. Laughing too hard at each other's jokes. The despair in the room was palpable to Paul as he panned the scene through his new lens.

Paul left the bar and returned to his room. He crawled into bed wearing his earbuds and drifted off to sleep—listening again to his soul reading.

Thirty-Four

"I have something to tell you, and you won't like it," Mary said, sitting across from Paul at their kitchen table at dusk on a Friday. Paul tensed, wondering what he was about to hear. He had just returned to their summer house from a week-long trip to several cities. All he wanted to do was sit by the pool, have a glass of wine, and ease into the weekend. Mary looked serious. Was it about money? Sometimes, she would spend money on something and then ask for forgiveness afterward—like the five-thousand-dollar Giacometti drawing on the wall behind her. Maybe it was about Simon. Or her mother bothering her again. He hoped it was not about the soul reader or Glastonbury. He brightened at the thought that he was calling Christine tomorrow. It would be the first time they had talked since the soul reading four weeks ago. He had so much to tell her.

She nervously rotated her coffee cup and wouldn't look up. "I'm embarrassed and ashamed, and I'm afraid of what you will think of me." Paul realized this was something more than an expensive painting she'd bought at a charity auction or a bad grade that Simon received. She looked like she could cry.

"What is it?"

Mary looked up from her coffee and tried to get the words out. "I'm closing down my business. The crash has killed it. No one can pay for my services. I'm losing money with the office rental and the admin help. I know it's pathetic that I can't cover the costs, but I can't. And it's depressing. I don't want to pretend I have a business when I don't."

Paul relaxed. He knew her business had dried up and she was left with the occasional lunch with former clients who could no longer afford to buy her services. "I understand. Lots of businesses are closing down. We're doing fine. Plus, I'm going to have a very good year—maybe the best in my career."

"I know, but I feel that you respected me because I worked, because I had a business. And now, I'll just be a housewife and mother. You don't value that in the same way."

"That's not true—"

"And I lose some of my financial independence. It worries me."

Paul came over to her side of the kitchen table and put his arm around her. "It doesn't make a difference. You don't have to work for me to appreciate who you are."

Mary buried her head in his shoulder. "I didn't want to tell you. I feel like a failure."

Paul's mind took over. He wanted to talk about the economy and the headwinds that everyone was feeling and the fact that all his clients were struggling. If it weren't for his idea of trivergence, he and his company might be suffering big time. But he stopped himself, realizing Mary was not looking for a rationalization. He ran his fingers through her hair. "I know you're disappointed. I do value you." He held Mary tighter. His mind went quiet, and the image of the waterfall in the Chalice Well Gardens appeared. He willed that image flow into her consciousness. *Bring her peace*, he thought.

Mary raised her head and looked at Paul, dark streaks running down her cheeks from her tears. "You're serious? You're not just saying that, are you?"

Paul kissed her on the forehead. "I believe in you." After a long embrace, Paul stood up and returned to his seat. He smiled and then sipped his coffee. "So that was easy. Are there any other secrets you want to tell me?"

Mary looked surprised. "What do you mean?"

Paul noticed her face turn red. "Nothing in particular. It just seems like you're in a confessional mood, so we should get it all out at one time." Paul saw a brief look of fear in her eyes.

"I think that's enough for one day," she whispered, staring into her coffee cup.

Paul stood up. "Should we take this conversation out by the pool with a glass of wine?"

Mary looked up and smiled. "What a great idea. Let me wash up, and I'll meet you down there. My face must look like I'm a member of Kiss."

"I'll get a special bottle from the wine cellar. Let's celebrate the end of an era and the beginning of another one."

Mary went upstairs to her bathroom. She smiled at herself in the mirror, relieved that Paul had taken the news so well—but she wondered about his question about other secrets. Did he know about Kevin? She thought about the lunch with Kevin and shuddered. What was happening to Paul? She did not get his new obsession, but the change seemed real and more than words. The whole experience tempted her to jump back in, to reopen her heart to him, to forget the past. But she remained guarded. The catalyst for it all was a fairy tale, and Mary did not believe in fairy tales. For the moment, she pushed her doubts into a dark corner of her mind. She wrapped a scarf around her shoulders and joined Paul out by the pool.

Paul put on music. The sun was setting, and the sky was a light red, as if lit by a giant flare ignited somewhere over the western horizon. The dusk light deepened the color of the gardens surrounding the pool, whose water matched the color of the gray slate patio. Paul and Mary sat side by side on reclining chairs.

"Here's to the future," Paul toasted. "This summer, you can spend more time out here, enjoying yourself."

"And we have a month in Italy! *And* I've signed up for a photography class."

"Photography?"

"You know how I like to take pictures with a real camera. I want to get better at it."

"Fantastic. Lots of photo ops in Italy."

"I know. I'm so looking forward to it. You are going to be there? You're not going to disappear on me, are you?"

Paul shook his head. "Despite Steve's threats, I'm going. I'll be there at least half of the time, maybe more. I have some day and overnight trips in Europe to deal with." At that moment, Frank Sinatra started singing "Summer Wind" over the speakers. They looked at each other and started to laugh. Paul held out his hand. "I think we're meant to dance now."

They got up and danced slowly.

"O-M-G, what gives?" Simon asked, standing at the opening to the pool area.

"We're pretending we're in Italy. Come here." Paul waved Simon over.

"No, you guys are having fun." He turned to go back to the house.

"Come on, dance with us," Mary said. Simon hesitated and then stepped into their dance. The three of them danced together, Simon bending over awkwardly, following the lead of his parents. Paul got a whiff of pot on Simon's clothing as he moved closer, explaining his son's willingness to join them. Even dancing with the parents can be funny under the right circumstances.

"That was special," Mary said as they finished. Mary's face revealed the look of a younger woman bereft of anxiety for once, happy to be with her family.

"Did you tell Dad about his Father's Day gift?" Simon asked.

"Oh no," Mary said. "I completely forgot! Simon, tell him."

Paul shook his head. "I forgot it was Father's Day this weekend. You guys don't have to do anything—"

"Well, Mom and I were talking. We know that you are, you know, going through some changes. And wanted a quiet place to be able to think and be alone. And Mom had said that you were commenting on how we don't use the woods area enough. Should we show him?"

Mary smiled and nodded.

"Follow me." Simon led them toward the woods in the back of the property. A miniature Chinese maple tree, previously buried behind larger trees surrounding it, stood alone in a small clearing in the woods.

"Oh my god," Paul exclaimed, looking at the small circular clearing. The sandy soil was freshly turned.

"We decided to make you a meditation spot," Simon said.

Paul stepped into the clearing and looked back toward the Chinese maple tree and the profile of the large house behind it, now dark as the sun had nearly set. "This is perfect. How did you do this?"

"Well, Mom talked to Ted, the landscaper, and he cleared it out."

"Ted said that he can work with you on putting something in the space—a bench, a large rock, whatever you would like," Mary said, beaming.

Paul noticed that half of the maple tree was patchy. For years, taller trees prevented light from getting to one side of the maple tree. But now it could grow back. Paul remembered the soul reader's words: *"Your soul is a tree. A damaged tree that needs to grow back. To become whole again."* Paul muttered, "I heard about this in my—" Paul caught himself. Not a time to reintroduce the soul reader.

"What?" Mary asked.

"Nothing, I really love this." He hugged Simon and Mary. "Thank you." Paul wanted to share all this with Christine tomorrow when they talked.

Thirty-Five

Paul woke up with a start, similar to his early morning risings in Glastonbury. It was a beautiful day in Quogue. The sun burned the moisture
off the grass, and a faint mist hovered over the lawn and gardens outside the bedroom window. He knew he wouldn't fall back to sleep, so
he put on a bathrobe and left the house, wanting to see the clearing
again. He went down the back stairs. The wet grass chilled his bare feet
as he walked toward the clearing. He paused and took a deep breath.
He remembered Mary and Simon's expressions when they showed him
the clearing. Gratitude washed into his heart like a wave crashing into
the shore and feeding into a tide pool, deep and calm. He neared the
clearing, visible behind the Chinese maple. Paul noticed something
in the middle of the clearing—it looked like a rock, which surprised
him. He did not remember anything being in the clearing the night
before. As he got closer, he realized it was a large snapping turtle. It
was breathing hard, and its head was covered with dirt. *Is it dying?* Paul
thought. He approached it cautiously, not wanting to startle it. The turtle ignored Paul, remaining motionless. Paul noticed that the ground
behind the turtle, at the very center of the clearing, was a different

color and had been disturbed. The turtle's head was covered in clay, and it was breathing heavily; it must have been digging up the dark patch. After studying the patch of land and the turtle from a safe distance, he figured that it was female and had just buried its eggs. He had never seen a snapping turtle on the property before. It was large and ancient looking.

He wanted to show Mary and Simon. He slowly backed away and hurried back to the house and into the bedroom. "Mary." He rubbed her shoulder. "Get up, honey. You have to see this!"

"I just want to sleep a little longer."

"You won't believe it!"

Mary sat up. "Is something wrong? Is Simon all right?"

"No, nothing's wrong. It's just a strange coincidence. I'm getting Simon up."

"Well, good luck with that."

Paul knocked on his door. "Simon, wake up. I have something I want to show you."

Surprisingly, Simon came right to the door. "What's up, Dad?"

"Put something on and follow me."

Mary and Simon both clutched their bathrobes, still groggy, and followed Paul. As they approached the clearing, they could see the turtle. She was still breathing heavily and had not moved.

"Holy shit," Simon said.

"I think it laid eggs. See where the soil is disturbed?" Paul pointed.

"I wonder what kind of turtle it is," Simon said.

"I'd say it's a snapping turtle," Paul said.

"We should Google it to make sure," Mary said. "And find out when they lay eggs. I think you're right, though."

"So cool," Simon said.

"Stay away from her, Simon. She just laid eggs," Paul said.

"I'm getting my camera." Mary hurried back to the house.

"This is turning into a big Father's Day weekend, Dad, eggs and all."

"I guess so." Paul put his arm around Simon.

Mary reappeared with the camera. "Let me take a picture of the two of you with the turtle. But not too close!"

After taking a few shots, they returned to the house. Paul went online in the kitchen while Mary started making coffee and breakfast. "What does it say?"

"It's definitely a snapping turtle. Look, here's a picture." They gathered around the computer. "It says they leave the water and go inland to lay the eggs. And they do this in late spring/early summer. That's exactly what's happening. They hatch forty-five to sixty days later."

"That's a shame. We'll still be in Italy." Mary went back to making breakfast.

"What a strange coincidence that the turtle showed up at that spot," Paul said.

"I don't think so. It's a clearing with freshly dug dirt and sand. It's a perfect place to lay eggs," Mary said as she turned on the morning news. Simon already disappeared upstairs. "They've probably been laying eggs back in the woods for years, and we just never saw them." Mary playfully covered Paul's eyes with her hands and yelled, "Simon! Come on. It's time to eat."

Paul wondered how Christine would interpret this; she had seen a turtle in his soul reading. He would find out in a few hours.

Thirty-Six

Mary paced in the kitchen. She had Janet on speakerphone. "I don't know what they're talking about. He's in his office, and the door is closed." Paul was on a call with Christine, the soul reader. "What am I supposed to do, put my ear up to the door and eavesdrop?" Mary fixed herself a cup of coffee. "We can't pick up and listen in on calls. Paul put in a new wireless, supersonic phone system with all these buttons and screens, and I can't figure it out." She opened the door to the dishwasher and started to put the clean dishes away.

"What good is a phone system if you can't eavesdrop?" Janet asked. "So what does a soul reader do, anyway?"

"I don't know. He said he kept his clothes on. It's better than having him with a masseuse."

"Be careful about that. She's French, right?"

"Yes."

"Well, you know those French women like to fuck. They think nothing of having affairs. Before you know it, she's reading more than Paul's soul."

"I don't think French women are any more promiscuous—"

"They're like bunnies. Why do you think they dress so well and don't eat?"

"She looks pretty good on the website," Mary conceded.

"And you say Paul's different?"

"He's been a little spacy. He doesn't want to play golf with his friends. He's not watching the news. He's spending time outside by himself. But he is also more caring, asking about things. I told him I'm closing down the business, and he was very understanding about it."

"Do you think she gave him some drug prescription?"

"No, I don't think so. In fact, he is drinking less, eating better, and going on long walks."

"He needs some serious therapy—midlife crisis."

"He was saying how he wanted to have a place where he could meditate. So we had a gardener clear a space in the woods in the back of the property. It was his Father's Day present."

"And what did he say?"

"He was so happy about it."

Janet muttered, "Maybe he *should* be taking medication."

"But here's the strange thing—the next morning, really early, Paul gets up and goes back to the clearing, and there's a big snapping turtle sitting there, and it turns out she had just laid and buried her eggs—right in the middle of the clearing! Isn't that unusual?"

"What did you want the turtle to do, drop her load in the pool?"

"Well no, but it sure is a coincidence."

"So the family sees a turtle laying eggs, how life changing."

Mary finished emptying the dishwasher and looked out the kitchen window, absent-mindedly wiping the kitchen counter with a hand towel. "Here's another one. Paul goes to visit his father last weekend. He goes into the attic and finds a box. There're letters from his first wife when they were dating. He calls her up and asks for forgiveness."

"Stop right there. Not good, not good at all. Cut that off at the pass. He wants to reconnect. Midlife crisis meets rekindling with the ex!"

"Are you a therapist or an investment banker?" Mary teased.

"Maybe I'm a soul reader." Janet laughed. "But if I had a cute client, I would ask him to take his clothes off."

"So anyway, he also finds a letter that he wrote to himself when he was Simon's age, before he was going to college. The letter is beautiful; he asks himself questions about life and what will happen to him."

"OK."

"It is so thoughtful. Like a young man talking to his older self. And it was exactly what Simon would say. The same words, the same cadence. We realized that Paul and Simon were exactly the same at that age."

"It's called genetics."

"No, I mean exactly the same voice. And the letter was sealed, and Paul doesn't even remember writing it."

"Mary, Paul doesn't remember my name; if it's not related to business, he doesn't remember." Mary watered the hanging plants in front of the kitchen window, enjoying the warm sunlight.

"In any case, it was another coincidence, and we shared it with Simon, and then Paul and Simon went on a walk and really connected."

Mary noticed a movement in the kitchen. Simon was standing behind her. "Simon! How long have you been here?"

Simon looked surprised. "What?"

Mary turned off the speakerphone and picked up the receiver. "Janet, I have to go. I'll talk to you later."

Simon was still in a bathrobe, even though it was the middle of the afternoon. His hair was standing up, and he still had streak marks in his cheeks, formed by the patterns in his pillow—he had just gotten out of bed.

"Were you listening to our conversation? Be honest." Mary's face reddened.

"No. I just came in. I think Snuffy needs to go out. She was scratching at my door." Simon smiled, pleased that he could be of service.

"OK, so take the dog out!"

"But I'm in my bathrobe."

Mary shook her head. "Get dressed then."

"OK. Maybe Dad wants to take a walk with me. I'll ask him."

"Don't interrupt him; he's on the phone."

Simon walked out of the kitchen. "Poor guy, always working, even on the weekends."

Mary thought about bringing a cup of coffee to Paul just to see what was going on. The red light on the phone indicated he was still on the line. What were they talking about?

Thirty-Seven

"How are you feeling?" Christine asked.

Paul lay on his office couch, his head perched against a throw pillow. He faced the window, and from his angle, he saw feathery clouds scattered across the sky. They looked like long threads of cotton candy thrown into the air. The sound of Christine's voice lifted him as if the law of gravity was suspended and he was floating in space. "I feel pretty good. I have so much to tell you."

Paul heard Christine exhale through the phone and could almost feel the moisture from her breath. "Paul, before you tell me anything, let's do a little exercise to slow you down and help you feel what is happening to you, OK?"

"OK."

"Close your eyes. Take a deep breath, and blow out slowly. I want you to imagine sitting on a golden orb. Now place your hands over your heart and focus on your breathing. Breathe in. And breathe out." Paul breathed, fighting the random thoughts coming into his head. What did Steve want to talk about? Where was Mary? Was she angry? Did anyone walk the dog?

As he listened to Christine's voice, all his thoughts and worries washed away, leaving him sitting on the golden orb, basking in its glow. Christine reminded him from time to time to think of the orb and the breathing. His arms and legs began to tingle on the outside but felt very heavy on the inside, as if the force of gravity was greater in this imagined world.

"Now I'm going to count to five, and you will come back to this moment, feeling calm and energetic." She counted, at each point telling Paul what he would feel as his body and mind came out of the trance. When she reached five, Paul opened his eyes. His body tingled, as if a mild electrical current was running through it. His surroundings, even the glass of water on his desk, were vivid in a blinding way. "I want you to take your time, have a sip of water, get comfortable, and tell me what happened."

Paul told Christine everything—the box in the attic, the call to his ex-wife, the letter to himself, the meditation clearing, and the snapping turtle. His voluble recounting and rising voice finally caused Christine to laugh. "My goodness, a lot has happened in a short period of time."

"I'm sorry. I guess I'm trying to cover everything quickly."

"No worries. The soul reading is working. You're progressing extraordinarily fast. Take care of yourself. Lots of change is good, but make sure you're eating and sleeping well. Drink lots of water, take walks. You're supercharged right now, OK?"

"Yes."

"The events you're describing are synchronistic. As you open up, your energy is becoming much stronger, and it attracts other energy in the universe."

"I've heard that word—*synchronicity*. It was a Police song, right?"

"Google it. It's a Jungian term. It refers to all these events that occur with no seeming cause—finding the box, finding your ex-wife, the turtle appearing. Yet they are not accidents. They're connections, and you'll have more such experiences, for sure."

Christine interpreted all his encounters for him. The connection with the ex-wife was a forgiveness ritual that he needed to do to remove his guilt. Finding his old letter and his interaction with his son suggested his son was an "old soul" and could be a teacher for Paul. The turtle laying eggs represented a rebirth archetype, relating to the change Paul was going through.

Paul listened intently. Everything Christine said, her voice having a soft authority to it, made sense. He did not take notes; he would remember every word.

"We covered a lot today, Paul. Is there anything else?"

Paul hesitated. "I'm a little worried about Mary." He looked at the closed door of his office and wondered if Mary was trying to listen. "I think she's worried that I'm going crazy."

"She did help with the meditation space. That seems supportive. And it sounds like you are experiencing more tenderness toward each other. Don't give up on her." Paul was silent. "Paul, listen to me. You're going through a profound change in your life. It'll have ups and downs, like a roller coaster ride. As you become more in touch with yourself, you will experience many emotions—happiness, guilt, despair, gratitude—and maybe several at the same time. Focus on this experience, and don't judge or try to make any big life-altering decisions, OK?"

The phone was silent for a minute. "OK."

"We are running out of time, and I have another call right after this one. As we discussed, I won't be taking any appointments until September. So we'll talk at the end of the summer, OK?"

Paul sat up, feeling panicked. "What should I do in the meantime?"

"You simply have to be and let life happen. The world is embracing you in an amazing way—look at all the wonderful things you've already experienced. Stay open. Listen to the reading. There's so much there. The time will fly by."

"But who will I talk to?" Paul sounded unconvinced.

"There are angels everywhere who will help you."

"That sounds farfetched." Paul felt like a child being thrown into the deep end of the pool and told to swim, only for the parent to walk away.

"Well, Jeanne's an angel who brought you to Glastonbury. You'll meet others. They're everywhere, and you're like a blinking beacon right now. They'll find you, and you'll find them. You're making amazing progress, but you need to slow down. It takes years, not weeks or months." The phone was silent, and Christine sensed his fear. "Let me give you a couple things to do—let's call them homework assignments."

Paul reached for a notebook.

"Mary. The next time you go out with her, I want you to imagine you don't know her. Have her arrive before you do. When you enter the room, look at all the people—their faces, their expressions, and their gestures—and scan the room until you see her. Watch her as if it were the first time that you saw her. Observe her. Ask yourself what kind of person she is. What does she like, what makes her laugh, what does she care about, who does she want to become? Make eye contact. She'll see you. When that happens, walk toward her, try to keep the eye contact. When you reach her, do something bold for someone you've met for the first time—kiss her on the cheek, hold her hand, or put your arm around her shoulders. Look into her eyes and think, *I've just met my life partner.* Will you do that, Paul?"

"I can try. We're going to a party tonight."

"Perfect timing then. See, synchronicity!"

Paul rubbed his forehead, suddenly tired from the conversation. "I know I'm too worried about getting somewhere fast—it's not a race."

"Exactly! Are you writing in your journal?"

"I am."

"Excellent. Maybe you'll have a book by the time we talk in September! So back to Mary. I also want you to think about love. What is love? What does it mean to you? This is something you can focus on this summer, starting at tonight's party. I believe you are capable of great love."

"I'm not sure Mary would agree."

"Just think about love. Become aware of the heart chakra. Listen to the reading—there may be clues there. Write about it. It will be good for you and Mary. We can talk about it at the end of the summer."

"What happens next?" Paul noticed that they had run over their time. "After the summer."

"We should have a retreat. You should come to Glastonbury for a long weekend and stay at my home. I've an upstairs guest room. We'll agree to a set of programs and rituals that would help you progress."

Paul brightened. "I'd love to do that." Paul caught himself. "I'm not sure how Mary would feel about that though."

"Bring her along. Maybe she'd like to have a reading. Or maybe she'd just want to observe. See what's comfortable. Anyway, I'm late for my next call. It'll all work out."

Paul's voice was tentative. "OK. Christine?" He thought about her in her house in Glastonbury. What she looked like. Her house full of sparkling talismans and the smell of sweet incense.

"Yes?"

"Thank you so much for everything you've done for me."

"It's my pleasure, Paul."

"I'm going to go to the clearing after this and will express my gratitude for meeting you. And I'll say a blessing for you and your book."

"That would be appreciated." She hesitated. "Goodbye."

Her voice disappeared, and Paul missed it already. He lay back on the couch, still holding the phone to his ear, staring out the window.

There was a knock at the door. "Paul?" It was Mary.

Thirty-Eight

The door opened, and Mary stood just outside with a mug in her hand. "I thought you might like some coffee."

"Thanks." Paul took the coffee and sat at his desk. He hit a few keys on his laptop and stared at the screen.

"That was a long conversation. How was it?"

"Good. She's very helpful."

"What'd you talk about?"

"She wanted to know how I was feeling. I told her about all the things that happened since the reading."

Mary eased onto the couch like a cat. "Isn't some of this stuff personal—your ex-wife, your son?"

"Well, that's what she does, Mary," Paul said defensively. "She reads your soul—that's pretty personal."

"Did you talk about me?" Mary asked.

Paul shut his laptop, sat next to her, and put his arm around her. "Yes, I did. She told me I should think about what love is and how to love you. Did you know 'What is love?' is the most popular question on Google, by the way? I just looked it up."

"You know, Paul, I'm not really sure I'm comfortable with you talking about our relationship with her—or talking about me at all. I don't know this person. She's not a licensed therapist. I think you should keep me out of this."

"Mary, we talked about a lot of things in my life. And like it or not, you're a big part of that."

"So what's next?"

"She suggested we have a retreat in her home in early fall. She has an extra bedroom, so I would stay with her."

Mary looked upset again. "Paul, you know that I'm very uncomfortable about that. She looks like a woman you had an affair with!" Mary realized she'd raised her voice and looked to see if Simon was outside. She lowered her voice, hissing, "There is no fucking way that you're staying with her for a weekend."

Paul said, "She invited you as well. You should come."

"I'm not going to be part of this. She just wants to get another client, another fee."

Paul pulled her down on the couch and tried to hold her, but Mary pushed him away. "We can work it out, Mary. I want you to be OK with this." They sat in uncomfortable silence.

Mary spoke evenly. "Paul, this woman could be a complete charlatan. You must agree not to book any trip to see her, pay her any money, send her any information—not without talking to me first."

Paul frowned. "Don't you think I'm a better person now?"

"I think you're different, but I don't know. Sometimes you seem to be in a trance. I think you're working too hard, too much stress. You're vulnerable. I don't want someone taking advantage of you."

Paul's phone started ringing. "I have to take this. It's my three p.m. call with Steve."

Mary shouted, "Dammit!" and stormed out of his office.

"Paul, I don't have too much time, so can we keep this short?" Steve said.

Keep it short? Paul thought. *You're the one who scheduled the call on a Saturday morning!* "Sure, Steve. Let me jump right into it. This is about Project Scratch. It's a stealth start-up backed by Kleiner Perkins and Andreessen Horowitz, and it has Vice and Barry Diller's IAC as strategics. I'm escalating this to you, Steve, because of reputational risk. They're looking for our help to do a technology assessment, design, business plan, ecosystem, the whole bit, but I'm not sure we should get involved."

"Why not? It sounds like a no-brainer."

"The product's a little unusual. It's in the trivergence space—another 'internet of things' application—but it's focused on sex. The application takes advantage of advances in haptic technologies. It uses them to simulate—"

"Slow down, Paul. I'm just a business guy here. What are haptic technologies?"

Paul realized Steve had not read the briefing deck. "It's about using technology to digitally translate body movements, replicating those sensations using sensors embedded in devices contoured to fit your sexual organs."

"So you have a device that helps you jack off? What's the point?"

There was a beep, indicating that someone had joined the call. "Who just joined?" Paul asked.

"It's me, Cynthia."

Steve said, "Hi, Cynthia. Thanks for joining on such late notice. Paul, when I read your email this morning, I realized that, if this about our reputation or image, Cynthia should be part of the conversation, and I invited her."

"I agree. Hi, Cynthia."

"Hi, Paul. Hey, Steve." Cynthia sounded unusually happy.

"Cynthia, I realize now the subject matter is a little risqué. I hope you're OK with that. I don't want another sexual harassment lawsuit at our company."

Cynthia laughed. "Steve, I read through the material this morning. I'm a big girl. Don't worry."

"Good. Now, where were we?"

Paul thought about repeating Steve's comment about jacking off but decided to play it straight. He needed an answer by tonight, and he had to get off the phone.

"We've been asked to propose, and I've been told that we have the inside track. They're familiar with our work around trivergence, and they feel that it ties nicely into what they're trying to do in the adult pleasure-enhancement segment."

"Adult pleasure-enhancement segment? Are they calling this APE products?" Steve roared at his own joke but then turned serious. "So what's the opportunity? How much?"

"It's a multibillion-dollar market. And they've raised thirty million so far. It'd be millions for us, for sure, assuming they like our initial work."

"OK. Give me more. What's involved?"

"Without going into too much detail, there is a male and female stimulator linked to the computer by Wi-Fi and connected to a common website that allows your partner to manipulate your stimulator. There're a lot of potential applications. For example, it can be used by couples who travel separately or who live in different cities."

"That's a good thing, right? Removes temptation."

"It can be used by people who want to be more intimate but not 'go all the way,' so to speak."

"Better than phone sex," Steve offered.

"And it has therapeutic applications for people who suffer from sexual dysfunction, people who are handicapped, and so on."

"Hell, I want to invest myself."

"But we think the dominant application right out of the box will be porn."

"Take me through that."

"The adult webcam market today is a one-billion-dollar market, growing very rapidly. One report says that twenty-five hundred new cam girls sign up every day."

"You're assuming that Cynthia and I know what you're talking about because we cruise porn sites."

"I've seen a few, Steve. Just for cocktail party conversation. Women watch porn too," Cynthia volunteered.

"Actually, about thirty percent of adult webcam customers are female. About five percent of the daily internet audience watches adult webcams."

"Holy shit. That's big."

"It's likely that one of the first and most lucrative applications of this technology will be an enhanced webcam experience where people can watch and stimulate each other."

"Sort of remote prostitution," Steve said.

"Exactly," Cynthia said. "Are we helping a client get into the porn/ prostitution business? And do we want to be associated with it? How could it affect our brand?"

"Can we carve out that application? Do the rest of the work?" Paul knew Steve was looking for an angle because he sensed a big opportunity.

"I thought about that, but a lot of our work around the design of the technology would be core to any application, and we need to consider all the sources of monetization to support the business plan. Their competitors would do that. We can't really carve it out," Paul said.

"Cynthia, what do you think?"

"If we could be sure our involvement would remain confidential, I'd say it's worth considering, but this is likely to get a lot of publicity, and our name could definitely get dragged into it. Some of our more conservative clients might get really uncomfortable."

"And it dredges up that damn tridget reference again. I can see the headline now."

"We also have to think about how our female work force might react to us working on this kind of project. They may be uncomfortable," Cynthia offered. "I could see us having brainstorming sessions about digital prostitution opportunities and some employees feeling harassed."

"This sounds like a ticking time bomb. Damn it, I've got to go. I'm gonna be late for golf. At least, now I've something to talk about—this week, it's digital prostitution. Man, Paul, you are coming up with some good material!"

"So you're saying no, Steve?" Paul asked.

"No, I'm not saying no. I'm saying you and Cynthia work it out. Talk to HR, talk to legal. Contain the risk so we can do this. We need the revenue this coming quarter. Cynthia, cover your ears. Paul, I could see me wanting to try the damn thing. I could think of a couple women I'd like to test it with. Anyway, come up with a solution. That's what you get paid to do." Steve hung up.

"Well, well, Paul. You certainly come up with provocative ideas," Cynthia teased. "My question is, if it's completely digital, does it redefine *in flagrante delicto*?"

"Well, it certainly opens the possibility of truly anonymous sex," Paul offered. "Two people could have sex, stimulate each other, and not really know who the other person is."

"That's a little creepy," Cynthia mused. "Or kinky, I guess, depending . . ."

"But think about it. You wouldn't know if it were a man or woman. What they looked like. What they did. And maybe then you would have to pay to find out more about them. Who did you have digital sex with? You could price the most attractive, skilled camsters higher."

"Or you could keep it anonymous. Would that be as good?"

Paul was silent for a moment, then finally spoke. "I don't think so. I think I'd want to know."

"You're seeing the market potential," Cynthia whispered. "I wouldn't pay at first, have the orgasm hopefully, and if I really liked it, then I would pay to find out who it is. If it was a powerful guy like you, I would probably come again." Paul heard her breath through the phone.

"I'm not sure we should be—"

"Hypothetically, I mean." She paused. "Do you think that would qualify as having an affair? I'm not so sure." There was silence on the phone. Paul was uncomfortably aroused. "I don't think we should do it."

"I agree completely," Paul said, releasing a long breath.

"I mean, take them on as a client."

"Of course." Paul hesitated. "I'll tell Steve."

"The rest is hypothetical, but I like the example. Have a good weekend, Paul."

Thirty-Nine

The party was a charity event being held outside at a beautiful water-front property just a few doors down from Paul and Mary's home in Quogue. They arrived at the party and split up. Mary joined her friends in the silent auction tent, while Paul walked down to the water and sat on the bulkhead, his legs dangling a few feet above the beach. The Quantuck Bay reflected the natural moonlight and the string of party lights, which added a festive air to the evening.

Paul breathed in the salty air and enjoyed the view. The bay was still. One lone motorboat glided through the water, leaving a slight wake. The boat was so far away and the music from the tent was so loud, Paul could not hear its engine. It skimmed across the water's surface like a bird. Fire Island was on the horizon—a dark shadow, separating the mainland from the ocean. If the music stopped, Paul would be able to hear the ocean waves, striking the island and the houses sitting on stilts. On a stormy night, the waves rose tall enough that you could see their white tops before they fell onto land. The white spray pirouetted in a frenzied dance, leaping into the sky, followed by the sound of the waves crashing into the dunes like the beating of tympani—an aquatic party. But tonight, the party was a manmade one, and Paul had to join it and be a social animal.

As he entered the tent, his eyes adjusted to the strong lights. Paul inched his way into the sea of people, scanning the faces, nodding hello to friends or people whom he should know. He was looking for Mary. In the distance, he saw her familiar shoulders, squared, and her back revealed in a V-shaped drop. Even though she was facing away, he knew it was her. She stood with a group of women in a vigorous conversation. Paul was a hundred feet away, but he could imagine her expression and the light in her eyes.

He remembered Christine telling him to remember the first time he saw Mary. It was more than twenty years ago. Paul saw her in a crowded bar in midtown—a watering hole for young business types. Mary wore the conservative business suit that women wore at the time, trying to look like men. When she turned in his direction, he could see her loosely clinging top. It looked like she'd opened another button on her blouse after work. The top of her white lace bra peeked above her blouse depending on the angle. Paul remembered every detail of what she wore. Her day-old makeup and tousled hair signaled her exhaustion from a long workweek. But when she noticed Paul across the room, picking him out among all the faces hidden in the haze of cigarette smoke, her look had a feeling of destiny. The light from her eyes washed across the room like the waves on the beach. As the waves pulled back, he was drawn to her, their eyes fixed on each other.

"Paul, let's get a drink. I need to talk to you." The man's voice brought Paul back to the here and now. He shook hands with him but ignored his offer. His eyes remained on Mary, and he slowly walked toward her. As in the bar so many years ago, Mary turned toward him, and he caught her eye. She smiled, and the years melted away. He contemplated her face, noticing the memorable landmarks when they first encountered—the turned-up nose, the bright-white teeth, the pale-blue eyes. Mary watched Paul as he approached. The tension was strong enough that her friends stopped talking and withdrew. As he reached her, the music and other voices retreated as well.

When they first met, Paul's opening words to Mary was a question: "Do I know you?" He used the noise in the bar as an excuse to lean forward to speak to her. His head next to her neck, he could smell her. He said, "I swear you look familiar." It was a pathetic line, but she was interested enough to continue the conversation and the dating that followed.

Tonight, he experienced that same excitement, forgetting the intervening years of neglect. He drew her hair behind her ear, touched her on the cheek, and gazed into her eyes like a mystic looking for a sign. He saw the same neck that drew him in years ago. He leaned into her shoulder, kissing her in the crevice of her neck and smelling the sweetness of her hair. "I love you." Mary's eyes moistened. She held his hand to her cheek and then moved it to her lips, gently kissing his palm. The touch reminded him of their first kiss outside the bar that night.

God, Paul thought, *it feels like we have been in a hurricane together since that night.* Tonight, he felt like they were in the eye of the storm, enjoying a calm moment.

When they walked home from the party, Paul insisted they visit the clearing in the backyard. "No turtles," Paul said. The dirt clearing was a ghostly white in the moonlight.

"What a crazy day." Mary had her arm around Paul and was swaying back and forth, feeling buzzed. "What was it with you at the party?"

"What do you mean?" Paul pulled her closer.

Mary rocked in his arms. "You were like a boy, coming up to me and asking me to dance."

"Really? I thought I was like George Clooney, hitting on the most beautiful woman at the party."

"Well, that too." She put her head on his shoulder. "It was nice."

"So what do you say?"

"What?"

"Is Clooney going to get the girl tonight?"

"I don't know, George. I hardly know you." They kissed and started walking back toward the house. "I can't believe we're going to Italy in a couple of weeks."

"You know George has a villa in Italy, don't you?" They punctuated every few steps with laughter, their voices trailing off.

Forty

Paul and Mary enjoyed their first afternoon in Orvieto, Italy, on their bedroom terrace. Their view took in a breathtaking landscape, overlooking a serpentine lake that disappeared into a mountainous horizon.

Paul focused on a tower ruin, rising from the forest on a nearby hill. The tower overlooked the junction of the Tiber and Paglia rivers below. From its position, men and women watched the flow of war and commerce for hundreds of years. The tower sat above it all like an ancient bird, reporting the comings and goings of soldiers on their way to victory or defeat.

The afternoon heat relaxed the tension in Mary's neck. Simon was arriving later in the week after finishing his music camp in Tanglewood, but for now, they were alone. She noticed Paul staring at the ruin. "What do you think that ruin was?"

"It reminds me of the tower on the Tor in Glastonbury."

Mary sighed. "Paul, let's enjoy being here, in Italy."

Paul hesitated. "Did you know that Umbria is the mystical province of Italy?"

"No, I didn't."

"Maybe we were drawn here for a reason." Mary looked crestfallen that Paul persisted with his New Age speak. Paul waved his hand in front of her, trying to make eye contact. "Mary, I'm here. With you. I'm not looking past our vacation—not thinking about going to Glastonbury again—"

"Jesus, Paul. I don't want to get into another fight about her."

"I'm not talking about her. It's just that I believe we're here for a reason."

Mary tried to change the subject. "To try the truffles?"

"There's an energy here, I feel it. Do you?"

Mary sighed. "Well, I'm all for energy . . . *and* truffles. Let's go to the farmer's market—maybe they have both there."

That evening, after a light dinner made from fresh ingredients from the market, Paul and Mary relaxed outside, observing the night sky. They watched the shooting stars, appearing like fish jumping in and out of the Milky Way. "It is a little magical," Mary whispered under her breath.

"What did you say?"

"Nothing. I think the jet lag is catching up with me." Mary got up to go inside. "I'm going to bed."

Mary propped herself up in bed and read a book. Paul joined her. "Should I leave the door shutters open? It's cooled off so much. We don't need the AC."

"I'd like that," Mary said. She put her book down. "Paul, thank you."

Paul crawled into bed next to her. "For what?"

"For taking the time off for us. I know Steve pushes you. This is really special." Her comment reminded Paul that Steve had left a long voice mail for him, but he did not want to listen to it now. "I wish I had more energy tonight," she whispered as she put her head on his shoulder.

"We forgot to buy some at the market," Paul teased. "Go to sleep—we've plenty of time." A large ceiling fan turned slowly. Paul could see the black night through the large sliding screen door that opened to the bedroom terrace. His eyes grew heavy. The combination of jet lag and a hot afternoon in the sun served as a super-Ambien, and they both fell into a deep sleep.

A breeze picked up outside their bedroom terrace. It originated from the Saharan Desert in Africa. This so-called *Sirocco* wind blew north across the Mediterranean, jumping the waves of the Tyrrhenian Sea, picking up moisture until it hit the coast of Italy. By the time it reached the hills of Umbria, it lost its intensity but held its moisture, cooling at the higher altitude. The air turned into white mist, as if Mother Nature dredged the Milky Way and poured it onto the Tiber valley. Pushed by the southerly wind, milky currents filled the valley and pushed upward toward the villa. It meandered among the olive groves and rows of grapevines until it overflowed the hedges surrounding the property, poured past the tall cypress trees, and climbed up the stairs to the bedroom terrace. The mist paused at the screen door.

Mary sat up, shivering. As her eyes focused, she saw a white fog outside their door. "Paul," she whispered, poking him until he woke up. "The mist." Paul rubbed his eyes as Mary looked for her robe.

Paul sat up and slid off the bed. He walked to the screen door and opened it. He carefully stepped down, feeling the contours of the few stairs with his feet, until he reached the terrace. "This is weird."

Mary gave up looking for her robe in the dark and followed him, naked. "I can't see you," she whispered.

His hand suddenly appeared in front of her, causing her to flinch. She took it, using it to steady herself as she stepped down to the terrace. Paul thought he could see the faint outlines of the three cypress trees at the end of the property, but he was not sure. He waved his arm in front of him and watched his hand disappear as it extended into the mist. "I can't even see my hand in front of me." He laughed. "Be careful." Paul moved his hand to the small of her back. It was warm to his touch, compared to the cool mist surrounding them. Mary was hyperventilating with excitement, drowning in the milky atmosphere. She trembled in the cold and turned to go in. "I can't see the door." They found the stairs by inching forward and touching the stairs with their feet, and then they made their way inside. By now, the inside of their bedroom was drowning in the white milky fog.

"Mary?" Paul's disembodied voice sounded distant. "Mary?" She felt his hand touch her shoulder, moving to the nape of her neck. He leaned forward to kiss her. His head appeared in the mist. She closed her eyes.

As Paul came closer, Mary appeared in front of him like a fairy emerging from a smoky forest. He kissed her, and their milky breath melted in their warm mouths. They fell on the bed, exploring each other's bodies hidden in the night fog. Paul kissed Mary's neck. Now he could see her dark hair falling down to her shoulders. His lips moved down her clavicle and followed the outline of her breasts, rising and falling, her nipples barely visible as light circles.

Mary watched Paul's head come in and out of focus, a hand appearing, a shoulder receding into the white shadows. She felt all of Paul moving on top of her. The wetness between her legs and the mist in the room melted into one as she warmed everything around her. Paul entered her. The lovemaking felt purposeful, an act of procreation. They rocked together, enjoying each other in this whitest of nights.

Forty-One

Voice Mail from Steve

I got a call from the chairman, and he read me the riot act. He knows we're facing a bad quarter, and he wants to know what we're doing about it. It's the second bad quarter in a row, and he said three strikes and we're out. I need your help. Trivergence is the only growth area right now. There's a very important client meeting in Rome. Can you be there?

I'm closing the quarter and trying to save all our jobs. The board is watching us closely. Don't lose the fire in your belly, Paul. It's time to show you still got it.

Paul was in the back seat of the car on a call with Roberto, his head of sales for Europe. Mary drove, and Simon was navigating their way to Assisi—a deadly combination. "The attendance at this meeting's fantastic. We've got the entire executive leadership of Conagra," Roberto said excitedly. "They're visiting our demonstration center for two hours."

"What's their agenda?"

"They definitely want to hear from you about trivergence. They want to see how they can use the technology in agriculture."

"OK. Do we have any ideas?"

"That's why I wanted to talk to you. Maybe we can brainstorm some ideas?"

Paul needed to keep it short. Mary and Simon were arguing about when to exit. "OK, let me just think out loud for a little bit, and then I have to go."

"Great, Paul. We're listening."

"They probably already have some sensing capability in their fields, with their animals, and so on. Some sensors for weather are spaced out on poles and fences. So they know temperature and rainfall and sunlight—basic stuff. But what's really going on where it matters—in the ground? What if you knew exactly what the plant experience was? What if we had seed tridgets? Little devices—the size of a seed—with primitive data storage and communications functionality." Paul noticed Simon looking back at him and motioning that his father is loco. Mary laughed. "When you plant seeds in the spring, you systematically drop these in . . . let's call it seedgits. Now you can track everything."

"That would be amazing. We'd know everything about the plants."

"We could talk to the plants, and they could talk to us at some primitive level."

"Seedgits—I love it." Roberto laughed. "You guys getting all this down?"

"Roberto, I have to go soon." Mary and Simon were now speculating they missed a turn for Assisi. As Paul listened, he checked Google Maps. They needed to take the next right. He motioned with his hand. Simon waved him off, and Mary jokingly gave him the finger.

"Roberto, right now we're driving past fields of sunflowers. Thousands of them in each field. During the day, the flower heads follow the sun. Depending on the time of day and the angle of the sunlight, they look happy or sad, excited or tired. They're alive."

Roberto said, "Plants with personality."

"Exactly." Paul laughed until he saw Mary's frowning face in the rearview mirror. "Let's go back to the seedgit idea. All I'm really suggesting is that we're getting to the point with the cost and functionality of technology that every plant could express itself digitally. Am I making any sense?"

"This is perfect. Just the kind of creative ideas we were looking for."

Paul smiled. "I have to go, Roberto. Let's talk later this week."

Mary pulled over to the narrow shoulder of the road. She fought with Simon for control of the map. "Give me that."

"And the same for animals, Paul," Roberto said.

"What?"

"Animals."

"Sure, sure." Paul put his hand over his phone, hissing, "What's the problem?"

"Animals can express themselves digitally," Roberto continued. "We'll be able to talk to them."

"This is starting to sound like a Disney movie, though."

"*Grandioso.*" Roberto chattered to his team in Italian.

Mary and Simon glared at each other as the car sat on the shoulder of the road, cars honking at them as they zoomed by. "I have to go."

"*Ciao, ciao, grazie, grazie.*"

Paul dropped the call. The car was moving again, easing onto the expressway. An oncoming car almost clipped them as it veered into the passing lane. "What's going on?" Paul asked.

"We found it, Dad." Simon pointed.

Nestled on the slopes of Mount Subasio, the town of Assisi shone with a rose aura in the morning sun. As they drew closer, its profile came into focus. A protective wall stretched along its entire perimeter.

The basilica cathedral towered at one end and a collection of medieval towers sprinkled the other end—like the skyline of a medieval Manhattan. Unlike many Italian hill towns, Assisi's geography welcomed visitors. Its embankment was relatively shallow; the approach resembled Oz as opposed to Mordor. It looked like God handcrafted a talisman of rose stones laid in gold threads and perched it on a hill full of dark-green forest. They joined the line of cars entering at the foot of the town—pilgrims in search of the saint.

Forty-Two

The angel startled Paul. She sat at a table in the piazza in front of the Basilica of St. Clare. Paul watched her out of the corner of his eye. Even from a distance, Paul could see the elaborate lace pattern of her bodice in contrast to the shiny silk body of the white dress. A white lace scarf covered her shoulders. A white chalky paste covered her skin from head to toe. White on white on white. Two large wings grew from her back.

Simon stood next to Paul, looking up from his phone. "Dad?"

"What?" Paul watched her nodding as tourists passed by.

"Is that a fucking angel over there?" Simon pointed.

"Simon, for Christ's sake, watch your mouth! We're standing in front of a church." Paul looked around to see if anyone was listening. "It's someone in an angel costume." The angel looked in their direction. "Damn. She probably heard you."

"No way. We're too far away. Look, she's waving us over."

"Just ignore her," Paul said.

"We can't, Dad. You can't ignore an angel. Come on."

"She's probably some sort of con artist, preying on tourists." Paul turned away.

"She's coming this way," Simon whispered. "She's—"

"*Buongiorno,*" said the angel. She looked puzzled. Up close, Paul saw she was an older woman. Her black pupils contrasted with her painted face, her eyes darting between Paul and Simon. "*Vuoi una benedizione?*"

"What did she say?" Paul asked. (For some reason, Paul expected Simon to understand any foreign language because he studied Spanish in school.)

"I don't know, Dad. Something about a prayer, I think."

"*Tu sei il padre? Questo è tuo figlio?*" the angel asked, first pointing at Paul and then Simon.

"I think she's asking if we are father and son." Simon nodded. "*Sì.*" A few people gathered around them, curious what the angel was saying. Paul wanted to walk away.

She put her hand on Paul's forehead. "*Via benedica sia benedetto il vostro viaggio.*" She nodded, and Paul caught himself nodding as well. "*Questo è buono.*"

Paul whispered under his breath to Simon, "Do you have any idea what she's saying?"

She put her hand on Simon's forehead and looked puzzled for a moment, then closed her eyes. She spoke slowly. "*Avete hai della saggezza oltre i vestry tuoi anni. Si deve Devi condividerla la vostra tua saggezza.*" She opened her eyes and removed her hand. "*Tu sei un profeta, uno benedetto, un Druido.*" The growing audience murmured as she backed away from Simon. She curtsied, spun around, and made her way back to her table.

"I have no idea what she just said." Paul shook his head.

One of the onlookers offered, "She said your son is a very wise old man."

"Don't tell that to his mother!" Paul said. They all laughed.

"She's pretty cool," Simon said.

"She's probably just trying to make some money. I'll give her something." Paul walked up to her table in the middle of the piazza and held out a euro.

She shook her head and laughed. *"La alla chiesa, alla chiesa."* She motioned toward the church. *"Dare alla chiesa."* No translation required.

Paul and Simon entered the church. St. Clare founded the women's order known as the Poor Clares, who paralleled the philosophy and lifestyle of the Franciscans. Similar to St. Francis, St. Clare dedicated her life to holiness and poverty. The basilica housed her remains and artifacts in its crypt. Simon, with his youthful fascination with the dead, hurried down the stairs to the crypt to see her remains. Paul found himself sitting in a pew in a side chapel along with other visitors.

A wooden crucifix hung from the ceiling, looking as if it were floating in the air if not for barely visible wires holding it in place. Paul closed his eyes and could feel a familiar energy coming from the cross. It was an object of veneration because St. Francis, while sitting in front of this cross, heard a voice tell him to reform the church. Paul looked at the visitors sitting near him. Some were on their knees in prayer and others, like Paul, looked up at the cross in anticipation. Paul imagined an energy crashing down from the cross like a waterfall, generating a cool mist in the air that he could almost taste. He lifted his hands up and drank in the cool spray, not caring what people thought. *Angels are everywhere.*

Paul lost track of the time. It was noon; time to go. Simon was nowhere to be found. His head spun as he stood up. The cross seemed to vibrate in front of him, pulling him in. He followed the exit signs, passing a small donation box sitting below racks of lit and unlit candles.

He remembered the angel telling him to give to the church. He fumbled in his pocket for a euro, finally pulling out a fistful of bills and coins. Paul was sweating as if he had just walked out of a sauna.

He picked at the coins, put one euro in the slot, then another, then a third—until there were no more coins. He could still feel the vibration of the cross from the chapel next door. He folded euro bills and started stuffing them into the slot. Paul tried to jam his last bill into the box as a guard approached him. "*Posso aiutaria?*"

"What?" Paul asked, startled.

"Can I help you?" The old guard looked at Paul with concern.

"I'm just trying to make a contribution. But there's no more room. I have more." Paul realized his hands were trembling. "More to give."

"You are very generous already." The guard put his hand on Paul's shoulder.

Paul put the rest of his money on top of the contribution box and rushed out of the church, nearly into the arms of the angel. She rose to her feet and held out her hands as if to embrace him, her wings at their full height. The sight of her in the bright light overwhelmed him, and he stumbled out of the piazza.

Forty-Three

Mary was already falling asleep upstairs while Paul and Simon finished cleaning up after dinner that night. Simon cleared the table while Paul rinsed the dishes. "While I was stuffing the collection box with your college tuition," Paul said, "you were meditating in a cave?"

Simon smiled. "I think Mom is worried about both of us. You giving all our money away and me becoming a monk."

"Should she be worried?"

"About me, yeah. I might as well be a monk. I never get laid."

"Tell me about this meditation place," Paul said.

"It's a hermitage. St. Francis would go there when he wanted to get away from everything. It's pretty cool. I was the only one there for a while."

"How'd you find it?"

"Wikipedia. I'm doing my summer paper for Western Civ on St. Francis."

"You have to do a paper during the summer?"

"Yeah . . . us overachieving private school kids are trying to keep up with our overachieving private school parents."

Paul motioned for Simon to join him in the living room. "Let's take a break. I can finish the rest in the morning. What are you going to write about?"

"I have some ideas," Simon said. "I think St. Francis was saying the world was out of balance."

"What do you mean?"

Simon picked up a book from the coffee table and started to turn the pages.

"The balance between man and nature, between the church and its flock, even between God and mortals. The average man felt disconnected, out of balance. St. Francis brought things back together."

Paul smiled. "What the hell have you been reading?"

"I even have this vision of what will happen."

"Let's not call it a vision, Simon. Your mother thinks we already have a little too much crazy floating around this family."

Simon laughed. "I know what you mean." His expression turned serious. "I think the world is still out of balance. If anything, St. Francis's message got lost in the noise of history."

"What do you mean?"

"Consumerism—that's the new religion. It's time to rebalance again."

Paul grinned. "I'm impressed. Maybe the tuition we're paying for is worth it."

"Actually, I get most of my ideas from the internet."

"Don't tell me that, Simon—humor me." Paul turned on the dishwasher and yawned. "What a day. I'm tired." Paul hugged Simon. Simon's skinny torso yielded a kind of vulnerability, and Paul enveloped it like a bear. "We leave early tomorrow, so try to pack some things tonight, and don't stay up all night on the computer." Paul turned out the lights and started up the stairs. "I'm going to have trouble sleeping, thinking about that angel. She's a crazy one, isn't she?"

Simon followed his father. "I thought she made a lot of sense."

Forty-Four

Several weeks after his vacation, Paul sat in Steve's office on a Saturday morning, waiting for him to get off the phone. He reread Christine's email from the previous evening:

Paul,
You invited Mary to the retreat for a reason. Imagine how she will enjoy her time here with you and me. She wants to join you, so try to relax.

Today, I saw a heart-shaped cloud. What a good sign!

Blessings,
Christine

Paul wanted Mary to be more comfortable with Christine and to see her work firsthand, but he also wanted to be himself and not have to worry about Mary. Paul suspected that Mary hoped to uncover that Christine was either a charlatan, a seducer, or a nut. Even so, they would fly to England in two days. He had to be positive.

"Don't even bring up that fucking deal," Steve shouted into the phone. "You've been promising it'll close for six months now. Stop the bullshit. It's over. Hit the numbers this quarter or we'll have a difficult conversation. You understand me? And never mention that deal again." Steve slammed the phone down. "He misses his numbers every quarter and drags me down with him. Has to stop." Steve looked at Paul for confirmation.

"Yep."

"Where were we?" Steve noticed the time. "Shit, I've got to go."

"We're almost through the plan." Paul relaxed because Steve was out of time and had already vented at someone else.

"That's right."

"I'll be in Europe next week, meeting with all the country heads in London. We'll set priorities in terms of which industry segments we target with which of our value propositions."

"We don't have jack shit without your trivergence story. Keep up the good work. What can I do to help? Stay out of the way, right?"

"I think your support is critical." Paul threw him a bone. "Everyone knows you took the risk and backed me on this." Paul noticed his phone buzzing—it was Mary. She was calling because he was late, or she had an errand for him to do, or Simon did something wrong. The phone stopped buzzing.

"That's my job—take risks, back my people." Steve leaned back in his chair and put his hands behind his head. "And you're the next new thing."

"Well, thanks—"

"Don't get a big head. Ideas come and go. But you—you're like a sorcerer, always looking for something new in the bag of tricks. Do you follow what I'm saying?"

Paul was not sure. "For sure."

"I know you want the brass ring," Steve muttered. Paul's phone buzzed—Mary again. Steve swiveled his chair toward the window and his fiftieth-floor view of the Manhattan skyline. Paul quickly texted

Mary: "Need ten minutes. Will call." Steve swiveled back to Paul and pointed his finger for emphasis. "You can't be a one-trick pony. CEOs pick horses and ride them. But they use the whip when they have to. You're bright, but are you tough enough?" Steve walked over to the window, lost in his own thoughts. "Everybody wants this job, but they have no fucking idea what they are getting into." Steve settled back in his chair. "Stick with me, Paul, and watch what I do. Learn to use the whip though."

"Use the whip?" Cynthia appeared in the doorway. "Sounds kinky. What am I missing?"

Steve frowned. "You working today?"

"We have a meeting now. I didn't mean to interrupt. Just wanted to let you know I'm here. I can come back."

"Yeah, I forgot. Let's keep it short, Cynthia." Steve waved at Paul, dismissing him. "Good luck in London."

Cynthia casually put her hand on Paul's shoulder. "London. Why does Paul get all the nice trips?" She smiled at Paul. "Do you need some marketing help?"

"I can always use your help, Cynthia." Paul noticed she kept her hand on his shoulder.

"While you both are here," Cynthia said, "remember the opportunity we turned down a couple months ago—the digital sex idea?"

"Who could forget it?" Steve chuckled.

"Weekend piece in the *Wall Street Journal* just ran. Talks about the company and the technology. They got hammered. Plays up the webcam prostitution angle. One shrink described it as a form of technological bondage."

Steve tapped on his keyboard. "Let me look up the article."

"Don't get me wrong," Cynthia continued, "the PR's great for the company—if they want to sell into the porn industry. But for our brand, it would've been a disaster, especially right on the heels of us winning the Catalyst Award for our initiatives for the advancement of women in our company."

Steve stared at his screen. "There it is. Jeez, look at that device for the men—looks like it could hurt you." Steve laughed. "So you're saying we dodged a bullet."

"Yes."

"And you saved Paul's ass," Steve muttered. "Paul's got a guardian angel looking over his shoulder these days."

"Paul and I agreed that it wasn't worth the risk." Cynthia moved her hand off Paul's shoulder.

"That's right." Paul stood up.

Steve looked at his watch again. "That's great. I've got ten minutes, Cynthia. Paul, talk to you next week."

Paul ran out of the office and called Mary as he hailed a taxi. "What's up?"

"I wanted to make sure you could join me tomorrow for brunch." Mary sounded excited.

"Sure. What's the occasion?"

"I just got a call from someone who stayed at my family's house as an exchange student almost thirty years ago! I saw her once in college and then we lost track of each other. Her name's Angela. She's Spanish, lives in Madrid. But she's in New York now visiting her daughter, who interned at a magazine for the summer. She Googled me and found my number. I want to see her before we leave for Glastonbury. Brunch tomorrow is the only time that works."

"You sure you don't want to go by yourself?"

"No. She wants to meet my family. Her daughter will be there; you and Simon should be there. I'll tell her we can meet them at the French Roast at eleven."

"Works for me."

"When are you getting home?"

"Minutes away, in a taxi. Do you need anything?"

Paul's phone buzzed. Steve's name appeared on the screen.

"No. It's quiet here. Angela's really a neat person. You'll like her."

The taxi pulled up to his building. Steve left a voice mail. *Screw it,* Paul thought. *I'll listen later.*

Forty-Five

The next day, the Moores arrived at French Roast for brunch with Angela and her daughter, Sophia, early. Mary fidgeted with Simon's collar. "Ah, there she is!" she said.

Angela appeared at the door of the restaurant. Mary ran to greet her, and they hugged. Angela was about five feet tall. She wore camouflage pants that ballooned around the hips and tapered to an elastic band around her ankles, simple leather sandals, a black T-shirt, and a thin necklace supporting a large gold circle. Her frizzy hair fell in long tangles to her shoulders, framing her small-featured face. When she smiled, her eyes grew bright and mischievous. *She looks like a pixie*, Paul thought as he shook her hand. Sophia was drop-dead beautiful, and Simon nearly lost his balance when she followed her mother into the restaurant.

Mary and Angela fell easily into a conversation, as if the intervening years had disappeared. Paul and Simon talked to Sophia about her time in New York. The teenagers amused Paul. Simon behaved like a typical American teenage boy smitten by Sophia's exotic looks and accent. Sophia looked up at Simon—a foot and a half taller than her—as if he was a baby giraffe.

"Paul." Mary waved her hand at Paul to get his attention. "You *must* hear what Angela does for a living."

"What do you do?" Paul asked.

"I heal people," she said in her heavy Spanish accent.

"How do you heal them? Are you a doctor?"

Angela smiled. "No. I'm a soul healer."

"What?"

"I touch people with my hands and read and heal their souls."

Paul looked at Mary in disbelief. "Did you tell her what we're doing?"

"No, you tell her."

"We're going to an English village called Glastonbury."

Angela nodded. "I know Glastonbury."

"We're having a retreat with a woman who's a soul reader. I did a reading a few months ago, and we're spending the weekend at her house."

"You must be excited," Angela said. Mary looked pensive.

Paul asked, "How did you become a soul healer?" Angela described how she fell ill and could not work as a designer in the fashion industry. Doctors were no help. In desperation, a friend recommended she visit a shaman in Ecuador. She ended up staying for months, studying with him. Soon after that, she became a soul healer.

Sophia yawned. "Mom, Simon and I are going for a walk." Simon looked pleasantly surprised.

"OK, dear, but just for ten minutes. We have to leave for the airport soon." Sophia grabbed Simon's hand and ran out the door. Angela smiled. "My daughter has a mind of her own. I hope your son doesn't mind."

"Are you kidding me?" Paul joked. "I'm sure he's hoping his friends see him cruising the city with such a beautiful girl. It'll give him instant cred."

Mary smiled. "I'm so glad we managed to get together."

"When do you leave for Glastonbury?" Angela asked.

"Tomorrow," Mary answered. A waiter cleared the table.

"Are you excited?"

"I wouldn't say excited," Mary said. "I'm there to observe what she does with Paul. I'm not convinced she's real."

"In what way?"

"Well, I don't know her. What if she's hypnotizing Paul? We're paying good money for this retreat. She can be brainwashing Paul to come back and spend more money." For some reason, Paul felt amused, not insulted, that Mary was talking about him as if he were not there.

"She has to make a living," Angela offered.

Mary hesitated. "I have been seeing some good things since Paul returned from his soul reading. He's more engaged with us. But I worry."

Paul interrupted, "But what about all the things that happened since the reading? The letters I found, the turtle laying eggs, the time in Italy?"

Mary frowned. "Paul, I know you think this is all related to the soul reading, but it could be coincidence."

"Or synchronicity." Angela reached for Mary's hand. "Things work together when the energy is right, even with no obvious cause." Angela smiled, massaging Mary's hand. "The fact that we're meeting right before your trip, is it a coincidence? But tell me, Mary, what are you really afraid of?"

Mary spoke quietly. "I'm afraid of what might happen to Paul if he sees her again."

Angela put her arm around Mary's shoulder. "You're not afraid of what might happen to Paul; you're afraid of what might happen to you. But don't be. Everything will be fine." Angela looked at Paul and Mary and laughed. Everyone relaxed.

Simon and Sophia returned. Angela glanced at her watch. "Sophia, we have to go."

Mary and Angela hugged. Sophia pulled Simon down so she could give his cheeks a kiss, leaving a trace of lipstick on both sides.

"Nice meeting you, Angela." Paul awkwardly held out his hand. "Goodbye."

Angela hugged him, standing on her toes. She whispered in his ear, "You're on the right path. Bring Mary along with you."

Forty-Six

Mary and Janet sat at a café sidewalk table on Broadway in the late afternoon. They nursed their carafe of wine while the waiter stared at them.

"That's unbelievable!" Janet was impressed. "A soul reader *and* a soul healer. I can't believe I'm having a glass of wine with my sister, who is hanging out with soul whatevers. Maybe I should go with you guys."

"I'm only going because I don't trust Paul with that woman. He stays at her house for three nights, just the two of them? I don't think so."

Janet nodded in the waiter's direction. "C'mon, let's order something, just to keep the waiter happy. How 'bout fried calamari?"

"I can't. Watching my weight. The soul reader looks skinnier than me. And that's in a picture."

"You can watch me." Janet motioned to the waiter. "Can we have some fried calamari and vegetables with hummus?"

"I'll pick at the vegetables."

"And another carafe, please."

"Janet, I have to pack!" The waiter scribbled down the order.

"Cut the guy a break. He needs his tables to spend money. I have a lot more empathy for waiters now that I'm dating one."

Mary's ears perked up. "Wait, did I hear you right? Is this the actor/waiter fellow you met?"

"Yes," Janet said sheepishly.

"Good for you! I want to meet him."

Janet watched the steady stream of Sunday-afternoon strollers walking down Broadway. "Yes, it's true. I could watch people walk by for an hour, and he would be the best-looking guy of the group. He's hot, I'm shallow, and I can't deny it."

"Don't be so hard on yourself."

Janet ignored her. "Sensitive in a dumb, helpless way. Good sex. Good sex parity, if you catch my drift. And that's important to me. I'm way too old for any other way."

"Does he have a name?"

Janet held her wineglass in front of her face, hiding her grin, and whispered, "Stefano."

"Not another Italian! Are you a glutton for punishment?"

"I think I am," Janet admitted sheepishly. "But this one is young, so he's not an asshole yet. We go to movies, read books in bookstores, go to plays. He talks about how he would play the role."

"Has he had any roles?"

"No."

"We grab a bite to eat, we make love, he goes to sleep, and I work on the computer. It is a very structured, civilized arrangement, and I don't have to worry about it."

"Do you love him?" Mary asked.

"There's no such thing as love. It's not love to be dating some boy toy. It's not love to be chasing your man across the ocean because you're afraid he's in a midlife crisis and will jump into bed with a soul reader." Janet saw Mary's expression. "I'm sorry, but who's really in love? There's temptation, infatuation, boredom, resentment, endings, and new starts. Love is this illusion that seems to thread it together, just long enough to hurt." Janet made a mock toast.

"Wow, you've figured it all out, sister. You should write a self-help book—*The End of Love*."

"God knows I have the experience to write one. And a mother that taught us well." This time they really toasted. Janet looked serious. "Can I be blunt?" Mary nodded. "Why didn't you just tell him, 'No fucking way. You're not going on a retreat. Hire a shrink.'"

Mary looked away. "I hesitate to say this after your love riff, but I must admit, we are getting along better since the soul reading. He even talks about love now." Mary was making circles around the top of her wineglass.

Janet realized she was serious. "So you want to see if you can get some of that love action?"

"No, I'm not participating in her treatments. I'm just there to observe her and Paul. Paul gets very excited whenever he talks about her."

"You're curious, aren't you? My god, my sister's going to come back wearing a robe with a garland on her head and hair under her arms."

Mary laughed and looked at her watch. "I have to go. I need to pack." Mary reached for her sister's hand. "Thank you for watching Simon."

Janet motioned for the check. "You go, girl. I'll be looking for pictures of you dancing with the fairies. Or chasing Paul with a club in your hand!"

Forty-Seven

"You have to listen to your aunt while we're gone," Paul said to Simon. They sat in the kitchen, waiting for Mary to come home. "Don't give her a hard time. I don't want her calling your mother while we are away, OK?"

"Sure, Dad." Simon nodded. "I'm not going to be around that much anyway. I have school stuff going on every night."

"That's fine, but you have to let her know where you are. We're used to you doing your own thing, but she isn't. She'll be worried."

Simon look amused. "Dad, I want you and Mom to have a great time. Relax. I'll take care of Aunt Janet. Send me some pictures of witches."

"I will."

"Are there really Druids there? Are you going to meet one? That would be cool."

"I don't know. It'll be interesting," Paul admitted.

Simon opened the refrigerator looking for something to eat. "Are we having something to eat when Mom gets home?"

"I'm thinking of ordering pizza, so no mess."

"Pizza's always good." Simon nibbled on a leftover quesadilla.

"Simon, you sure that's still good? Mom made that a week ago!"

"Tastes fine," Simon said, contemplating it as if examining a rare diamond. It smelled OK too. He tore it in half and offered Paul a piece. Paul hesitated, but he was hungry.

Paul tried it. "I guess it's not going to kill me."

They gobbled the snack down. "I wish there was more," both said, catching themselves before laughing out loud. "Should we order now?" Simon asked.

"Let's wait until Mom gets home. Maybe she already had something to eat." Paul looked at the clock and got up to leave. "I have a call. You should clean your room before your aunt gets here in the morning."

"What do you think Mom's going to do in Glastonbury?"

"What do you mean?" Paul asked.

"Remember when Angela said that Mom was afraid of the retreat?"

"Yes."

"What did she mean by that?"

"I think it can be scary sometimes not knowing what to expect."

"I guess. But I think that sometimes, not knowing what's going to happen is the best thing," Simon said.

Paul contemplated that. "Interesting thought."

"Besides, you're not scared."

"Sure, but I was already there."

"That's true. I just don't understand what people are afraid of." Simon opened the refrigerator again, looking to forage something else. "Nothing happening to you is scary."

"What do you mean?" Paul's phone buzzed.

Simon closed the refrigerator door unsuccessfully. "You're trying to figure out what kind of life you want to lead. I'm in the same boat."

Paul properly closed the refrigerator door and smiled. "Well I can help you with that—you should do what you want to do."

Simon wasn't smiling. "That's not what you did, though. I read that letter you wrote to yourself when you were my age. You asked yourself questions you've never answered."

Paul fingered the phone in his pocket, but he couldn't abandon this conversation.

"But at least you're figuring it out now," Simon continued. He found a package of cookies in the cupboard and offered one to Paul. "And I think it's great. It's cool."

Paul had no words to respond.

"I'm home!" Mary burst into the kitchen. "Let's order pizza tonight." She sensed the stillness in the room. "Did I interrupt something?"

Paul's phone kept buzzing in his pocket, but he ignored it.

"Is pizza OK?" she asked. They both nodded.

Forty-Eight

Mary contemplated her wardrobe for the trip late that night, long after Paul and Simon were asleep. Her outfits hung from lamps, doorknobs, and chairs in Paul's home office. What to wear? There was the cheery floral sundress, but she wore it at the lunch from hell with Kevin. Maybe blue jeans with a loose T-shirt—casual and good for walking. She needed something to wear at night.

Would they go out? The black single-shoulder dress was casual but maybe too New York and too sexy. Maybe the beige slacks with the embellished black top with heart-shaped crystal studs along the V-neck? Mary worried about overdressing. But she wanted to look good. Who knows what the soul reader would wear. She lay on the couch, her head propped against the pillow, and looked at her options, each outfit hanging like a wall tapestry. She smiled to herself. She had never packed for a retreat with a soul reader before. The sundress was the closest to a New Age outfit that she had. She should pack it, regardless of the bad association with Kevin.

Paul gave her the soul reader's instructions for preparing for the retreat before he went to bed. It was on his desk, and she decided to read it. He scribbled a note in the margin: "I know you don't plan to participate, but this is what Christine asked me to do before the retreat. In case you want to try it." *This is such hocus-pocus,* she thought. "Imagine you are lying on a blue orb. Feel the coolness fill your body. Listen to your breath. Say to yourself, 'I surrender to my heart and soul.' Repeat this as you fall asleep."

Mary was tired. She put the page down, closed her eyes, and listened to her breath. She tried to imagine the orb, having never seen one. Is this what Paul did before he went to sleep tonight? She saw herself lying on a blue orb. The circumference of the orb—originally the length of her body—spread its borders to the ends of her world. She sank into its cool embrace. What were the instructions? Heart and soul? What should she repeat? She forgot the words; she even forgot to breathe.

Like a moving stage, the orb rolled, pushing her body forward to a standing position. She faced a tower on a hilltop. As she walked, the blue orb released her and rose into the night sky, hovering above her like a crystal ball. She entered the arched doorway to the tower. Her eyes adjusted to the darkness inside, dimly lit by the blue orb hanging above the roofless tower. The orb's light revealed shapes standing along the three walls facing her. It was an armory. Suits of armor stood in rows glowing a light-blue color, the polished steel reflecting the moonlight—except for a black suit of armor directly in front of Mary. Its oxidized surface absorbed the moonlight like a black hole. Decorative gold patterns etched in the armor reflected a pink-white glow and provided shape to the armor's elegant contours—from the armet helmet to the chest plate to the sabatons covering the feet. The gold accents sparkled like stars, implying motion, a shimmering being hovering in front of her.

Did it just move? She heard breathing—someone was inside the armored suit. The knight slowly raised its right gauntlet toward her. Its glove touched her cheek, a soft caress, but of cold, hard steel. The glove moved down her chest and stomach and reached under her dressing gown, settling between her legs. She took a breath. She felt the steel fingers through her underwear, now warmed by her own body heat. The knight leaned against her. She was shaking and short of breath. Now her head was next to its helmet, and she could hear its breath more clearly. It was a man's breath, careful and deliberate. Though she could feel the cold armor against her body and the warmth growing underneath her nightdress, she saw nothing of this man, even though she lay against him like a lover.

Like a blind person, she touched the helmet in front of her with her hand. She lifted it upward, pulling the visor back. The knight stared ahead, his pale face reflecting the moonlight as if a flashlight was under his chin. It was Kevin. She gasped and stumbled back, holding her arms in front of her as if protecting herself from a blow. Light sparkled on the tower walls, reflecting the bright steel suits. The effect was disorienting, like a mirror ball suspended high above Mary. Kevin's face floated toward her, his eyes looking beyond her toward the doorway, his right gauntlet still motioning as if he were touching her. She could hear his breath quicken. She turned to run and stumbled, falling toward the stone floor, holding out her hands to cushion the impact. As she lost consciousness, the blue orb appeared before her, and she fell into its soft embrace.

Forty-Nine

The raven watched her from the tree in the garden. Christine moved through the rooms of her townhouse waving a stick topped with burning sage. She was preparing the house for Paul and Mary's arrival. She ended up at the sliding glass doors to her garden. Rain fell hard outside, creating large puddles on the patio. The dark sky rumbled with distant thunder. She saw her reflection in the glass and almost laughed out loud. The raven watched her standing at the door, wearing a bathrobe and a red wig, its long hair hanging down to her waist. She slid the door open and looked outside. She extended her arm, and the rain soaked the sleeve of her robe. She untied the belt to her robe and let it drop to the floor. The rain beckoned, and she stepped outside, dropping her sage stick on the ground.

She closed her eyes and spread her arms toward the sky, drinking in the storm. The raven flew down to the birdbath in her garden. The trees provided some shelter from the downpour. The lightning came closer and was followed by the thunderclaps, whose vibration relaxed her body. Lightning flashed, and she glowed in its light like a goddess come down from the heavens. The sky fell silent momentarily.

The raven cawed for her attention, and Christine opened her eyes and smiled at it. She stood, perfect in her beauty, from her long red hair to the aura around her naked body. The raven cocked its head, trying to recall an ancient memory. Christine held out her arms and turned her palms toward the raven as if to embrace it. Then the raven remembered—Brigid, the goddess of fire and healing, now stood in the garden. Every flower strained to touch her healing nature. Her hair burned bright as she reached forward and lifted the raven in her hands. The sage stick ignited spontaneously, despite the pouring rain, and its smoke filled the garden with its scent.

Fire and healing were everywhere.

The Retreat

Fifty

When Christine opened the door, Mary's heart sank. Christine was a beautiful woman, taller and thinner than the photos on her website. And Paul was right—her eyes glowed. Her hair looked like naturally braided yellow rope—attractively wild. Mary held the handle of her trolley suitcase tightly; she felt like a refugee looking for handouts. *Paul has no idea what is going on here*, she thought to herself.

"Welcome, everyone!" Christine said, ushering them into her home. Christine and Paul looked very comfortable when they hugged.

"It's so good to see you," Paul said.

"And you must be Mary," Christine said. Mary tensed. She was dirty and uncomfortable from the plane trip.

"Yes."

Christine held Mary's hands and smiled. "You *are* Mary." The way Christine said her name gave Mary pause. "You must be tired."

"Exhausted." Mary smiled weakly.

"Let's send Paul upstairs with the bags, and I'll fix you a tea, OK?" Christine held Mary's hand and walked her downstairs to the kitchen. Mary followed, unsure why she took her lead. "Please have a seat." As

Christine fixed the tea, Mary looked out the sliding doors to the patio and garden. "Here you go." Christine sat across from Mary. "How was the trip?"

"It was OK. I can't sleep on planes."

"I can't either. I really don't like flying at all. If God wanted us to fly, he would have given us wings." Her eyes twinkled. "And I don't think I've grown any wings yet." Christine stirred her tea. "I think it's wonderful that you came with Paul."

"Well, it's good to get out of New York. And to see Jeanne and Edward," Mary said too casually.

"I know you're here as an observer. But I want to make sure you're completely comfortable and you don't feel excluded from anything. Tell me if you do."

"Thanks. I know Paul is excited to be here."

"And how do you feel?"

"Honestly?" Christine nodded. "I'm very uncomfortable. I don't believe in these sorts of things." Mary waved at the bookshelves lining the dining room wall full of crystals, statuettes, and colored glass. "Paul's been behaving strangely, and we don't really even know you—and we're staying in your house!"

"I can tell you more about me."

"I already read your website." Mary sipped her tea, staring down at the table, too uncomfortable to look at Christine.

"Mary?" Mary didn't look up. "Perhaps I can tell you how I became a soul reader?"

Mary felt vulnerable, sitting alone with Christine. "Where is Paul, anyway?" Mary shouted, "Paul!" A dog barked. It sounded like it was in the basement.

"That is my dog, Lourde. He's in the basement. He's is very friendly but gets nervous around new people, and Paul mentioned that you were afraid of dogs."

Mary frowned. "Oh did he?"

"I think he mentioned it because he wanted to make sure you were comfortable."

"Well, he didn't say anything to me. Where is he?" Mary pushed out her seat to get up.

"I'm afraid of a lot of things. I'm afraid of crowds. Noise. Noisy crowds." Christine smiled. "I feel safest when I'm doing my treatments. It's so peaceful and rewarding."

Mary stayed. "What led you to do this?"

"Well, I really didn't choose to do it. I was always a little different as a girl. I knew what people were thinking; I could feel their feelings. But my mother told me that's what little children did, before their senses turned to mush as adults. Then a car struck me as I was bicycling. I was daydreaming and didn't see it coming around the corner. I remember seeing a large shadow appearing in the corner of my eye as I drifted into the intersection. By the time I focused, I was staring at the right headlight of a car—that's all I saw before I closed my eyes. The impact went through me like a set of knives being pushed into my legs and hips. The bike shot forward, the car stopped, and I flew in space for a moment. I don't remember anything after that. I hit the ground headfirst and suffered a concussion and a skull fracture. I was in the hospital for six months, and for a lot of that time, I was in a coma."

"That's terrible!" Mary said.

Christine smiled. "One day, I regained consciousness. Everything looked different. People—my mother, doctors, and nurses—floated in front of me. I saw through their bodies. Spirits surrounded them. They hovered, silently participating. With my new lens, the world lost its disguise. I looked into people's souls." Christine stared out at the garden as if she had forgotten about Mary. "Strange. I feel cold right now." She reached for a blanket and wrapped it around her shoulders.

Christine stared at Mary. Her smile had disappeared, and she pulled the blanket tighter around her body. Mary felt uncomfortable. What was she looking at? Why did she stop talking?

Christine finally spoke. "My mother told me that I was only conscious for a few minutes that day. The doctors had to induce another coma to treat the swelling of my brain." Christine sat down. "I'll never know what I really saw or felt."

"Sounds horrible."

"In any case, I did recover."

"Did you become a soul reader after that incident?"

"No. I was an accountant at a bank for a long while. But I never felt normal. I knew I had a gift, but I didn't know what to do with it."

"I see. So when did you?"

"I'll finish my story, but then you have to tell me about yourself. More tea?" Mary nodded. Christine prepared another pot. "My supervisor was the typical strung-out guy at a corporate job. But then he changed. He became more relaxed and happy. I told him I noticed the change. He acknowledged it. He credited a class he was taking. He learned meditation and visualization techniques. I did the training and then taught others."

Mary yawned. Christine looked concerned and said, "I'm boring you."

"No, not at all. I'm sorry; I'm just a little tired. And your voice is—well, it's very soothing. So you taught visualization techniques?"

"Yes. Are you familiar?"

"Well, Paul gave me your instructions for getting ready for the retreat. He thought I should try it, even if I wasn't participating."

"How nice of Paul." Christine said his name in a very familiar way. "And did you do the technique?"

"I tried but ended up having a nightmare, to be honest. I fell off a couch and hurt my shoulder. Not sure if it was helpful," Mary said nervously.

"I should have told Paul not to share it with you."

"What do you mean? Paul shouldn't keep things from me," Mary said testily.

"That's not what I meant. It was an exercise for him. Clearing out his fears before the retreat."

"What fears?"

Christine smiled. "I really can't share that with you."

Mary bristled. "We're married, you know."

"I know, but I can't do my work if my clients don't feel safe. You can understand that, can't you?" Christine reached across the table and put her hand on Mary's. "Tell me about your nightmare."

Mary looked down at the table. "Oh, it was stupid."

"Remember when I said I felt cold a moment ago?" Mary said nothing. "I saw you in a dream. Let me share it with you." Mary looked as if she wanted to run away.

Christine went into the kitchen and returned with a black tray. She took a bowl from a shelf. It was filled with round stones, some clear and some opaque. She placed the tray between them on the table. "In my vision, I saw a square room. People—or maybe statues—stood in the room." Christine placed stones on three sides of the tray. "You stood alone at the entrance here." She placed a white stone for Mary. "Facing you was a man." She marked the man with a black stone. "And I sort of floated in the middle, observing." She placed a clear red stone in the middle. "That's what I saw." As Christine talked, the room darkened from the overcast sky outside. Christine's voice took on an edge. "I see this person coming toward you, but I remain between the two of you. Does any of this make sense?"

"Yes," Mary whispered, feeling goose bumps on her skin.

Christine looked up from the tray. "This figure walking toward you and me—you know very well. You waver between desire and fear. You want to take it in. You want to run away. Is this familiar to you?"

"Yes."

"The figure is a man with very strong masculine energy, and you don't know what to do with it. It's like playing with a snake. You will not embrace it, and you will not run away. Finally, you fall to the ground."

Christine put the stones back in the bowl. She returned the tray to the kitchen. Christine poured more tea. "This is what I do. I have a lens into the soul." Christine sat down across from her again, staring at her intently. "Do you understand why I must have secrets? With you? With Paul? With anyone I work with?"

"Yes." Mary's voice quavered, beads of sweat appearing on her forehead. She looked down, refusing to look into Christine's eyes. She heard the scrape of a chair push back. She shook, and tears trickled down her cheeks. Christine moved around the table. Her hands gripped Mary's shoulders firmly. Mary desperately wanted Christine to put her arms around her. Shocked by her own reaction, Mary closed her eyes, hoping it would all go away.

Christine said, "Now let's go find Paul."

Fifty-One

Christine and Mary walked up the stairs to the third-floor bedroom. Paul lay on a futon, fast asleep. "That's strange," Mary whispered. "Paul never sleeps after a red-eye. He stays up to reset his clock for the new time zone."

"Maybe he feels comfortable here. It's not unusual. People sleep a lot on my retreats. Why don't you take a nap with him? I'll wake you up in a couple hours."

Mary shook her head. Christine hugged her. "Rest, Mary," Christine whispered in her beautiful accent. Mary lay down next to Paul and fell into a deep sleep.

Christine woke them at lunchtime. They had a late lunch in the village, visited the shops on the high street, and met Edward and Jeanne for an early dinner. Christine had asked Paul not to drink, as the retreat would officially begin that evening with a meditation. The dinner conversation was light as the four of them caught up, but they steered away from Christine and the reason for their visit.

Finally, Jeanne could not resist, and she whispered to Mary, "What do you think of Christine?"

Mary felt foggy from the jet lag, the red wine, and her deep sleep. "What do you mean?"

"You know. Do you like her? Does she put you off?"

"She seems fine. A little strange."

"A little strange? My girl, I'd say a lot strange." Jeanne laughed. "Even the way she looks."

"She's got a great body."

"Come on, so do you."

"Not like hers. She looks like my yoga teacher."

"Was she what you expected?"

Mary thought about the question. "I'd say she was friendlier than I expected. Not so mysterious. Her voice is hypnotic."

"I know. It's special, isn't it?"

"Do you think she hypnotizes people?"

"No, I don't think so, but her voice is definitely part of her package."

Mary hesitated. "Of course, her eyes—"

"Yes?"

"Well, her eyes glow. And the glow feels like it touches you."

"I know what you mean."

Mary's voice rose. "I don't know if I trust her. But she has something—there's an energy."

Jeanne whispered to Mary, "How is it staying in the house with her? I've only been there for a short visit, but I'd think it would be very mysterious."

"The house is very comfortable. Lots of interesting objects all over the place. It feels like, I don't know . . ." Mary sipped her wine. "I know it makes no sense, but it feels like the home that a child wishes for—very safe." Mary looked over to Paul and Edward, who were laughing about something, and then whispered to Jeanne, "I worry she knows what I am thinking."

"Why do you say that?"

"Well, she told me about something I'd dreamed last night. How would she know that?"

"She's intuitive," Jeanne suggested. "She has that ability." Jeanne whispered into Mary's ear, "Are you going to have a soul reading?"

"No! Absolutely not. I'm here to observe." Mary glanced at Paul, still chatting with Edward. "And to make sure that she doesn't seduce Paul."

"Oh, don't be silly. I've seen how she behaves with my guests. I trust her. Otherwise, I wouldn't have recommended her to Paul. And Paul's a gentleman." Mary said nothing. Jeanne whispered again, "I must admit though, you do sort of fall in love with her when you have a reading, whether you're a man or a woman."

"Really?" Mary's eyes widened. "That's a little scary."

"Oh, don't worry about it. She's very professional." The waitress walked over with a bottle of wine. "How about another glass?" Jeanne asked.

Mary shook her head. "No, I can't. I'm having a meditation session with Christine and Paul tonight after dinner."

"You are? That's great!"

"Not a soul reading. Just a meditation. I thought, what the heck, it might help me sleep."

Jeanne held up her refilled glass of wine. "Here's to a good meditation and a soul reading to follow!"

Edward jumped in. "What? A toast without me? Bloody Paul is nursing his Pellegrino all night. Let me jump in on this one. Here's to what now?"

"Nothing, Edward. Mind your own business."

"How's that nasty dog of Christine's? Is she going to put him down finally?"

Mary tipped her empty glass. "Actually, Edward, I think he's the friendliest dog; he put his head on my lap while we were talking with Christine this afternoon."

"Watch out, is all I have to say." Jeanne glared at her husband, but Edward continued: "I hope you're getting something out of this retreat. So far Paul has no horse tips for me. What's the point of talking to a fortune-teller?"

Jeanne said, "She's not a fortune-teller, Edward. You know that!"

Paul noticed the time. "Well, this has been fun, folks, but we have to get back to the house."

Edward said, "Is it a school night or something? Do I need to write a note to Christine? 'Please allow Paul and Mary to stay out past nine p.m. and have an alcoholic beverage in a pub.' I'll even deliver it in person," Edward said sternly. "We'll have to tie up the dog though."

They all laughed and then said their goodbyes. Paul and Mary left the pub and walked to Christine's house, arriving a little late. Christine hurried them to her treatment room. Paul smiled, recognizing the room where the soul reading occurred a few months ago.

"OK, I want you to lie down on your backs next to each other. Move around until you feel comfortable." Mary and Paul lay silently on the floor. "I'm going to cover each of you with a light blanket in case you become cold. Now close your eyes and listen to my voice. The purpose of this exercise is to help you relax. Restore your energy. Recharge your batteries. Have a restful sleep. There's nothing to do. Just listen to my voice. If you drift off, that's fine. Are you comfortable?"

The ritual began. Christine talked about Mother Mary and drawing on her energy and the angels surrounding her. She talked about being cradled by a yellow orb. "Listen to your breath." Christine breathed through her mouth, breaths of growing duration. Mary lost track of Christine's words but followed her voice and breathing. She could hear Paul snoring slightly, succumbing to her spell. Mary drifted off as well.

Christine rose and walked to a table against the wall. She dipped her fingers into a bowl of water, crouched down above their heads, and touched their foreheads with her fingers, brushing them back and forth.

She moved to the other end of the room and tucked their feet in the blankets covering them. Then she slowly rubbed the soles of their feet.

"Now I'm going to count to three. When I reach three, you'll be conscious. One. You begin to feel yourself—your hands, your feet, your head—and you can begin to move very slowly. Two. You're fully conscious. You can move your arms, your legs, your torso. Three. Now open your eyes. You are in my home, in this room. You feel awake and refreshed. Take your time. Lie there and enjoy how you feel. Relax. I'm going to get some tea for us. Take your time in rising." The door opened and shut quietly.

Paul and Mary slowly rose to sitting positions. They pulled the blankets around them, both suddenly feeling cold. Christine returned with piping-hot cups of chamomile tea, which they gratefully sipped.

"Did that feel good?" asked Christine. They both nodded. "Good. You must be tired. You should sleep well tonight. I'll make breakfast for us tomorrow. Paul and I will do a ritual walk. It will take the morning, and then I thought we could meet for lunch in town. Mary, you are welcome to stay in the house, or you can visit some of the sites, OK?"

"Sure," Mary said dreamily.

"We can talk again in the morning." After finishing their tea, they went upstairs to their room. The sleeping arrangement in Christine's guest room was a little awkward. Futons lined two walls, so the couple slept separately. Paul and Mary lay in their respective futons in silence, still feeling the effects of the meditation. Paul felt waves of joy; this retreat was working its magic on him already. But he worried about Mary. She lay in her bed, her back toward him. "Good night, Mary."

"Good night."

They were both exhausted. Glastonbury energy filled the room and soaked into their bodies like a magical salve. Even a wakeful state was dreamy in this village. The hours passed by. Paul and Mary both moved from time to time.

Paul whispered, "Mary, are you still awake?"

"Yes."

"Are you OK?"

"I'm a little afraid."

Paul said nothing, but he moved to Mary's futon, pulling his blanket with him. Together, they fell into a deep and restful sleep.

Fifty-Two

"Follow your heart." Christine and Paul stood in front of her house. He hesitated. "Let it steer you in a direction, any direction." Paul took a couple tentative steps, unintentionally putting his hand over heart. Christine laughed. "You'll have to pick it up a little or we'll never get to the village. Release yourself from work, all worries, anything that ties you down. Come on!" Playfully, she skipped ahead of him. He picked up the pace.

As they walked up the high street, Paul worried about Mary, despite Christine's advice. Mary looked unhappy when they left. Christine suggested that she visit the abbey and meet them for lunch at the Blue Note Café. Paul did not know what to do. If he pressed her to be part of the rituals, she would resist; if he respected her wish not to participate, she would feel hurt.

Just as they passed the Speaking Tree bookstore, a woman called from across the street, "Christine!" She ran up and gave her a hug. "I haven't seen you for so long. Where have you been hiding?"

"Numi." Christine looked nonplussed as she disengaged from her. "I'd like you to meet Paul."

Numi looked at Paul and said, "Oh, I see where you've been hiding."

Christine blushed. "No, Paul is a client of mine."

"And where are you from?"

"New York City." Paul stared at Numi. Her long black hair, streaked with red highlights, framed a pale face. A dark dress clung to her petite body.

"New York's a long way from Glastonbury." Her eyes receded beneath thick eyelashes and dark mascara. It was a seductive look when she smiled, a threatening one when she pursed her lips.

Christine, embarrassed by the innuendo, elaborated: "Paul had a soul reading a few months ago, and now he's returned to Glastonbury for a retreat. We've got to keep going, though; we're in the middle of a morning ritual."

"Where're you staying, Paul?" Numi was unshakeable.

"At Christine's house."

"Charming. It's such an intimate setting for a retreat. Powerful energy," Numi mused.

Christine blurted out, "His wife's here."

"What?"

"His wife. She's staying as well."

Numi frowned. "Oh. Well. Where is she?"

"She's not really participating. She's not really—" Paul stammered.

"I get it, Paul." Numi grinned. "It happens all the time. Partners on different paths at different speeds. She doesn't want to be left behind."

"Numi, we have to go," Christine insisted. Paul sensed the tension between the two.

"Of course." She hugged Christine again and then turned to Paul. She placed her hands on either side of his head as if she was about to kiss him. "You're in very good hands, Paul."

"Thank you," Paul said awkwardly.

Numi looked over at Christine. "I sense this is a special one. Good-bye." Numi ran across the street, nearly being hit by a grocery delivery truck, and said, "Call me after the retreat. I want to catch up!" She laughed as she disappeared into the crowd of morning shoppers.

"Now where were we?" Christine said.

"Who was that?" Paul asked.

"Someone who wants to be my friend."

"What does she do? She seemed to be a little different."

"The village is full of people who are different, Paul—normal peo-ple like you are the exception! Some people are spiritual. Some are charlatans and crazies. Numi is a witch."

"A witch?"

"A black witch, meaning she helps people gain power to control their lives."

"She's very charming."

"She's a bit of a rascal. She cast a spell on you. That's why you stood there like—" Christine blushed. "Like a little boy. It's her version of flirting, and it's not nice. She tried to cast a spell on us, but I wouldn't let her."

"What do you mean on us?"

"Never mind. Do not take up with a dark witch, Paul. You need to be careful." Christine resumed walking, and Paul followed. "You opened very quickly to the energy of Glastonbury, but you're still a babe in the woods."

Fifty-Three

Mary stood in Christine's house with nothing to do. She could walk around the village but wanted to avoid running into Paul and Christine. The whole situation was awkward—like going on one of Paul's golf outings but not playing golf. Christine's house spooked her; the walls and shelves were alive with things that shimmered and vibrated in the morning sunlight. They stared at her like rows of mystical nanny cams.

The door to Christine's bedroom was partially ajar. Through the opening, Mary could see a shiny silver quilt on her bed. She went inside. The bedroom was pristine and had a few pictures of Christine and her family. Interestingly, unlike the rest of the house, the bedroom was bereft of spiritual paraphernalia. A dressing table held trays of jewelry and cosmetics. A long silk scarf hung off the back of the dressing table chair. Its bright-red colors and floral pattern drew her eye. She slipped into the chair and looked in the mirror, draping the scarf on her shoulders. Mary noticed a jar of herbal lipstick—*Christine's red lips*, she thought. She opened the jar, dabbed her finger without leaving a trace, and then put some on her lips. Voilà, a new Mary with plump scarlet lips. Then she noticed it and almost cried out. The red wig on a hook on the back of the closet, hanging like a wild animal pelt. She could not resist and held it, feeling the texture of real human hair. She put on the wig and walked downstairs, a daytime sleepwalker.

The raven grew restless on the birdbath, waiting for her. The door slid open, and Mary walked out, holding her hands together in a prayer gesture. The long red hair and bright lips were familiar, but the raven knew it was a different woman. The raven flapped its wings as if to warn her away. She put her cupped hands in the birdbath and poured water on her face, and it trickled down her chest. The raven cawed, surprised by the splashing water, ready to fly away.

Mary laughed, unafraid of the large raven sitting inches away. She settled in Christine's chair and drew her bright-red scarf close around her shoulders. She wore a smug smile as she closed her eyes, enjoying the warm sunlight. We all keep secrets, and Mary will uncover Christine's secret self. Her long red locks covered her chest. The raven waited for the fireworks to begin.

Fifty-Four

Paul and Christine stood on the road that led to the Tor, facing a pair of blue wooden doors. "I'd like to go in."

Christine smiled. "This is a special place, but unfortunately, it's not open."

"What is it?" Paul asked.

"The White Spring Temple. It was a reservoir in the 1800s. The Chalice Well Gardens are over there," she said, and she pointed across the road.

"I went there after our soul reading," Paul said.

"Do you remember the red water at the well?"

"Yes, I drank it!"

"The red water represents the feminine energy."

As they stood outside the temple, Paul watched people filling large bottles with water from spigots extending from the Chalice Well wall and the White Spring Temple. "The White Spring produces a chalky white water. It comes from springs inside the Tor. It's said to be a source of masculine energy."

"Oh? And what's the scientific cause for the colors?" Paul asked.

Christine laughed. "Of course you have to ask! They say the red water is created by iron oxide sediment and the white spring water feeds through calcium-rich rocks."

"Quite a coincidence that they end up in the same place," Paul murmured.

"You think it's a coincidence?" Christine asked.

The blue doors opened, and a woman emerged. "Can I help you?"

"Hi. I'm Christine. My friend is visiting and asking questions about the White Spring. Can we peek inside?"

"I'm Alicia," the lady said as she squinted in the sunlight. She was caked with dust. She tried to wipe her hand on her blouse and offered it halfheartedly. "I'm sorry. The work is very dirty inside." She brushed the dust out of her hair, assessing the couple in front of her. "This is a construction site right now, not really safe for anyone to enter."

"Paul's come all the way from New York. I'm sure he'd love to hear what you're doing. We're all so excited about the project."

Alicia beamed. "We like to say it'll be the world's only active water temple." She motioned them in. "You can step inside, but stay near the entrance. It's not really safe."

The interior was dimly lit by two electric lamps hanging from the ceiling. It looked like a manmade cave with a stone ceiling composed of three domed vaults high above a red brick floor. The floor was slightly concave, and water gathered in shallow troughs sloping down to outside drains. The roar of water crashing down the far wall explained the heavy moisture in the air. Paul felt he was inside the belly of a giant whale.

"Right now, we're building pools that will be fed by the spring water entering along the far wall," Alicia explained. "The space centers on a shallow half-moon pool. Against the wall in that corner will be a much deeper pool. Pilgrims can disrobe and immerse themselves in a cleansing ritual—if they can bear the cold!"

"Oooh . . . I so look forward to that, feeling that spring water against my skin," Christine said. Her eyes twinkled in the dim light. Paul imagined her naked, sliding into the pool.

"We're building shrines in the corners of the temple. There'll be a shrine to the King of the Fairy World in the back. It's a portal to the Tor's interior, where the fairies live. Over here, by the plunge pool, Our Lady of Avalon, the earth mother." Paul could barely follow what Alicia was describing. "Finally, in this near alcove, we have the shrine to Brigid, keeper of the flame."

"Brigid . . ." Christine said under her breath.

"We already built part of her shrine when we consecrated the space. Brigid is the guardian of sacred springs. You can see her portrait over here."

She pointed out a painting with a small table in front of it. The table held a lantern, which illuminated the painting—a woman in a red dress, rays of light rising from her head, standing on a red moonlit landscape.

"Wow." Paul found the place to be irresistible. Alicia then described the conversion of a nineteenth-century reservoir into a twenty-first-century temple.

"I wonder," Christine asked, "would it be possible for us to spend a few minutes at Brigid's shrine?"

Alicia shook her head. "This isn't open to the public yet. You really shouldn't be inside."

"Just a few minutes. We won't tell anyone," Christine suggested with her hypnotic voice.

"Let me talk to the crew."

While Alicia moved away and whispered to the other workers, pointing toward Christine and Paul, Christine whispered, "I feel we should spend some time here."

"OK." Alicia reappeared. "The crew is ready for a break. We'll leave. I'll close the doors and douse the light, so the only light you'll have is Brigid's candle. You must sit at this shrine." She pointed to two wooden benches facing each other in front of the painting. "And don't move, OK? It's too dark and dangerous to walk around."

"Of course, we'll stay here," Christine said. Alicia gave Christine a serious look, and then she and the other workers left the temple.

Christine and Paul sat down, facing each other. The doors closed with a thud. The temple was pitch black, which heightened the sound of the water smashing onto the floor, creating a deafening echo. Paul noticed mementos—dried flowers, stones, and folded notes—strewn on the table. "People left these?" *Apparently, Alicia breaks the rules often*, he thought.

Christine nodded. "Should you leave something? Perhaps one of the heart stones?" Before they left the house, Christine asked Paul to pick three heart-shaped stones from her collection to take with him on the walking ritual. Paul selected one that had a gash running across its surface, as if someone had tried to smash it into pieces with an ax. He held it next to the candle. "Does that stone have significance for you?" Christine asked.

"It looks like a broken heart to me." Paul turned the stone in the light. "This is going to sound strange. In my soul reading, you saw that I was betrayed by my friends. Do you remember?"

"Yes."

"I didn't know what you were referring to at the time. But now I remember. Something did happen. I was maybe twelve years old, and there was a girl in my class who was cute. Back then, boys and girls didn't really talk to each other, but I was sure she liked me. Something was up, anyway." Paul put the stone down. "This is silly."

"Nothing about the heart is silly," Christine said.

"My friends encouraged me to test the waters. I wrote a note, and they acted as the go-between. She quickly wrote back. When I saw her—in class or the hallway—she'd smile at me. We enjoyed our secret together."

"A paper romance. Kind of like texting," Christine offered.

"Yes! Then I took the next big step. I asked her to meet me in the hall during a break period. It was time to have an actual conversation."

"How brave!" Christine chuckled.

"I showed up. She wasn't there. But my friends were, and they looked sheepish. They admitted the whole thing was a practical joke. They never forwarded my notes, and they wrote her responses themselves."

"That's horrible," Christine said softly. She picked up Paul's heart stone with the gash in the middle.

"There was nothing there. I was devastated." Paul laughed nervously. "I can see that girl's face as if it were yesterday." Christine was silent. "Why am I talking about this? With this"—he looked up at the painting and shrugged—"goddess, whatever, standing over us. It's crazy."

Christine reached out, took Paul's hands, and gave him the heart stone. "Maybe this stone reminded you of the damage to your heart. Unrequited love breaks hearts, Paul." Christine wrapped her hands around Paul's hands and the stone. "Close your eyes. I will ask Brigid for a blessing."

Paul closed his eyes and became aware of his breath. Christine's voice faded into the dissonant sound of the water falling. Paul's mind drifted to a place, years earlier. He saw her, sitting at a desk, several rows in front of him. She looked back and smiled at him as the teacher wrote on the board. Everything they wrote to each other rushed back into his memory. Now he stood in the hallway, nervously anticipating the moment. They would finally talk, and he had so much to say—if he could get the first word out. The shock—that everything shared was not real—hurt so badly. He fell for a practical joke. His friends watched his reaction, and he laughed along with them, but all the while, he thought, *Never trust your heart.* Paul carried that mantra with him.

"Paul?" He opened his eyes. Christine wore a quizzical smile. Paul still clenched the heart stone, and tears filled his eyes. He placed it by the candle, relieved to leave it behind.

The temple doors cracked open, and a ray of outdoor light splashed across the floor. Alicia peeked around the corner. "I'm sorry, but we have to get back to work."

"Your timing's perfect, isn't it, Paul?" Christine said. "I can't thank you enough. Brigid's shrine is so moving."

"I'm glad to hear that. I love her energy," Alicia whispered conspiratorially. "I believe every woman has a Brigid inside."

Christine gave Alicia a banknote. "Here's a small contribution to the work you're doing."

"That's not necessary," Alicia protested.

"Please, use it for the Brigid shrine." As Christine and Alicia hugged, Paul exited. The bright sunlight disoriented Paul as he stepped off the curb onto Well Lane. He had trouble finding his footing, bobbing and weaving among the pilgrims as they bottled their water, red and white.

Fifty-Five

Christine no longer had to tell Paul what to do—he just followed his feet. They reached a wooded area highlighted by two enormous oaks, twenty-five feet high with trunks five feet wide. The ancient trees were dying a slow death. Their branches and roots sprayed into the air as if they were prisoners escaping from the misshapen trunks full of pockmarks. In a few cases, the cavities formed by the tree's erosion contained large stones set as tightly as a jeweler sets a stone in a gold ring. It looked like an excavation site for a prehistoric dig, yet some of the trees' branches grew green leaves, suggesting that the oaks clung to life, despite being surrounded by their own decay.

"You've said nothing since we left White Spring," Christine said.

"I'm enjoying the walk."

Christine sat on a fallen branch of one of the giant oaks and patted the spot next to her. "Why do you think she smiled at you?"

"Who?"

"The girl in your class. You said she smiled at you whenever she saw you. Why'd she do that?"

"I don't know," Paul said, joining her on the branch. "She probably thought, *Why's this boy smiling at me?*"

"I doubt that. I know I didn't smile back at boys just because they smiled at me. I'd ignore them. Or give them a look." Christine made a face. "Like 'Stay away from me.' I wouldn't have smiled to be nice—not day after day."

"What're you saying?"

"What I'm saying is that your friends played a cruel trick on you, no doubt. Your first true love—the first time you turned that switch on—was based on an illusion. It had to be a devastating feeling." Paul nodded. "But perhaps there was a mutual feeling, an attraction between the two of you. Perhaps your feelings were justified—she smiled because she liked you. She wondered why you didn't talk to her, and in her confusion, she grew shy and might have thought it all was an illusion as well." Paul relaxed to her singsong voice. "She's somewhere today, possibly holding on to her version of this distant memory—this smiling boy teasing her heart. Not as dramatic an experience—she wasn't betrayed by her friends—but in a way, the whole experience was even more deceptive." Christine smiled. "I'm sure you had a real puppy-dog look when you smiled at her."

"I remember her smile. It was real," Paul said.

"This girl—let's call her Annie—grows up and forgets about you, your smiles in the classroom, the glances in the hallway. She stores this first love in a file called 'Unrequited Love.' Make sense?"

"I hadn't thought about it that way," Paul said.

"Annie's grown up now. She thinks she's happy. Her husband is a good man. She wishes she could let go of something that's holding her back, but she doesn't know what it is. You *do* know what's holding you back because you met this nutty soul reader," Christine teased.

"Now you're making me feel guilty!"

Christine smiled. "I'm going to ask you to do something. You'll think it's crazy, but I know it will be helpful."

"OK."

"I want you to close your eyes and listen to your breath and push your mind out of the way. Visualize this young girl, Annie." Paul closed his eyes. "Tell her what you were feeling at the time, from your heart. I'll be quiet."

Paul closed his eyes. Within minutes, he found himself back in the classroom. Annie was expecting him. They found themselves in the stairwell, finally having the encounter they longed for. They looked like young kids circling each other, but their conversation was an adult one. He told her the story of deception, explaining why he never spoke to her. Paul said he loved her, if children their age had that capacity. "It was real," he said, not knowing what else to say.

She broke into a wide smile as what he was saying sunk in. "Thank you, thank you," she repeated again and again as their young love rose like a balloon into her heart. They held each other like awkward twelve-year-olds and relished the feeling. Finally, they wiped their tears away as the encounter faded away.

Then Paul watched Annie standing in a kitchen, years later. Her children were eating breakfast while she prepared their lunch. Everyone was running late. She stopped wrapping a sandwich and blushed. For some reason, that boy—her first infatuation—came into her consciousness. She placed her hand on her teenage son's head, absentmindedly brushing his hair. He ignored her, trying to eat his cereal as quickly as possible. Annie looked out the kitchen window at the trees in the backyard. She touched her heart, warmed by a newfound memory. Her children did not see the single tear running down her cheek.

Annie's husband paused at the bottom of the stairs, even though he was late for work. He watched Annie—the tear rolling down her cheek, her hand caressing their son's head. She looked different, he thought. It was the smile. How was it possible he had never seen that smile before? It was as if it had arrived from a different time and place, misplaced until now. *Hold onto that smile*, he thought, *in this time and place, with me.*

A bird's cry startled Paul, and he almost fell off the branch. "Are you OK?" Christine called out. Paul nodded, feeling groggy.

Christine was circling the giant oak trees. "They think these trees are about a thousand years old. Some claim they are drawn from the roots of older trees. The trees have names, you know."

"Really." Paul slid off his seat.

"Gog and Magog. They're the last of the oaks that lined the road to the Tor. Legend has it that King Arthur left a tribute under the trees before he fought a rebel chieftain for the control of the Tor. Many pilgrims leave tributes under the trees."

Now Paul understood why the gnarled trunks of the giant oaks were littered with dried flowers, stones, ribbons, photos, and little notes. Paul stooped under Gog, pulling something from his pocket. "What're you doing?"

"I'm putting my second heart stone under this tree." Paul kneeled by the tree. "The meditation really worked. I can't even tell you what happened. It was like I was transported to another place, but it didn't feel like a dream. More like being in a movie."

"This is a magical place." Christine picked up her bag. "Let's return on this path. It takes us more directly to the village."

"I thought I was supposed to follow my heart," Paul teased.

"Not anymore—unless you want to be late for lunch with Mary."

Fifty-Six

Mary opened her eyes when she heard a bird call. She was sitting in Christine's garden. Her cheeks were burned pink from the sun. She licked her crusty lips, which were covered in dried lipstick. She touched her head. What was she wearing? It took a minute before she knew where she was. Suddenly, she remembered all of it—the red wig and scarf and the raven, who was gone. She looked at her watch. It was late. She hurried back in and returned everything to where she found it. Then she ran out to meet Paul and Christine for lunch.

Fifty-Seven

"Isn't a goddess temple for women?" Paul protested.

Christine laughed. "Goddesses like the company of men as well."

Christine and Paul arrived early for their lunch and were standing in a courtyard behind the Blue Note Café. Paul had noticed a banner hanging from a second story railing—the Glastonbury Goddess Temple. He made the mistake of asking what it was, and now he was going to find out, like it or not.

"Take off your shoes," Christine whispered as they entered the temple. It was a simple room with a high cathedral ceiling. The walls were plain white; rose drapes hung from tall windows. Natural light poured into the room, which, along with burning incense, created a hazy atmosphere. The walls were lined with white wool blankets and cushions of all shapes and sizes resting on a deep-blue carpet.

A female figure, created from wood branches, wore a red robe draped over her frame and guarded the entrance to a bowered enclosure. The figure stared at Paul, her face a beautifully sculpted wood mask, painted in flesh colors with two dark crystals for eyes. Behind her, two women slept on blankets on the floor under the bower.

A life-size ceramic statue of an Indian goddess stood along one wall, every inch of its surface hand painted, like a kaleidoscopic figurine. Other goddess figures stood or sat in poses—a fat primitive goddess kneeled on the ground holding her large breasts, a somber gray-haired woman in a silver gown held a staff topped with a stuffed owl.

Paul's eyes were drawn to a large painting on the far wall. It was a goddess standing on a lake with the Tor and other landmarks in the background. She wore a red flowing gown with armor covering her torso and hips. Long coils of hair snaked down her body and into the faux landscape. She leaned on a sword as high as her shoulders, as if it were a walking stick. She bore an angry expression—glowering eyes, pursed lips, and hollowed cheeks—underscored with fiery war paint. Paul feared this woman warrior goddess. She was the Lady of Avalon. He felt she could walk out of the canvas at any time.

Christine guided Paul to some unoccupied pillows where they both could sit.

A young man sat across from him. He sat in the lotus position, eyes closed. He looked as if he was floating peacefully in space. Christine had already entered a meditative state. Paul was too curious to close his eyes.

A young woman walked purposefully to the altar in front of the frightening Lady of Avalon, holding the hand of a young boy. Her hair, brown with streaks of green and wrapped into a bun, was held together with a collection of colorful hairpins. She wore a brown robe that touched the floor, covering her bare feet. She wore two nose rings. Her eyebrows were green, and her already large eyes, framed by black mascara, took on the shape of orbs. The cutout in the front of her robe revealed a tattoo of a forest goddess sleeping next to a brook, plant tendrils wrapped around her naked body. She wore a collection of bracelets on each wrist and a simple twisted leather necklace.

Paul would have dismissed her as a New York Lower East Side goth if he saw her walking in St. Mark's Square, but in this goddess temple, she took on a singular beauty. Perhaps it was her unmistakably positive aura, or her little partner clutching her hand, or the half-moon profile of her belly blooming underneath her loose gown. The backlight from the window behind her teased the sharp features of her face as she closed her eyes and smiled, rocking with the boy and her unborn baby.

Paul suddenly felt drowsy and closed his eyes. The atmosphere in the temple grew heavy, and he heard ringing in his ears. He fell into a trance.

Paul was a child at a playground. Children circled a maypole, painted like a candy-striped barber's pole. Paul joined them. They chanted rhymes and tried to twirl as they ran around the maypole, sometimes falling to the ground. Shrieks of laughter filled the air. Paul, deep in his trance, had no idea he was grinning from ear to ear. He heard the laughter of a single child emerge from the noise. Drifting back into consciousness, he realized it came from within the temple. He opened his eyes. The little boy stood in front of the shrine, pointing up at the Lady of Avalon and laughing out loud. His mother motioned for him to stop, looking around the temple, embarrassed by the distur-bance. She pulled him closer to her belly, almost muffling him, and he calmed down.

The young man across from Paul now lay on his side—eyes closed—his head propped against a pillow. *He looks so peaceful,* Paul thought. The little boy nestled in his mother's lap, his eyes closed, suck-ing his thumb. Paul embraced the differentness surrounding him.

"It's time to go," Christine whispered.

Fifty-Eight

Mary slid in next to Paul at a picnic table in the courtyard behind the Blue Note Café. "So how was your morning?"

Paul was smiling at Christine, and his ecstatic expression startled Mary. *This is ridiculous,* Mary thought. *Paul is obsessing about Christine.*

"It was great. We went for a long walk. We ended up at a goddess temple right behind this café."

"Oh," Mary said. Paul was grinning at Christine again, as if there was an inside joke. "Did you find it beneficial?"

Christine gestured. "Look at Paul's eyes. Can you see the difference?"

"He looks happy." *He's fallen in love with you, that's what I see,* Mary thought. "I'm glad you had a good morning."

"I'm going to leave you two alone. I've got some errands to run this afternoon, and it looks like it will be a beautiful day to walk around the village."

"Join us for lunch," Paul said too enthusiastically. Mary was quiet.

"No, I need some time on my own. These retreats take a lot out of me. I might just crawl into bed and have an afternoon nap. Tonight, we're having dinner with Jeanne and Edward at seven. You guys have a good time this afternoon." Paul watched Christine leave, looking as if he wanted to follow her home.

Paul and Mary ate lunch in silence. Mary picked at her veggie burger. "What did you do this morning?"

"We walked around. I followed my heart."

"Did you see anything?"

"We had a lot of interesting experiences."

As Mary asked questions, Paul reluctantly answered. He seemed uncomfortable. He was afraid to tell Mary what happened; she would just think it was all hocus-pocus craziness, and Paul did not want her to spoil the spell he was under. He never felt more alive and in tune with the world. But she persisted to ask questions, painfully drawing it out of him. As he described the goddess temple and the pregnant goth girl, she finally lost it. "Paul, this is crazy. Do you know what you sound like? Where, exactly, is this goddess temple?"

Paul pointed reluctantly. "But don't go there, Mary."

"Why not?"

"You won't get it. You'll think it's crazy."

Mary shook her head. "What, only you and Christine understand? Maybe it is crazy."

"I must admit, at first, I was uncomfortable. But Christine was right. I had to let go of my fears, my inhibitions."

"Paul, you can't spend any more time with this woman. You're falling in love with her."

Paul looked angry. "No, I'm not."

"You're looking at her like an infatuated boy, hanging on her every word."

"Mary, you don't understand."

"Did you touch each other during this . . . walk?" Mary said the last word with sarcasm.

"We hugged at one point. We held hands as part of a ritual—"

"Ritual! Are you going to fuck her as part of a ritual too?" Mary's voice rose, and others could hear her. "Is that what happens next?"

Paul got angry. "Don't make fun of something you don't understand."

"Don't you be condescending toward me. I understand exactly what's going on here! Either *you* don't understand, or you're playing me for a fool." Mary jumped up, drawing more attention to them. "I'm going into this goddess temple."

"Mary, don't go. You won't understand, I'm telling you."

"Let me be the judge of what I can or cannot understand." Mary stormed off.

Paul smiled at nearby diners to reassure them that everything was OK. He paid for lunch and sat waiting in the courtyard. Mary ran down the stairs in a huff. "I'm leaving. I'm going to the airport now."

Paul followed her onto the high street. "What's wrong?"

"What's wrong? My husband's losing his mind!"

"That's unfair."

"You think so? Really? You think it's normal to spend time in a temple full of these . . . goddesses and all these strange people? It's insane." Mary started crying and walked faster. Paul tried to keep up.

Paul realized why Mary might be uncomfortable, and truthfully, he wasn't sure why he was so calm. Christine seemed to be the bridge. But he couldn't bring up her name in front of Mary now. "Mary, I'm really OK." Paul tried to use his well-honed skills of persuasion. "Even you've said that I've changed for the better."

"I'm leaving, and you'd better come with me if you want to save our marriage, Paul."

They continued up the high street. Eventually, Mary slowed down and let Paul put his arm around her shoulder. She seemed too tired to fight anymore. They neared the entrance to the path to the Tor. "Let's climb the Tor," Paul suggested. "You've never been."

Mary acquiesced. "Any place is better than Christine and her weird house."

As they climbed the hill, she appreciated the view of Glastonbury below. It looked like any other quaint English countryside village. In the glare of the bright afternoon sun, the Tor looked harmless as well.

They reached the top of the Tor and sat together on a grassy bluff. Paul realized he could not convince Mary by appealing to logic. He looked at Glastonbury below and thought about the last twenty-four hours. "I'm really thankful that you agreed to come here," he said.

"Are you sure? You look like you're having a good time without me." Mary picked the weeds out of the grass and tossed them in the air.

"This is all new to me. I get caught up in it, almost like I'm high. But I understand why you could get upset." Paul took her hand.

Mary appreciated that the *new* Paul was trying to understand her feelings; before, they would fight and go into opposite corners, licking their wounds. Mary said, "I'm sorry I blew up like that. It's a struggle not to be jealous—I have reason to be." She patted the ground next to them. "So this is the Isle of Avalon?"

"That's what they say. Thousands of years ago, the surrounding farmland was a lake and marshland, except for the village itself. The Tor was an island. People have been looking for Avalon ever since."

They watched as a line of people in red-and-white gowns and capes passed them on the way to the tower. Paul looked at Mary, and they both started laughing.

"It's crazy, right?" Paul admitted. "But you know what? I think I needed something really crazy to shake me up. I was so frozen, Mary. Empty inside. I needed a whack across the head with a baseball bat to wake me up. That's what I like about this place. It's so different that I can't ignore it."

"What about Christine? Why her?" Mary asked.

"I don't know. Jeanne recommended her? Mary, she's amazing."
Paul grabbed her arm excitedly. "You should have a soul reading."

Mary pulled her arm away and frowned. "That's not going to happen. You don't know Christine that well."

Paul realized he said too much. *Your partner will sense your
change, and it will change her . . . not in the same way—differently.*

Fifty-Nine

Jeanne and Edward had returned from dinner with Paul, Mary, and Christine at the Who'd a Thought It Inn, ready to retire for the evening. Jeanne read her newest romance novel while Edward brushed his teeth in the bathroom. He poked his head into the bedroom, his toothbrush sticking out of his mouth. "I think Paul behaved strangely. He had nothing to drink."

Jeanne put her book down. "You know that's because he's on a retreat, and he wants to keep his head clear."

Edward joined Jeanne in bed, wearing his reading glasses and holding a *Daily Racing Form*. "I felt like the drunkard at the table just because I had a few drinks."

"More than a few, Edward. You shouldn't have ordered for Paul and then had his drink as well!" Edward rustled his paper, ignoring her. "That's OK, I thought it was a very nice dinner," Jeanne said, continuing to read. "Nice to see Christine getting out for a change—I don't think she gets out much at all."

"Thank God the dog wasn't with her—that menace to society." Edward removed his reading glasses. "Paul looked like he was in a daze. Do you think he's ill?"

"I thought Mary looked uncomfortable."

"At least she was drinking."

"But she barely touched her food. And she wouldn't look up from the table. She and Christine have a very awkward relationship."

"I can't blame her. Christine doesn't drink, you can't hear what she's saying half the time, and she dresses like a gypsy."

"Listen to my fashion critic!" Jeanne sat up in bed. "When Paul looked at her . . . I don't know. I hope he's not getting in too deep."

Edward frowned. "Let's not go there."

"You know how men fall in love with Christine—women too, for that matter. She has that effect. You've seen it."

"Not with me, darling. I'd be afraid to lower my pants for fear of what she or her damn dog might do."

"Of course, my darling Edward. You're never going to fall for a soul reader." She patted Edward's belly. "More likely, you'll chase that barmaid tart at the Rifleman."

"She chases me, the little wench."

"Sure, sure, you say she's just chatting you up for a tip. She's the only one you do tip! You don't think I notice?" Edward looked absorbed in the paper. Jeanne sighed. "I'm glad Mary agreed to go to the Holy Grail ritual with Paul and Christine tomorrow."

"Yes, I was a little surprised too. What a depressing idea," Edward muttered. "Looking at a wine decanter that's been empty for two thousand years." He shut off his light.

"Edward!" Jeanne slapped his arm with her book. "I think it helped when I described the ritual to her. It's quite affecting. She's here—why not? Few people have the opportunity."

"I'm jealous." Edward rolled onto his side.

"I think participating in one ritual might break down the distrust between Mary and Christine, which would help everybody. Remember, Mary's leaving in the morning to fly home, and Paul is staying another night. He's got meetings in London on Monday."

"Let's have dinner at the Rifleman," Edward said, his voice muffled by his pillow.

"I can't blame her for insisting Paul move out of Christine's house versus staying there, alone with her. Too much temptation. I wish we had room for Paul. But he's staying at Little St. Michael's House at the Chalice Well, and that experience could be a terrific ending to his retreat." She patted Edward's hand. "I'm not sure I'd trust you alone with Christine for a night. You might be tempted to have more than a soul reading." Jeanne smiled at her own joke. The snores from Edward's side of the bed suggested he missed it.

Jeanne turned off the bedside lamp. Lying in the dark, she thought about the dinner. It looked to her like Paul was pushing forward on his journey. Mary reserved judgment, observing Paul and Christine. Sometimes, she frowned when something was said. Jeanne had never seen Christine so animated—not at all the reserved, shy soul reader that Jeanne remembered. When Paul talked, she leaned forward, laughing at his jokes and listening intently when he was serious. Jeanne did not know Christine that well, but if she had to guess, she might be falling in love with a married man.

Sixty

Paul, Mary, and Christine sat upstairs in Little St. Michael's House on the grounds of the Chalice Well Gardens with the caretaker of the Chalice Bowl. Little St. Michael's House was an inn and a place for spiritual retreats, including Chalice Bowl ceremonies. The Chalice Bowl was said to be the Holy Grail that held the wine Jesus and the disciples drank during the Last Supper.

They sat around a wooden box on the floor. A few steps led to a higher floor with a table and thirteen chairs. The table was set with china and a row of unlit candles. Jeanne explained to Mary at dinner the night before that sometimes a group would hold a Last Supper ritual. They would have dinner at that table, drink wine, and pass the Chalice Bowl. Many participants reported visions of one sort or another.

The caretaker, Beth, opened the wooden box. A deep porcelain bowl—blue and white—lay inside. It rested on a white satin material that padded the box like the interior of a coffin. Beth lifted the bowl and held it in front of each of them in turn. Then she put it on a short table and returned to her seat.

For the next half hour, they sat in silence, observing the Chalice Bowl. Mary stared at the bowl until her vision blurred, and she felt faint, forgetting to breathe. Her heart quickened as she watched things unfold.

She heard a distant rumbling, like the vibration from a subway train. The bowl filled with water in front of her eyes. Like ants pouring out of an anthill, dolphins miraculously emerged from the water, leaping into the air. They circled in the bowl like a flock of birds, slipping in and out and over and under each other. The chalice grew to fill the floor. Mary floated above the seething cauldron of dolphins. The dolphins swam faster and faster until they turned into crystal objects, frozen in an aquatic transubstantiation, achieving eternal perfection in her vision.

In the distance, she saw the faint light of candles in the upper room—crystal people sat at the table. They moved with a studied motion like robots. Mary did not belong in their world. She stared at her folded hands, wrinkled and colored with hints of age. Mary wanted out of her world, full of decomposing people and disappointing memories. She yearned for the crystal life.

A hand touched her knee, startling her. She opened her eyes. "Would you like to hold it?" said the caretaker. She kneeled in front of Mary, holding the Chalice Bowl.

"Yes, please." She cautiously took the bowl in her hands. It was empty. She could see the bowl had been repaired, its surface full of blemishes, yet it glowed like a full moon. It was a thing of beauty. Mary gripped the bowl as if it were the answer. How could such a fiction feel so real and perfect? The caretaker retrieved the Chalice Bowl and returned it to its box. Mary wiped away her tears, avoiding eye contact with the others.

"Thank you and bless you," Christine whispered to the caretaker, and everyone stood. They left the meditation room and went into the gardens. No one spoke.

It was Mary's first visit to the gardens. She joined a short line of visitors at the lion fountain and drank the cold water quickly, realizing how thirsty she was. Mary caught up with Paul at the Chalice Well. He sat on the stone bench circling the well with others, deep in meditation.

Christine sat on a bench nearby. She watched Mary watch Paul. Mary looked lost. Christine caught her attention, waving for Mary to join her. "Would you like to sit down?" Christine motioned to a space on the bench next to her. "It's called the Angel Bench," Christine whispered, pointing to a stone angel statue behind them. "How did you find the ritual?"

Mary looked down at the ground. "It was interesting."

"What did you see? Is there anything you want to share?"

Mary hesitated. "Why share? Don't you already know what I saw?" Christine smiled, but Mary got angry. "Why are you smiling at me?" she hissed. "I saw a bowl full of crystal dolphins, a table of crystal people—I saw perfection, and I felt horrible." Mary began to sob. "And I'm tired of trying to be something I'm not. Now I have to deal with *you*."

Christine put her arm around Mary. Mary cringed, not looking up. She brought her lips so close to Mary that they brushed against the fine hair of her ear. "You have a beautiful, perfect heart." Mary wanted to pull back, uncomfortable with the intimacy, but whether it was the sound of her voice, purring like a cat, or some sort of spell, Mary relaxed instead, letting her head rest on Christine's shoulder. She smelled the faint scent of Christine's perfume, reminding her of the red scarf and wig and her nap in the garden.

"Think of the ritual as a kind of play being performed on your behalf. The story told is you speaking to yourself," she whispered in Mary's ear. "I'm so glad you joined us."

"Where's Paul?" Mary asked dreamily.

"He's nearby. Do you want me to get him?"

"No, that's OK. Let him do his thing." Mary lifted her head reluctantly and watched Paul sitting by the well, his eyes closed, his hands on his knees in a meditative pose. Mary hesitated. "Christine, I know it's been difficult having me here. I'm skeptical; it's my nature. And I'm *still* skeptical. But I can't deny that Paul has changed thanks to you, mostly in a good way."

"He's opening up very quickly, faster than almost anyone I've worked with." Christine smiled.

Mary stood up. "I don't understand what you do. Or how you do it. That's probably what bothers me more than anything. You're not a doctor. Jeanne says you have a positive impact on many people. Yet here you are, by yourself, in this little town in the middle of nowhere. What's your story?"

"I trust the universe." Christine saw the look on Mary's face. "I know you think that's corny." Christine took a dry flower from the foot of the stone angel and twirled it in her fingers. "What's out there for me that I should leave Glastonbury? I have this." She waved toward the gardens. "And I have this," she said, touching her heart. "I struggle like you. But Glastonbury is my friend in that struggle. That's why people come here and never leave." Mary sat down again. "Think about it. You just sat in a room and witnessed the Holy Grail. Crazy, right? But you let yourself go, and how do you feel now?" She placed the dried flower in Mary's hair and let her hand rest there for a moment.

"Confused," she confessed. Mary sat still.

"Look, you said you don't understand what I do, so let me explain it—I help people love themselves." Christine smiled and removed her hand from Mary's hair.

Sixty-One

Paul lay on the slope of the Tor, enjoying the sunny afternoon. Mary had left that morning for the airport, and Paul moved his bag to Little St. Michael's House. In staying there, one had access to the gardens twenty-four hours a day. Christine suggested Paul book a room there on the final night, as it sits on the Archangel Michael ley line, and he could walk the gardens one last time. He was taking the train into London the following morning for his European management meeting. Mary was strangely quiet when they said goodbye. "This was a draining experience," she said. "Let's talk about it when you get home." They all were exhausted. Christine pushed Paul out the door, suggesting they could have a coffee later. Paul stopped by Turnips to say goodbye to Edward and Jeanne and turned down their offer of dinner that night. He wanted to be alone with himself.

He closed his eyes and contemplated the meaning of the last few days. He fell into a dream and hovered above his sleeping figure on the Tor. He noticed several ravens slowly circling around him. A silver line appeared from the horizon, shooting through the top of the Tor down into the Chalice Well below, crackling with sparks as if an electric current flowed in its path. The ravens cawed and flapped their wings, transforming into giant dragons, roaring at the line. Paul returned to his body, where the deafening roars faded and the line disappeared. All was silent for a time.

Their voices woke him up from his slumber. He sat up and looked behind him. To his surprise, dozens of Druids gathered on the top of the Tor in their white robes, many with green sashes. More Druids arrived every minute. The men covered their heads with hoods. The women wore headdresses made of antlers or green garlands. When they reached the tower, a man and woman, in full regalia, guarded the entrance. As each Druid approached, they bowed and said a greeting as they entered.

Paul joined the crowd, curious to see why they gathered. Paul asked a long-haired hippie standing next to him, "What's going on?"

"It's a Druid ceremony." He handed Paul a one-pager.

We are the order of Druids, ovates, and bards celebrating our fiftieth anniversary. We have a reverence for the Earth and nature and a love of myth and story. Druids believe that all natural phenomena, from stones to trees and stars, have much to teach us and that one of our most important tasks as human beings is to get back in touch with the rhythms of nature, to listen to her, and to protect her.

The Druids had collected on the top of the hill, forming a large circle. Paul joined the group. As people filled in behind him, he found himself in the inner circle. He was an obvious outlier, dressed in jeans and a windbreaker, but it was too late to pull back. A Druid stepped into the center of the circle, carrying a thick branch. He put the end of the branch to his lips, and a deep sound emerged, like the sound of an elephant trumpeting, no doubt audible to the village below.

Paul stepped back reflexively at the sound and bumped into a girl behind him. He whispered an apology. He motioned for her to take his place, and she happily stepped in front of him. She was a beautiful girl, probably the same age as Simon. Long brown hair fell down her back, held in place by a flower garland on her head. She wore a long dress tied on the side with a string, a rose sticking in its knot. Her bare feet peeked out from underneath the dress. Paul thought that she looked like a nymph.

The horn stopped, and another Druid strode in from the tower. He stood nearly seven feet tall. He held a walking stick that was another foot higher, topped with a large silver symbol. The tall Druid walked slowly around the circle, nodding to the crowd. As he passed Paul, they made eye contact, and Paul involuntarily nodded. The nymph girl in front of him hopped and waved, and the Druid acknowledged her with a smile.

A shorter Druid walked into the circle. He wore a white robe covered with a red cloak. His face was partially obscured by a red hood, but it did not entirely hide his anachronistic wire-rim glasses. He was a pale American and middle-aged. He smiled, held a sword toward the sky, and said,

> Before me are the diamonds of light.
> Their sword is in my hands,
> With the long rays of dawn.
> I have spoken.

Paul watched this man call the Druids to order with a nonsensical pagan poem. Who was he? What does he do when he was not at Druid festivals? Did his friends know of his pagan celebrity status? What does his family think? Is his wife with him? The Druid turned east toward Paul. Everyone, including the nymph girl, raised their hands as he spoke to them. Paul found his hands leaving his side as well, soaring toward the sky and bringing an inexplicable smile to his face. Two men from America, staring at each other, arms flung upward. Paul saw the joy in the Druid's face as he spoke the ancient truths.

The gathering triggered his memory of attending Davos earlier in the year. He laughed to himself at the juxtaposition. Davos was a modern ritual, only a few decades old. The Druids have gathered for millennia. Which is more meaningful? In Davos, leaders gather every year to talk over and over again about how the world is changing. In Glastonbury, Druids gather to repeat over and over again an ancient story about man and nature, unchanged for thousands of years. Which will survive the next millennium? Davos or the Tor? Davos men and women or Druids and goddesses?

As the crowd started chanting a song, a single raven, perched on top of St. Michael's Tower, cawed as if it was singing along. Then the tall Druid reappeared in the center of the circle and pointed a thin metal rod at his fellow Druids:

At this time of highest light,
I hold this blade that was born in fire
As a bridge between heaven and earth.

And then Paul joined them in their vow:

We swear by the peace and love to stand,
Heart to heart and hand to hand.
Mark our spirit and hear us now,
Confirming this, our sacred vow.

The tall man continued in the circle, dipping the rod and blessing the gathered Druids. When he finished his circle, he bowed his head for a moment in silence. He embraced the nearest Druid, signaling the end of the ceremony, and the band began to play again. The nymph child smiled at Paul and held out her arms. She was radiant. The top of her head, ringed by the colorful garland, was sprinkled with colorful speckles. Her face was painted with gold spackles, and below her sharp blue eyes, a green symbol was painted on each cheek. Paul hugged her like she was his own daughter.

As the circle broke, the girl ran toward the cluster of senior Druids. She hugged the tall Druid, coming to his waist. He patted her head, breaking into a wide smile. The music emanated from St. Michael's Tower, now surrounded by a crowd of Druids and hangers-on. *This music has a more mesmerizing beat than the Skrillex concert at Davos,* Paul thought to himself, amused. He felt a tap on his shoulder.

"Hello." It was the nymph girl. "I'm sorry I ran off."

"I'm happy you came back," Paul shouted above the din of the music and chanting.

"Let's find a quieter place." She turned and walked, confident Paul would follow her. They sat where the hilltop began to slope down. "What a beautiful day for the celebration! I'm Brigid, by the way." She held out her hand.

"Brigid? Really?"

"Yes, an Irish girl named Brigid. Not that uncommon, is it?"

Now Paul detected the slight Irish accent with the softened vowels and hardened consonants. "That's a special name for me."

"She's a special goddess. My father named me after her. He said I would, with others, help the world heal itself."

"And I'm sure you will."

"Where are you from?"

"I'm from America. My name is Paul."

Brigid slapped the ground. "I knew it! My father asked me if I knew where you're from, and I said you looked American."

"Which one is your father?"

"That beautiful tall man who led the ceremony." Brigid smiled. "How did you like your first Druid ceremony?"

"At first, I thought it was crazy, but then I tiptoed my way into it."

She hugged him again. "I have to go, Paul. My father worries about me. Even when we're celebrating." She disappeared into the crowd. Paul looked around. By now, it was dusk, a fire was started next to the tower, and bottles of wine were being opened. The Druids danced to the steady drumbeat. Paul suddenly felt very tired and out of place. As he started down the hill, the tall Druid noticed him departing and tilted his staff toward him, as if to say goodbye. Paul waved at him and continued. He reached the bottom of the Tor and looked up to the tower. The crowd was a collection of shadows flying by the fire, and the Tor itself sounded like a beating heart.

Sixty-Two

Light shone through the bottom of Paul's door. He lay in bed in his room at Little St. Michael's House. The light finally went out, signaling that all the residents had retired for the evening. He was having difficulty falling asleep; he did not want to leave Glastonbury and return to work tomorrow. He found it hard to imagine sitting in a conference room in London, talking about business plans.

What if he moved to Glastonbury? He would be able to see Christine all the time. What would it be like to be with her every day? She had never contacted him about coffee—she was probably too tired. He missed her already. He had her mobile number, and it was well before midnight, so he pulled out his phone.

Thank you for everything. I already miss talking to you. Paul.

A *harmless good-night text*, he thought. Minutes passed by, then a buzz.

I miss talking to you as well. The retreat went too fast. I'm still absorbing everything. Good night.

Paul responded:

Perhaps the retreat was one night too short.

Then another buzz:

Perhaps.

He lay in bed with his eyes open. No point in trying to fall asleep. A half hour passed; it was nearly midnight. He had to talk to her again:

Hopefully you'll read this in the morning. I can't sleep. I'm lying in bed at the foot of the Tor. The Chalice Well is a stone's throw away. You were right; the energy at St. Michael's is intense. It's poking at me. There's little between me and the dreamworld. Between me and the well. I can taste the red water.

Minutes ticked by.

I can't sleep either. I'm sitting in my garden. The sky is clear right now, and the stars never looked brighter. You are being filled with the feminine energy.

Paul replied,

I want to soak in as much of it as I can. It feels like this is the last time I'll be able to, and every minute is precious.

Christine suggested,

Perhaps we need to do one more ritual at the Chalice Well. Are you up for it? I'm exhausted, but I don't think I am finished with you.

Paul's heart pounded. He replied yes, and then Christine replied,

I will come to the cottage. Wear something warm. We will go back to the well. Night at the Chalice Well has its own power and attraction. See you shortly.

Paul quickly dressed and waited by the window. When he saw her walking up, he opened the door. He smiled and held his arms out. Christine smiled and hugged him briefly. She carried a large shoulder bag with her and handed it to him. She put a finger to her lips, signaling he should be quiet, and they quickly walked through the living room to the back door, which opened into the gardens.

The moonlight was sufficient to see the stone path to the well. They passed the healing pool and the lion's head fountain and arrived at the wellhead. It was pitch black under the dense trees, which formed a natural ceiling over the well. Christine lit a candle and placed it on the ring wall of the well. The candlelight illuminated her face.

"There, now we can see each other." Her eyes sparkled, and Paul shook with excitement. "You're freezing, aren't you? I told you to dress warmly. Here." Christine reached into her large bag and pulled out several blankets. "Help me with these."

In a few minutes, they sat on the ground and leaned against the round stone bench that circled the wellhead. They covered up with the blankets, and their eyes reflected the candlelight. Their shoulders and hips touched, and Christine seemed completely comfortable; in fact, she looked at Paul and broke out laughing.

"What?"

"I don't know. You look so serious."

"Oh." Paul looked at Christine carefully, drawn to her abnormally bright-green eyes and her smile, richly drawn with red lips and a bright row of teeth. Her cheeks were slightly red, whether from the cold or makeup, Paul did not know. While continuing to look at Paul, Christine removed a band holding her hair in a bun and shook her head, allowing her curly golden hair to fall to her shoulders. *She truly looks like a goddess*, Paul thought.

"I'm sorry I laughed." Christine looked back at the well, breaking the tension of the moment. She closed her eyes and leaned her head against the bench. "I was so glad when you texted me. I couldn't sleep. I felt like we really didn't finish today. This is the right place to do that. The divine feminine energy is strongest here." Christine faced Paul. "You hunger for this kind of energy, don't you, Paul?"

"Yes, I think I do."

"It's something lacking in the work you do. Everything is so logical. Numbers doling out power and power doling out numbers."

Paul laughed. "I've never thought of it that way, but it's a great description." Her eyes lingered on his face, and then she sat back again, looking pensive.

Christine noticed Paul was still shivering. "Here, let's get closer. The stone conducts the cold." They pressed closer, shoulder to shoulder, her arm entwined with his under the blanket. "There, that's better, isn't it?" Christine looked at the well, avoiding eye contact with Paul. "Remember in your first reading, I saw you writing a book, drawing from your journal? Are you still writing in your journal?"

"Yes, I'm writing entries about this retreat."

"Good." Christine exhaled slowly, her breath turning to mist in the cold night air. "The world is full of seekers, and you can reach them with your words."

"I'm beginning to realize that. Christine, I have to ask you something." Christine dropped her hand from his shoulder. "I think I have feelings for you."

Christine slowly stood up. Paul wanted to take his words back. She circled the wellhead, rubbing her hand along its wall. "That's not a question," she said.

Paul raised himself to the stone bench across from the well. "Well, you see everything, right? Am I falling in love with you?"

Christine continued circling the wellhead. "You need me to tell you that?"

"I don't know. I'm so confused."

"You're married, Paul."

"I know. But you know how difficult our marriage has been. I'm changing. Will Mary change too?" Paul could not stand the awkward silence. "Is there anyone in your life?"

Christine still avoided looking at Paul. "Men find it hard to be my partner. They don't like the fact that I can see inside of them. It scares them to have no place to hide. To be 'naked' in every way possible . . . that's a lot to take on for any partner. Plus, I see and feel people's truth so deeply, it makes it hard sometimes to be around others. Solitude is so much easier." She looked at Paul. "I had a partner when I came to Glastonbury years ago."

"What happened?"

"He fell in love with someone else."

"I can't imagine that."

Christine leaned over and looked into the well. To Paul, it seemed like she wanted to jump in. "His name is Javier. One night we came to this very place. The caretaker was our friend and helped us set up that special night. We drained the well to the point that we could enter a little antechamber below the water line. We climbed down using a hook ladder. It was a very hot summer night. We sat on blankets and enjoyed the cooler air below. Javier dared me to jump into the water. Being down there, the energy . . ." She stared into the well, lost in thought. "Everything felt possible." She glanced at Paul, then continued to circle the well. "I took off my clothes and jumped into the water. It was so cold but felt so good. Javier pulled me out of the water almost immediately, afraid I might sink to the bottom. I was shaking uncontrollably from the frigid temperature. Of course, he was so warm by comparison. One thing led to another, and we made love on our blankets, not even bothered by the hard stone floor." She finally sat down on the wellhead wall, her back to Paul. "Can you imagine the energy we attracted? The feminine and masculine drawn to each other, overcome by lust."

"Sounds beautiful."

"It was a special evening, one of our last evenings. I knew it was over. He left for Paris and didn't return. I frightened him away. I do that to men." Christine turned to Paul, her gentle eyes now intense and serious. "How about you, Paul? Doesn't it scare you?"

To say he was not afraid would have been a lie. And she already sensed his fear. So he said nothing but felt everything, and it panicked him, as if he swam too far from shore and suddenly realized that he could drown.

Christine walked over to her bag and started to place tea lights along the circumference of the wellhead.

"What are you doing?" Paul asked, hoping Christine would come back and sit with him.

"I'm lighting up our secret little world," she said.

"Aren't we trying to hide?"

"No one can see the light from here. It's late. I think we have the gardens to ourselves." She lit the tea lights one by one.

"Have you ever loved again?"

"No. Sometimes I think it may not be possible anymore."

"Don't be silly, Christine. How can you say that?"

Christine finished lighting the candles and sat next to Paul. She rested her head against his shoulder. "I've no business sharing this with you. I'm sorry. I guess it's been an intense retreat."

"Christine," Paul whispered in her ear, "I want to share more with you."

"You want more of what I can do for you," Christine said. "And that's not love." Christine slowly rose to her feet and returned to her bag. She retrieved a long stick with sage leaves bundled on the end. She lit it and walked around the well, letting the smell of sage fill the air. The smoke settled within the overhanging trees. She bent down in front of Paul again. "Paul, look at me. You're married, and marriage is sacred. Your infatuation is just that—an infatuation. You are falling in love with yourself, not me. I'm just helping you through your journey."

Paul was crestfallen. "But I feel such a strong attraction to you, to this place. Look at the synchronicity that occurs when we are together— or even when we're apart. Isn't this different?"

Christine stood up, turned away from Paul, and continued waving the sage in the air. "Yes, it's different. I've tried several times in the past to enter the White Spring and was turned down—until I was with you." She leaned on the wellhead. "But we cannot be together." Paul looked defeated. She motioned all around them. "What you're feeling is from the divine feminine energy." She put the smoldering sage on the wellhead. "But it's everywhere. Now that you've opened up, you'll recognize it; perhaps you'll find it in Mary. She's changing as well."

"I don't want to leave here."

Christine looked at her watch. "It's late, and I still have one last ritual here tonight. I may be making a mistake, but I want to show you who I am. Now close your eyes and listen to your breath."

Paul closed his eyes and tried to concentrate on his breath, but his mind filled with questions about Christine and Mary, about going back to work after a weekend like this. What happens next?

"Keep your eyes closed and drink the well water." She held a glass against his lips, and he sipped the cold. He finished the glass and then felt her touch his mouth and cheeks with a cloth. "Feel the water slide down your throat, down your chest, settling deep inside your soul."

Paul heard Christine moving. "Keep your eyes closed and listen to your breath." He pulled the blankets tighter around him as the cold water chilled his body. Christine continued to talk, but Paul drifted into his own world, forgetting where he was and whom he was with. He heard her voice again.

"OK. Now I want you to open your eyes."

For a moment, he could see nothing. There was a thick screen of smoke, and there were many more candles. The light from the candles was blinding. As his eyes adjusted, he focused on a large candle in front of him, its wick-sputtering red light sparkling like a firework gone awry. Then he saw her standing in front of him. Her eyes shone bright, like a pair of green sunsets. Dark-red hair hung to her shoulders, and she wore nothing but a red scarf draped around her shoulders, which descended to her hips. She was a painting come to life. Steam rose from her body. The world blazed red. The air crackled, the red spring gushed forth, and the bloody earth groaned in Glastonbury.

The divine feminine flowed into Paul until he could not breathe. He stared at Christine and understood the sacred love between them. Desire gave way to gratitude. Paul closed his eyes, and he felt his heart expand until it filled his entire body. He felt like he was floating, being drawn away from Brigid, the goddess of fire and healing. He hovered above the fiery scene, feeling a mad joy.

* * *

The raven sat at the top of the tallest tree in the Chalice Gardens, drawn to the light at the well. It watched the man stumble out of the garden. The red-haired goddess remained. She held her arms above her head as she circled the well. She danced and skipped, her pale skin reflecting in the light as she passed through the rooms of the gardens. She came in and out of view like a forest nymph—a goddess trying to find a pair of arms to rest in.

Sixty-Three

The train picked up speed. Paul looked out the window as the countryside slid by and Glastonbury disappeared into his past, somewhere between memory and myth.

He grimaced as he opened his laptop, expecting the worst. Christine made him promise he would not check his email or voice mail during the retreat. The commitment was much easier to keep than he had imagined. Now it was payback time. He squinted at the mailbox and quickly scrolled. There were fewer than he expected. The lack of news from work was almost ominous, as if he had not been missed. The first email that caught his attention was a personal one from Mary. The subject line surprised him—"My First Journal Entry."

> Paul, I don't know why, but I wanted to share my first journal entry with you and thank you for a memorable weekend. I always thought I would share adventures with you that I would otherwise not experience. This trip ranks among the most unexpected. And least understood! Here goes . . .
>
> It is time for me to get back home. As the car drives off, I watch Paul and Christine in the doorway of her house from the back

window. The car speeds through the narrow treelined roads of the countryside on the way to the airport. It seems like a film is playing for me in fast motion.

I start to see everything differently. Christine is not a sorceress trying to tempt my husband into an affair. She is a fragile soul attempting to share insight into the lives of others with compassion and honesty, not easily found elsewhere. Paul is not out of his mind. Perhaps he has never been as close to his true self as he is right now.

Flying home over the Atlantic, I close my eyes and continue drifting away from doubt and guilt to a better place. I picture the ocean below and imagine myself swimming home like a dolphin, feeling the great cleansing power of the sea wash me free.

Paul looked out the window and thought about his wife. Maybe Christine was right. *Your partner will sense your change, and it will change her . . . not in the same way—differently.*

He continued scrolling through the emails. Cynthia sent a cryptic note asking if he could call her in the morning, New York time, saying only that it was important. Nothing from Steve. Paul had a sinking feeling in his stomach. The train raced forward like a thoroughbred horse under the whip. Paul watched the countryside recede as if it were running away from wherever Paul was going to. The retreat in Glastonbury had been too perfect. Will everything come crashing down on him this week? Did he take his eye off the ball one time too many?

Paul noticed an email from Simon as well, which was an unexpected surprise. The subject was "My Letter to Myself."

Dad,

While you and Mom were gone, I decided to write my version of a letter to myself—something to be opened at a future date. I'm sharing it with you because you shared yours with me, and I appreciated that. In case I lose it, will you keep a copy for me? Here it is:

Hello, self. You are an older Simon now, reading a letter from a seventeen-year-old Simon finishing high school and getting ready to go out into the world. I wanted to ask you some questions and tell you what I hope for.

The very first question that I can remember is one that our father asked me when I was five years old. The question was "Do you believe in fairies?" I didn't remember my answer until my father told me recently. My answer was "I believe in everything." I still do.

So my first question to you is, Do you still believe in everything?

My second question is, What kind of girl did you marry? I believe she will be from a place far away. Maybe she will be a fairy! I hope she is your lifelong friend; you need one. How many pixies do you have? I hope more than one.

My final question is, What will I be when I am grown up—what do you do? Do I follow in my father's footsteps? My grandfather's? Will I be a profiteer or a prophet? I hope a prophet.

Simon, October 2009

Paul wiped away a tear, put in his earbuds, and began to play his soul reading. He closed his eyes and listened: *Your son is an old soul and a window into yourself.*

The Offer

Sixty-Four

Paul sat in the conference room in Ascendant's London office with his European management team as his deputy, Roberto, walked them through Ascendant's plans to connect the world, one company at a time. Coming from a weekend in Glastonbury to a planning meeting was like jumping into quicksand. He could barely breathe. The voices droned. The air was heavy. He wanted to sleep.

His phone lit up with a text from Cynthia:

I need to give you a heads-up.

Paul held his phone under the table and responded,

In a meeting but can text. What's up?

Paul could see the Tower of London across the street from their office, which was in the Old Mint Building. Gray-white stone walls lined the tower's perimeter, reminding him of the Glastonbury abbey. His mind drifted back to the previous night at the Chalice Well. How will he ever forget seeing Christine as the blazing goddess? He found it impossible to concentrate on the subject at hand. His team might as well be reciting the phone book. They would have to set the room on fire to get his attention. Paul wanted to go back to Glastonbury.

Very exciting but confidential news. You did not hear from me, OK?

Sure.

You will get a call from Steve shortly—the board is promoting you to president! Congratulations!

Paul felt a chill.

That's a surprise. Where's Steve on this?

Where do you think? He looks like a walking dead man. You're the heir apparent. It's just a matter of time. I'm drafting the press release now. Goes out tonight. Sound surprised when he calls. Then call me, and let's celebrate!

"Paul, do you think we should take a break?" Roberto realized Paul wasn't paying attention.

"Umm, sure. I think that's a good idea," Paul said, dazed by the news. "Let's take an hour break. I need to do a call." He threw on his jacket and left the room, avoiding his colleagues' puzzled looks. He needed to find a place to think. He exited the building and found himself staring at the tower. *Why not?* he thought, and hurried to the entrance.

"We close in less than an hour, sir," the man in the ticket booth said. Paul muttered under his breath and slid his money under the ticket window. The man shook his head, questioning Paul's judgment in paying for a ticket with so little time left to visit.

In the Tower Green, a yeoman warder regaled the last tour group of the day with stories of famous grisly executions at the site of the scaffolding. Paul's phone rang, drawing the eye of the disapproving warder. Paul found a quiet alcove. "Hi, Steve."

"Paul, I need to brief you on something. Are you alone?"

"Yes."

"Paul, the board and I met and agreed that we need a strong number two to work with me to turn the company around, and you're their choice. An internal and public announcement goes out tonight. You're now president of Ascendant and will join the board as well. Congratulations."

Steve's unfriendly tone and matter-of-fact delivery told Paul what he needed to know. Steve disagreed with the decision—while thinking that Paul had potential, the timing was too soon, and now Paul was a threat. "Thank you, Steve."

"Obviously, this sets you up to take the CEO slot, but I'm not planning to go anywhere anytime soon. We need to work closely together."

Paul wondered if working together meant a fight to the death. "Sure."

"They want you to take all the operating units. I keep the staff functions, and you still report to me, whatever that means. I cannot lie to you, Paul. This setup feels a little uncomfortable to me, but it's what the board wants."

"I look forward to working with you," Paul said carefully, his mind spinning and his stomach churning.

"I'm sure." Steve paused. "I have to give you credit. You've upped your game lately. And it's like you're not trying, but it all goes your way anyway. I don't get it." Steve added sarcastically, "Maybe I'm too good a teacher for my own good."

"I'm not sure I want it," Paul blurted out.

"What?"

Paul hesitated. "I've been thinking about—"

Steve started to laugh. "Christ, Paul, don't bullshit a bullshitter. You've wanted my job since the day we met. You used to get away with the puppy-dog look, but now you are a full-blown pit bull, and I know you would rip my face off in a minute if it got you a step closer to the top."

"I'm serious."

"No, I'm serious." Paul could hear voices in the background. "I have to go. Not a word to anyone for the next few hours. No one. The chairman will call you shortly to tell you. Try not to twist the knife in my back too deep on your first call with him," Steve said bitterly. He hung up.

Paul took a deep breath. The late afternoon air turned cool in the long shadows created by the castle walls. He walked aimlessly until he reached the Bloody Tower, where many prisoners died. While awaiting execution, they could see the Thames, but Traitor's Gate blocked them from escaping to the river. Many entered the tower by boat through the gate. Very few ever left.

The sun edged toward the horizon, and the breeze coming off the Thames picked up. Paul shivered, dreading the next call.

The tower's ravens sat on the wall above him, staring at him as if he were a condemned man. He waited for the chairman's call. A yeoman walked past, ringing a bell, bellowing instructions to leave the tower. It was closing its doors.

Paul thought back to that spring day when Edward dropped him off in front of Christine's house. He remembered standing in front of the red door, the brass knocker in the shape of an angel. He knocked. No one came to the door. He had second thoughts. Perhaps the soul reading was a bad idea. Perhaps he should leave. Then she opened the door. *He walked inside and fell in love with the world. With Mary and Simon. With himself.*

The ravens' caws brought Paul back to the present. They lined the wall like restless soldiers on watch, looking down at the visitor staring at his phone. Should he call Christine? The wind laced the Thames with wavelets lit sunset red. *Christine knows nothing of the business world*, he thought. Christine was an angry goddess and would lay waste to everything he has worked for—his career, his money, his belongings—to save his soul. He could see her in front of him. On the other side of the gate. Banging on the iron rods as if she could will them away. The Thames blazing red behind her. Fire and healing everywhere.

Paul waited for the phone to ring. What would Mary say to him? This promotion will change their lives. They could move up to the penthouse in the city and the beachfront in Quogue. Things to fill the void between them.

His phone rang. The chairman's name filled the screen. "Paul, John Owens." Paul listened as John congratulated him on his promotion. The ravens continued to stare at him, expressionless. The warder came toward him, shouting something he could not hear, his ornamental keys hanging from his wide belt. Paul tensed.

"I appreciate your trust and support, John," Paul said, barely able to utter the words. "I'm in." The call ended.

Paul's heart pounded like the drums on top of the Tor. Now he got first dibs on the corporate jet—including the annual trip to the World Economic Forum. *He* would enter the stage as a *real* Davos man—leader of Ascendant, one of the most influential companies in the world. Soon he would have it all, including his "fuck you" money. Then he could retire to Avalon, a happy man.

A raven cawed, sitting directly above him, and Paul looked up. He thought back to the day he asked his son if he believed in fairies. Paul felt his little Simon tugging at his leg and looked down. It was so cold. Snow was falling. Simon smiled at his father, his breath visible in the air, his heart filled with the joy of discovery. "I believe in everything." Such a journey. But does believing make it true? Fairies, Druids, and goddesses? *His imagined soul?*

"Come on," the warder said softly, feeling sorry for the disturbed man. "It's time to go." The warder led him by the arm. The ravens were silent.

Paul's phone chimed, again and again, the congratulatory texts pouring in. It sounded like an arcade game, the pinball sitting in a hole, ringing up a score.

Ching, ching, ching.

Acknowledgments

Although *Journey* and its characters are fictional, I want to thank Sacha Knop, whose soul readings and coaching started me on my own journey and inspired this story.

I wrote a large portion of *Journey* as part of Charles Salzburg's writing class and am grateful for the support and feedback from him as well as from my fellow classmates.

Jane Friedman helped me navigate my way through this crazy business called publishing and provided sound advice and useful introductions.

Kurt Flamer-Caldera and the Radius Books team, including Mark Fretz and Evan Phail, helped the book take shape through the editing process, and Rodrigo Corral captured *Journey* with his brilliant cover.

I've had the privilege of working at four outstanding businesses—PwC, idealab, Accenture, and frog design. I hope my colleagues enjoy my portrayal of being human in an increasingly digital world.

Through its fellowship program, the Thomas J. Watson Fellowship Foundation gave me my first opportunity to write full time following my college graduation. I traveled with circuses in Europe and never finished my book, so this novel is a very late homework assignment.

And thank you to my parents, who have always encouraged me to pursue my love of telling stories. I am finally listening to them.